CONTEMPORARY PARANORMAL

REAPER SERIES
Dark Alpha's Claim
Dark Alpha's Embrace
Dark Alpha's Demand
Dark Alpha's Lover
Tall Dark Deadly Alpha Bundle
Dark Alpha's Night

DARK KINGS
Dark Heat (3 novella compilation)
Darkest Flame
Fire Rising
Burning Desire
Hot Blooded
Night's Blaze
Soul Scorched
Dragon King (novella)
Passion Ignites
Smoldering Hunger
Smoke and Fire
Dragon Fever (novella)
Firestorm
Blaze
Dragon Burn

Constantine: A History (short story)
Heat

DARK WARRIORS
Midnight's Master
Midnight's Lover
Midnight's Seduction
Midnight's Warrior
Midnight's Kiss
Midnight's Captive
Midnight's Temptation
Midnight's Promise
Midnight's Surrender (novella)
Dark Warrior Box Set

CHIASSON SERIES
Wild Fever
Wild Dream
Wild Need
Wild Flame
Wild Rapture

LARUE SERIES
Moon Kissed
Moon Thrall
Moon Struck

Moon Bound

EVERWYLDE

THE KINDRED

DONNA GRANT

This is a work of fiction. All of the characters, organizations, and events portrayed in this novel are either products of the author's imagination or are used fictitiously.

EVERWYLDE
© 2018 by DL Grant, LLC
Cover Design © 2018 by Charity Hendry

ISBN 10: 1635760860
ISBN 13: 9781635760866
Available in ebook and print editions

www.DonnaGrant.com
www.MotherofDragonsBooks.com

ACKNOWLEDGMENTS

Writing is a solitary business where writers can immerse themselves in the worlds we create as characters come to life. But getting a book ready to hand to a reader takes a team. I'd like to take a moment to thank the wonderful people that make up my team.

The beautiful covers and all the gorgeous graphics posted on social media are the work of Charity Hendry who never fails to deliver amazing work.

The multiple reads of the book for editing and copy editing all falls in the very capable hands of Chelle Olson who always finds the small things.

Next is formatting who is done by the amazing Frauke Spanuth at Croco Designs who puts in the beautiful touches at the end.

I need to send another shout out to Charity and Chelle for our meetings were we toss ideas around about the series. Thank you for understanding the vision I first saw for this series and for joining on the ride with me.

Last but not least is you. Yes, you, the reader. You're part of the team. I might dream up these worlds and character, but you help breath life into them. That makes you an important part of the team. So thank you for coming along on the journey.

October 1349

This wasn't war. Carac fought against the rising tide of anger that rolled violently through him as he watched the army fighting his men die in droves—without his men lifting a finger.

He drew his sword and prepared to ride into battle to...hell, he didn't know what he'd do, but he couldn't stand by and watch a slaughter.

"Hold."

He clenched his teeth and slowly turned his head to stare at Lord John Atwood. "You called me here to fight for you."

"And you did." John's brown eyes met Carac's before the lord adjusted his horse's reins in his hands. He then glanced at the woman beside him.

Carac had taken an instant disliking to her. While she was pretty enough with her golden blond hair and clear blue eyes, there was something about her that rankled him. She hadn't said more than two words in front of Carac, but John seemed to turn to her for every decision.

And the way she watched the carnage on the field before them, with a smile of enjoyment, sent foreboding snaking down Carac's spine.

"It does not appear as if you needed my men," he stated.

John's brown head turned to him. "You question me, Sir Carac?"

This was one of the times that Carac wanted to shout the secret he kept buried. It was his choice to keep his true identity hidden, but the longer he was in John's and Lady Sybbyl's company, the harder it was to hold back.

Before he could think better of it, Carac said, "I do."

"A pity." Boredom contorted John's face as he turned his attention back to the battle.

"You're butchering men. Men, I might add, who are simply fighting for their lord. You promised Lord Randall the five hundred acres between your holdings."

John sighed loudly as irritation laced his words. "I changed my mind."

In other words, Sybbyl changed his mind. Carac didn't understand how the woman had such a hold over John. In fact, had anyone asked Carac three months ago, he would've said John preferred the company of men.

Carac looked at the spot between his stallion's ears as he struggled to get his frustration and disdain under control. It was the jingle of a bridle that drew him out of his thoughts.

Sybbyl moved her mount between him and John. She stared at him a long while before Carac finally acknowledged her. Only then did she ask, "You do not care for me, do you?"

"Not particularly."

She smiled shrewdly. "A man who speaks the truth, regardless of whether it will benefit him or not."

He was in no mood for such talk. Especially with her. The need to put distance between them warred with his desire to get to the root of why he disliked the woman so. "What is it you want, Lady Sybbyl?"

"Carac," John admonished.

"It's fine," Sybbyl said and laid a hand atop John's arm. Then her gaze slid back to Carac. "John told me you were a man of war, that you served him well once."

Carac looked back at the field where not one of his men had so much as a scratch on him as they cut a swath through their enemies. "Aye, I did. When it was a fair fight."

"Fair?" she asked with a laugh. "Are you suggesting your men are not more skilled than their adversaries?"

He hated when people twisted his words. "I've fought alongside some of those currently being butchered, my lady. I know just how skilled they are."

"Apparently, your men are more so," she replied.

"That would be rather difficult since I've trained some of Lord Randall's men myself."

Something dark flashed ever so briefly in Sybbyl's eyes. "You are making this difficult, Sir Carac."

"How so?"

"Enough," John snapped.

Carac looked between Sybbyl and John. "Aye, I do believe it is enough."

Without another word, he turned his horse and rode back to his tent where his squire rushed out to meet him. Carac dismounted before his horse had even come to a stop. He strode into his tent and began yanking off his armor without waiting for the young lad to help.

When he was free of the armor, Carac shoved the flap aside and walked outside to find Simon waiting for him astride his bay gelding.

Carac walked to his stallion that stood munching on grass. He rubbed the animal's sleek white neck and eyed Simon. "Say it."

"You normally hold your temper better."

Carac looked into the dark brown eyes of his best friend and shrugged. "There is something going on here. I feel it in my bones."

"I, as well, old friend. But we can do nothing."

And that's what infuriated him. Carac got on his horse and nudged him into a run. He had to put some distance between him and John before Carac did something stupid.

He didn't slow his mount until they reached the village. Carac halted his stallion before the tavern and dismounted with Simon following only seconds behind him.

They shared a grin before entering the building. Carac made his way to the back of the pub and took an empty table. Once Simon sat, and they ordered, Carac ran a hand down his face and sighed.

"This is wrong. What is happening on that battlefield is wrong."

Simon smiled at the barmaid who brought their ale and flipped her a coin. He took a long drink after she left before wiping his mouth with the back of his sleeve. "Remind me again why you choose to hide who you really are? This is one of those times I wish others knew."

Carac shook his head and lifted the ale, but he didn't let it touch his lips. Not after watching his father sink into his cups every night. "You know why."

"Explain it to me again. Because I think now is a good time for John to find out who he's been speaking to so insolently. Innocent men are being killed."

"Men are always killed in battle." While Simon's words were true, they still didn't sit well with him.

The men dying might not be innocent, but that didn't mean their deaths didn't matter. There was something at work here, and Carac wanted to figure out what it was. Because he might enjoy a victory—but only those he truly won.

When Simon raised a dark brow, Carac nodded. "I know. I know."

Simon quickly finished off his drink and switched his mug with Carac's. "Tell John who you are."

"I hide my identity so I did not receive special attention. And you, above all others, know that I wished for a simple life."

Simon sat back as his lips compressed. "That was a long time ago, Carac. We were skinny lads then. You earned your knight's spurs quickly, proving that nobility is not a birthright, but something some men have. And most do not."

Carac scratched his temple. "Everyone said I was too old to be a squire."

"You were," Simon replied with a grin. "But you have always gone after the things you wanted. Being a knight was all you talked about. You trained harder and longer than even I."

"I would not have made it without your friendship."

Simon let out a guffaw. "This I know."

Damn, but it was good to have friends he could trust. Carac knew the acrid taste of betrayal all too well. It was what made him choose his friends—and the company he kept —carefully.

"You can stop this. Tell John who you are," Simon urged.

"After all the years I deceived people, there will be fallout. Especially among our men."

"*Your* men. And you've always known this. However, I do not believe it will be as bad as you fear. Some will not like discovering that they treated nobility so...wretchedly."

That was all true, but Carac preferred for people to treat him in a way befitting who he was rather than for his title. But something was holding Carac back from revealing his identity at last. If only he knew what it was. "If I do tell John, it might end this battle. Maybe. Then what?"

Simon lifted the mug of ale. "You return home."

"And you?"

"I accompany you, of course," Simon said with a wink before taking a big gulp of ale.

The idea of going home had entered Carac's thoughts more and more over the last three years. Thanks to Simon's visits there and the steward in place to run things, Carac wasn't missed. But he had begun to long for the moors and all the bleakness and wildness that came with them.

"You know I love a good battle, but that is not what is happening out there. There is something else at work here," Carac said in a low voice as he leaned his forearms on the table.

Simon nodded, his face cut into lines of distress. "I agree."

"I could stop the massacre," Carac agreed, his gaze moving to the side. "Then we would leave, but I know it would begin again."

Simon leaned close and glanced around to see if anyone were listening. "You think John wanted this?"

"As peculiar as he is, he's never gone back on his word before now. The truce between him and Randall was agreed upon weeks ago, with John returning the land his grandfather took from Bryce's."

"John's honor will be in question now."

Carac nodded. "Exactly. No man would purposefully do that unless he had a bigger plan already in place."

Simon's face went slack as he sat back and snorted. "He wants Bryce's land."

"It would double John's holdings. Randall does not have an heir, which means, if he dies, his title does not pass on."

"That still does not explain why John is doing all of this."

Carac heard the laugh of the barmaid, who bent to show off her ample cleavage to a patron. "Sybbyl."

Simon gave him a flat look. "I will be the first to admit that a woman who can work her wiles can get a man to do many things. But we both know John is rarely seen with females."

"Maybe he likes both sexes. Or perhaps there is something else she can give him."

"Like?"

Carac shrugged. "Information."

"You think she knows something about Randall John has not shared with you?"

Carac drummed his fingers on the table as he slowly sat back. "Actually, the more I think on it, I believe Sybbyl is the one with the plan, and that she is using John."

"No woman has that kind of power."

"Men have long feared the minds of women. It is why females are used as nothing more than chattel, but that cannot last forever. What if Sybbyl found a way?"

Simon frowned and drew in a deep breath. "What is in it for her?"

"I have not worked that out yet. It could be anything. But look at the facts. She arrived with only one maid and no other escort. Within a few hours of her appearance, John sent for me. Instead of allowing me to plan the battle as I usually do, he and Sybbyl did that."

"That is a shite load to muddle through," Simon muttered. "How did you discover all of this?"

Carac shot his friend a smile. "I asked around the keep.

John's men like to talk. Especially to those they think they can trust."

"You make it sound as if you believe Sybbyl is the cause of all of this."

"I think she is."

Disbelief fell over Simon's face. "You cannot be serious."

"I have known a few women intelligent enough to do this. Can you honestly say that you do not believe females capable?"

"I have not thought about it. I will certainly be looking at women differently now," Simon said, a deep frown marring his forehead.

Carac chuckled at his friend's response, but the laughter died. "It would be easy for me to stop John, but I am more concerned with Sybbyl. She has power over him somehow, and I need to figure out why."

"What do we do?"

"We find out what it is she is after. Because whatever it is, it is on Randall's land."

Simon rolled his eyes and blew out a breath. "And you want me to go to Bryce Castle to find out."

"You read my mind," Carac replied with a grin.

Simon raised his mug in salute. "You owe me a barrel of ale when I return."

Carac watched his friend drain his mug. They exchanged a glance, but no more words were needed. They had been down this particular road before. No one could infiltrate an enemy camp like Simon.

2

The village was like all the others she had seen before. But this time, Ravyn was close to locating the woman responsible for wiping out her loved ones.

Every time she closed her eyes, she dreamed of the night her family was killed.

And she heard the witch's laughter.

"This is a mistake," Margery muttered for the hundredth time.

Ravyn looked at her traveling companion as she maneuvered her horse to a stop. "I told you not to come."

"As if I would let that happen after what Leoma went through."

"She was not alone."

Margery sighed loudly. "Braith does not count."

"Oh, I would not say that," she replied with a smile before dismounting.

"Do you ever think about anything other than lying with a man?" Margery asked irritably.

Ravyn came around the front of her horse and raised a

brow at her friend. "Let us find you a man tonight so you can rid yourself of your maidenhead and learn the truth for yourself."

Margery's russet-colored eyes quickly lowered to the ground as she adjusted her skirts and smoothed her hand along her sandy blond braid. "Nay."

"I was terrified my first time." Ravyn tied her mount to a post and ran a hand down the mare's neck. "You need to find the right man. Someone who knows what he is doing, and who will make sure you feel pleasure, as well."

"Enough," Margery said and turned her back to Ravyn.

She came up alongside her friend. "Stop being a prig. I have seen the way you look at men. There is nothing wrong with being curious about your body."

Margery nervously licked her lips before shooting her a glance. "I am not like you, Ravyn. You have always been confident in yourself and your abilities. Men recognize that and flock to you."

"They come to me because I let them know I am interested," she said with a laugh. "And once you have a taste of pleasure, you will, as well."

"I want what Leoma and Braith have."

Ravyn ignored the small pain in her heart at the mention of love. She didn't wish for such things because she knew it would never find her. "Then I wish you luck."

"You speak as if you do not want that."

She clasped Margery's hand and gave it a squeeze before releasing her and facing the village. "I only want one thing."

"Revenge."

"Justice," Ravyn corrected.

Margery shrugged. "Same difference."

"You came to Edra as a baby without any knowledge of

your family, so do not think to tell me there is no difference," Ravyn declared as she walked past her.

She didn't slow until she came to the tavern. If there was one place to learn what was going on in a village, it was a pub. Ravyn nodded to the serving girl as she entered and took a seat.

The establishment was full with patrons. The noise that bordered on chaos might put some off, but she found it comforting. It reminded her of home, of her large family before it had all been taken away.

"I apologize," Margery said as she stood beside the table.

Ravyn motioned to the vacant chair. She'd been in a foul mood for the past two weeks, though she couldn't explain why. It wasn't Margery's fault that she didn't understand the need for justice. Though, honestly, few at the abbey could.

They were the lucky ones.

Then again, Ravyn knew how fortunate she was to have been found by Radnar and Edra. The witch and her knight took in many homeless and abandoned children. The abbey deep within the forest was hidden by Edra's magic, and for years, it was the only place Ravyn felt safe.

With Radnar's help, Ravyn turned that fear into strength. He'd offered to train her to be a Hunter. At first, the thought of going after witches from the Coven terrified Ravyn, but the more she trained, the less afraid she became.

The day she'd helped track down a witch from the Coven was the dawn of a new era for Ravyn. She recognized the power she wielded, and she knew then that she could find the witch responsible for ruining her life—and finally get justice for her family.

Ravyn might not have magic of her own, but that didn't stop her. She was a skilled Hunter, the best at the abbey. Each arrow she used with her specialized crossbow was imbued with Edra's magic to help kill witches.

Because it took more than a weapon to bring them down. It took magic.

It was one reason everyone feared witches. They were nearly impossible to kill. It was also why the Hunters were needed. Someone had to bring the Coven under control. Because whatever it was they wanted couldn't be good.

Leoma and Braith had stumbled upon the Blood Skull, the head of the very first witch. Braith was now the Warden of the skull.

While they knew very little of what the relic could do, it had brought Braith back from the dead. And the Coven wanted it. That was enough for Ravyn to want to keep it away from them, regardless of whether the skull could help the Hunters or not.

Ravyn pulled herself from thoughts of the past and focused on the conversations around her. She glanced at Margery to find her friend talking. While Margery was a good Hunter, she worried about everything and wasn't always comfortable in her role.

No one was forced to become a Hunter. It was their choice. Anyone could stay at the abbey, but they had to pull their weight. Whether it was being a Hunter, forging weapons, training others, or caring for those who sought shelter, there was always work to be done.

After ordering drinks and food, Ravyn sat back, nodding as Margery continued to talk. But she wasn't listening. Her attention was on the others around her.

It took her less than a minute to learn that the lord of the keep near them, a John Atwood, had gone back on his word to the neighboring baron, Randall Bryce, over a plot of land between their two estates. Now the two were at war.

And the battle was not going well for Randall. In fact, based on the talk, it appeared that after only half a day, John's force had somehow annihilated Randall's.

Ravyn smiled at those around her. She flirted with one man while listening to the conversation at another table. It was a skill she'd learned from Edra, and it had saved her life multiple times. A discussion caught her attention, and she stopped flirting.

"Did ye see Carac in here earlier?" The man shook his head. "What kind of man leaves his army to come in here for a drink?"

What kind indeed, Ravyn wondered.

"His army was the clear victor," another retorted. "Without a single one of 'em dying."

This Carac was either an imbecile who happened to have capable men—which wasn't likely—or he knew he would win so didn't bother to stay around and watch.

"The summons that took him from his drink did not please him," someone said with a smirk.

Another man said, "He will return. He always does."

The table laughed, but Ravyn knew she needed to find this Carac. He could lead her to the witch.

"Careful," Margery murmured before their food was delivered.

Once the server walked away, Ravyn slid her gaze to Margery. "What is your meaning?"

"I heard their discussion, as well. Everyone in here did. You think Carac is working with a witch."

Ravyn tore off a piece of the bread and nodded. "Did you miss the part where they said the army won without a man being killed?"

"Aye."

"Magic has to be involved."

Margery nodded slowly. "I honestly hoped you were wrong."

"The blond witch was seen near here, and now this news. Without a doubt, we have her."

"You just need to find her. She's likely in the castle with Atwood."

Ravyn grinned. "I came prepared for that."

Margery looked at the ceiling as if praying for patience. "Pléase tell me I get to play your maid. I much prefer that role."

"What? You're not up to seduction?" Ravyn teased.

"I do think I hate you sometimes."

Ravyn laughed and took a bite of the stew. "You would not turn your nose up so quickly if you would let me find you a man."

"How many have you taken to your bed?" Margery asked in a whisper.

"Not nearly as many as you believe I have. Most times, I merely flirt and show a bit of cleavage. I have no idea why men seem to lose their senses when they see breasts, but it is a fact that it loosens their tongues and addles their minds."

Margery glanced down at her flat chest. "I will not be able to do the same."

"Sure you will. It is not about what assets you do or do not possess. It is how you hold yourself, the way you talk, and how you look at them. They need to believe that you have eyes for no one else, nor will you ever."

A frown marred Margery's brow. "So, you lie."

"You call it a lie, I call it a skill to gain information. Not only do I use my crossbow, but I also use my body. I do not like harming anyone—unless they are witches. Yet there are those out there who protect the Coven. I can either make them bleed or give them false hope that I will share my body."

Margery swallowed. "I wanted to be a Hunter."

"But your heart is not in it." Ravyn had known for a long time. It was time for her friend to realize it, as well.

Margery shook her head and pushed away her platter of food. "I do not have the drive you or even Leoma have."

"You know how to fight, and I can use someone watching my back. Once we return to the abbey, you can decide what to do."

"I will always have your back."

Ravyn smiled and looked away, only to find a man staring at Margery. She tapped her foot against Margery's. "You have an admirer. Are you sure you wish to remain untouched?"

"Find me a skilled man, and I might rethink it," Margery replied with a grin.

Ravyn laughed, accepting the challenge. "By the time we return to the others, you will be a woman in all ways."

"You assume a man would want me."

"Look around," Ravyn told her. "Men are looking at you."

Margery shot her a hard look. "Nay, my dear friend. They look longingly at you."

Ravyn sat back and ignored everyone in the pub. She took a drink and slowly lowered the tankard of ale. "I was very much like you once."

"You were never like me," Margery said with a shake of her head.

"You were still a babe, but I would hardly leave my chamber. Edra would spend hours coaxing me into the sunshine. It took months before I felt that I could walk about the abbey safely. I feared everything."

Margery folded her hands in her lap. "Because of what happened to your family."

"You might not have suffered such a tragedy, but that does

not make your anxiety any less genuine. You know what we fight. You have seen them."

"And what they can do."

Ravyn drew in a deep breath. "Not all witches are evil. Edra taught us that, but any witch who joins the Coven strengthens their power. We cannot sit idly by and wait to see what happens."

Margery's lips twisted. "I was hiding behind the door when you gave that argument to Edra and Radnar a few days ago. While you have a point, we both know why you came here. And so does Edra."

"Justice." Ravyn touched the inside of her left wrist.

Beneath the sleeve of her gown was the image of a Norse rune. She'd had Asa tattoo it onto her skin after her first training lesson.

"Radnar's right. Killing this witch will not return your family."

Ravyn dropped her hand and met Margery's russet gaze. "I'm a Hunter. I take out any of the Coven, so no other innocents are harmed. The justice I seek is not only for my family but also for all the other families who do not have a voice."

3

He was going to kill someone. With every step Carac took toward the keep, his fury festered and escalated until it was all he could think about.

The last time he'd encountered such rage was when he learned what his uncle had done to his younger brother. The result hadn't been pretty, but it shaped the man he was today.

Carac didn't like the way the anger made him feel as if he weren't in control, but there was no getting away from it this time. He was right in the middle of whatever this mess was, and he would have to be careful how he stepped through it lest the damage fall to his friends or his knights.

His men cheered as he made his way up the steps. Carac paused and turned to look at them. He wanted to silence them, but all they knew was that they had won the day. So, he lifted a hand in a wave before turning and entering the castle. He didn't have the heart to tell them that he had nothing to do with their victory, mainly because he didn't yet have an answer for what was going on.

But he planned to get one.

He strode into the solar where John inspected a map he had unrolled on a table. Carac took a few moments in an attempt to calm himself. Losing his temper would gain him nothing.

Without looking up, John said, "Great battle today. Too bad you left before you saw the finish."

Carac rested one hand on the hilt of his sword and fisted the other at his side as he looked up and slowly released a breath to get some semblance of control over his mounting fury.

"I had no idea of the riches Randall had on his land. I cannot wait to begin reaping those rewards."

Carac narrowed his gaze. Whatever little control he'd acquired in those few moments snapped. "Your honor is in tatters."

John slowly straightened and looked at him. "I imagine no one said such a thing to Charlemagne."

"I imagine that's because Charlemagne did not give his word and go back on it," Carac retorted.

John's nostrils flared, an indication of his mounting anger. "Your name is tied to a great victory."

"And that sickens me." He wasn't worried about John attacking him because the lord barely knew how to handle a sword, let alone fight.

"I do not understand you, Carac. You have spent your entire life earning your reputation. This will only increase that tenfold. You should be thanking me."

Carac's hold on his sword tightened. "It is a lie."

"A lie?" John asked with a bark of laughter.

"I've been in many battles, and not once have my men come away unscathed."

John's smile was smug and much too confident. "They do if you know the right person."

"Meaning?" Carac realized that Sybbyl was not in the solar, which was odd since she never strayed far from John.

"Nothing for you to be concerned with. You fulfilled your task."

If he didn't know better, Carac would think his army had merely been there for the sake of appearances and nothing more. Carac could have given a young girl a sword, and she could have achieved the same outcome.

Though he wasn't sure why he was so confident of his conclusions. Having witnessed and been involved in numerous battles—places where there was a disastrous amount of bloodshed, and others with hardly any—he knew there was something else at work here. But his mind couldn't grasp what it could be.

"Are you dismissing me?" In many ways, Carac hoped that was the case. Another part of him knew he couldn't leave just yet.

John turned back to the map. "I think it better if you remain for the time being. The fee I paid you was for a fortnight."

That gave Carac just over twelve days to figure out what was going on. "Where is Lord Randall?"

"Sybbyl is with him now," John replied as he bent to look at something on the map. "I do not want him running off or thinking to take his own life before I have everything I need."

"As you wish." Carac turned and was about to walk out when John's voice stopped him.

"I summoned you for a reason."

Anger spiked in him, and Simon's urging about telling John who he was briefly ran through his mind. But Carac knew there would be a better opportunity.

He faced John and waited. Minutes passed as John continued to examine something on the map. Patience was usually a skill Carac mastered easily, but it was all he could do not to yank the map from the table and throw it into the fire.

Finally, John straightened. "You are a knight, Carac. A well-known one at that, but you do not know your place. Never again speak to me as if your rank is equal to mine. And never again leave my side in battle."

It would be so satisfying to tell the prick just who he really was, but Carac somehow held his tongue. He knew better than to respond to anything when he was furious.

"I think perhaps I will return your coin and take my men and leave," Carac replied in a soft tone.

John's head cocked to the side. "Do you really think you could?"

"Without a doubt. I already have requests from three other lords. You do not need my men any longer. Nor, I suspect, did you ever."

John clasped his hands before him, the large ruby on his left pinky flashing. "I do believe I struck a nerve."

"I will have the coin in your hands forthwith, minus the costs for today." Carac hid his smile when John's gaze narrowed.

"Wait," John said before Carac could turn to leave.

Carac heard approaching footsteps behind him as John dropped his hands and looked over Carac's shoulder.

A servant appeared and bowed to John before turning to him. "For you, Sir Carac."

Carac took the missive and unrolled it. He was pleasantly surprised to find a note from Braith. It had been almost two years since he last saw his friend, and Carac had yet to pay his respects to Braith over the loss of his nephew.

He rolled up the missive and raised his gaze to John. "Did you have something else you wished to say?"

"Who is that from?" John asked instead.

Carac clasped his hands behind his back. "As you said, I am well known. I am also sought after because my army is one of the best."

John began to pace while nervously fisting his hands. "I am not supposed to tell anyone."

"If the order came from the king, then you should obey it."

"Of course it did not come from the king," John snapped.

Intrigued, Carac waited.

Finally, John stopped and faced him. His chest expanded as he huffed out a breath. "While I am wealthy, my status never equaled that of Randall's. Rank is everything, as you know."

"So you are jealous."

John made a face. "It does not matter where you are in life, you always look to those ahead of you and covet what they have."

"Is that why you dishonored yourself?"

John slammed his hand on the table. "I am after power!"

"How much more of this do you think can occur and have the king look the other way?" Carac questioned.

John sliced his hand through the air. "Not even the king will stand in my way."

Worry slivered its way through Carac. "Careful with your words, my lord."

John's brown eyes met his before he burst into laughter. "Oh, Carac, if you only knew the power within my reach. It could be within yours, as well, but you should show Sybbyl more respect."

Now that got his attention. "Lady Sybbyl? What does she have to do with anything?"

"Everything," John said in a whisper.

Before Carac could open his mouth, another servant entered the solar. "My lord, you have a guest."

John came up beside Carac and put a hand on his shoulder. "Stay and watch what happens over the course of the next few days. I will put in a good word for you with Sybbyl, as well. Hopefully, she will allow me to tell you the rest of it."

Carac turned and watched as John walked out. When he heard a feminine voice, he made his way into the great hall and stared transfixed at the beauty clad in a deep blue cloak curtsying to John.

"A pleasure to meet you, Lady Ravyn," John said and lifted the back of her hand to kiss it.

Ravyn straightened and dropped the hood of her cloak, showing a wealth of glossy, midnight hair. A single gold chain sat atop her head and rested on her forehead.

Large eyes a deep, tawny color slid to him. The mesmerizing bronze orbs ensnared him. There was fire in her gaze, carefully hidden, but there for anyone who looked closely enough.

And he was looking.

Her oval face was something straight out of his dreams. Smooth, unblemished skin except for a mole near the left corner of her mouth. He nearly missed it as he gawked like a randy lad at her full lips.

She stood demurely, her chin lowered just enough to give the illusion of meekness, but Carac wasn't fooled. In fact, he was utterly intrigued.

Because along with the fire he glimpsed in her gaze, he also saw strength and wildness.

His body heated at the thought.

"I do apologize for arriving unannounced, but this seemed the safest place with the war that rages. I have already taken a great chance by traveling with only my maid," she said.

Carac barely held back his groan at the sound of her sexy voice. The woman was a walking seduction.

"You are more than welcome," John stated with a wide smile.

Carac saw the way John gazed at her with lust. With his ire already up, Carac needed little to spur him into action. He took a step toward John when Ravyn's gaze returned to him.

Whatever he had been about to do was forgotten as he became lost in her eyes. His anger was tempered as if doused by her presence.

She shifted toward him, her cloak falling open enough for him to spot the hilt of a dagger. He would keep that to himself since she was going to such extremes to hide it.

"Ah," John said, his displeasure at seeing Carac evident in his tone and the set of his jaw. "Lady Ravyn, let me introduce Sir Carac."

"A pleasure," he said as he bowed over her hand.

Her lips curved ever so slightly. "Are you the one I hear is responsible for crushing the army that invaded Lord John?"

Carac released her hand and straightened as he drew in a deep breath. He glanced at John, but refused to take credit for what happened on the battlefield. "I do lead the army that is here at the lord's request."

"Then I suppose I should say congratulations," she replied.

The anger Carac experienced earlier came back with a vengeance. "No one is ever really a victor in war, my lady. Good men died today fighting for their lord. Whatever side they were on, it is a great loss."

"Carac, really," John said, his lips compressing.

Ravyn stepped toward Carac and bowed her head. "I agree with you, Sir Carac. It is a loss indeed. There are families grieving right now."

There was something in her words that caught Carac's

attention. He saw the honesty in her eyes, and after a few moments, the glimpse of frankness in her gaze was gone, as if a wall were erected as she turned to John with a smile.

Carac didn't hear the words that were exchanged as he tried to figure her out. There was something not quite right with Ravyn. While she certainly dressed and acted the part of a lady, she was hiding something. Of that he was certain.

Because he, himself, hid something important, he was able to recognize it in others.

"My word," John whispered as he came to stand beside Carac when a servant walked Ravyn and her maid up the stairs. "She is something."

"It is not right that she is traveling alone," Carac pointed out.

John shrugged, seemingly indifferent. "It gives me reason to help her. I do need to continue my line. Perhaps it is time I think of taking a wife."

For some reason, that statement made Carac want to ram his fist into John's nose.

4

"You are playing with fire," Margery admonished in a whisper once they were alone in their chamber.

Ravyn faced her friend. "The only way we're going to get answers is to be in the thick of it."

"I know." Margery let out a long sigh and squatted next to the hearth to build a fire. "I just have a bad feeling about this."

She put her hand on Margery's shoulders. "We are Hunters. This is what we do."

"You are not telling me anything I do not already know," Margery said as she turned her head to look at Ravyn. "But I cannot shake this feeling within me."

"I suspect we will only be here a day. The witch is here. I'm sure of it. Once I find her, then I will take care of things."

Margery shook her head as the flames caught and began to devour the wood. "And if she is not here?"

"Then our hunt continues," Ravyn said with a shrug. "Either way, we are only here for a night."

Margery stood and dusted off her hands. "I suppose you better get to work, then."

She grinned when Margery winked. "See—"

"What I can find out from the servants," Margery interrupted with a grin. "Aye, I know."

Ravyn could do this mission alone, but she was glad to have a friend with her. It was easier to do such work when there was someone watching your back, someone to confide in. But Margery's anxiety worried her.

After Margery left, Ravyn remained in the chamber for another few moments, thinking over her friend's words. It was a dangerous game she played. But it was the same for every Hunter on every hunt.

Ravyn knew in her bones that the witch she sought was near. She couldn't explain why. It was just a feeling that had led her straight to this location. Of course, the rumors of a pretty blonde being seen right before horrible deaths occurred also helped.

Ravyn knew that in order for her to find the witch, she had to mingle with those below. Talking instead of fighting. Thankfully, she was good at both.

She exited the chamber and made her way down to the great hall. As she descended the stairs, she saw Carac shake his head in irritation as he walked away from John. The knight appeared to have no affinity for the lord. It was obvious by the way the two looked at each other that the feeling was mutual.

Why then was Carac here? And why had John brought him there? More importantly, did it tie in to the witch?

While at the tavern, Ravyn had discovered a great deal about Lord John. Most people didn't have anything negative to say about him. He was known to be fair, if not ambitious. His recent dishonor with Lord Randall shocked everyone enough that it was all they could talk about.

Which made learning about the plot of land that led to the

battle easy. It had also been fairly simple to discover that Randall Bryce was far wealthier than John Atwood. And more powerful.

Because John acted so out of character, it was best to look at those around the person in question. Upon her arrival at the castle, Ravyn saw how the army celebrated their victory. They either didn't care what took place, or they had no knowledge of it.

She was betting on the latter.

The servants seemed on edge. Their gazes darted about, and any little sound made them jump. That could be because of John's deceitfulness. It seemed the correct choice, but until Margery returned with a report, Ravyn would keep that verdict up in the air.

As for Carac, the knight's words about war and death made it appear as if he didn't agree with the battle earlier. The way John rolled his eyes showed the line in the sand that had been drawn between the two men.

If a witch were helping John, getting close to him would be difficult since the woman would be suspicious of anyone new. But Carac was another matter altogether.

Ravyn stilled, waiting for John to walk away before she continued down the stairs. Once at the bottom, she went out the door to search for the handsome knight.

Talking, even flirting, with Carac would not be difficult. She stood at the top of the steps and let her gaze move over those in the bailey until she found him.

He was easy to spot with his blond hair that shone as brightly as the sun. It hung to his neck, windblown and in disarray, something that she somehow found endearing.

She grinned when he raked a hand through the thick length as he spoke with one of his men. He stood straight and tall, as if carrying the heft of an army on his shoulders weighed no more than her cloak.

His face had the look of a man who saw and experienced much. It showed in the laugh lines around his eyes and the creases of worry on his forehead. The two-day growth of a beard only showcased his strong jawline and rugged features.

By the small crook in his nose, it had been broken at least once. The scar on the right side of his neck was most likely only one of many hidden beneath his fine leather tunic. At first glance, the garment looked to be modest, but upon closer inspection when she met him, she had noticed the expert craftsmanship and the intricate design around the neck, shoulders, and hem.

She let her gaze wander from his broad shoulders to the strap around his narrow hips that held his sword then to his black boots.

When she raised her eyes, his green depths were locked on her. For just an instant, her stomach fluttered, but she quickly halted the seeds of desire that attempted to sprout.

It didn't matter that his eyes reminded her of a stormy sea churning violently with so many different shades of green that she lost count. She didn't care that his blatant interest caused her pulse to quicken.

Or so she tried to tell herself.

Carac didn't take his eyes from her as he said something to one of his men before making his way to her. Ravyn tamped down the quell of nervousness that rose the closer he got.

"My lady," he said, stopping below her and bracing a foot on a step above him. "I thought you would be resting after your journey. If you are here to make sure the gate is guarded, you have no cause to be frightened of Lord Bryce coming here."

She looked out through the gate to the road beyond. He

spoke with such deference that she wondered how he would react to seeing her in her normal attire instead of the gown. "I am sorry to disappoint you, Sir Carac, but I am not one to be easily alarmed."

"That does not disappoint me."

Her gaze jerked to him as her pulse quickened. She searched his face but saw only truth reflected there. "Are you not like other men who believe women should be shielded, unable to make decisions on their own?"

One side of his mouth lifted in a grin. "I can see that you are a woman who decides things on her own. And, nay, my lady, I am not one of those men."

"That pleases me," she said before smiling. It pleased her tremendously.

"If you do not scare easily, what brings you here, knowing there is conflict?"

She glanced down, her mind immediately conjuring Carac as he might look in armor riding into battle with his sword raised. "I am simply prudent. I have no wish to die, and I learned the roads may not be safe."

"I commend you for taking action, though I do have to wonder why you did not travel with, at the very least, a male servant for protection."

Ravyn didn't want to like Carac, but she appreciated how he attempted to gain information without coming right out and asking. "You think that is unwise."

"You did point out the dangers. You never know what awaits you on the roads."

"I am capable."

"If you can use the dagger at your waist or the crossbow I saw attached to your saddle before your horse was led into the stables, aye, I would say you are."

She raised a brow. Perhaps she'd underestimated Carac.

Instead of admonishing her belief that she could defend herself, he was asking more. How...curious.

He grinned, a challenge in his eyes. "Afraid to respond?"

"What would you say if I told you I could use both weapons?"

"I would say it is good that you can defend yourself. Then I would ask who taught you such things?"

Ravyn turned her head away as she thought of Radnar. "My childhood was unusual. I was fascinated with the weapons the knights around me used. One day, I picked up a bow." She swung her gaze back to Carac. "One of them told me that if I were going to hold it, I'd better know how to use it."

"They taught you?" he asked, surprise evident in his voice.

She nodded, smiling as she remembered that first day of training. "With any weapon I wanted."

"And your father? He approved of this?"

Her smile died. "My father was killed. Murdered. Along with my mother and siblings."

"My apologies," Carac said, a sincere frown furrowing his brow.

She swallowed and forced a smile. "It was a very long time ago."

"But you still carry the pain."

Her gaze dropped to the ground as she heard the distant screams of her sisters in her mind. "Always." After a moment, she pulled herself from the past and looked back at Carac. "Forgive me. Sometimes, the memories pull me along whether I want to go or not."

"There is no need to apologize. I am well acquainted with how the past keeps a firm hold on a person." He looked around before his head swiveled back to her. "Would you like to stretch your legs?"

"I would."

He turned and waited for her to come alongside him before continuing down the stairs. Ravyn observed how Carac's men greeted him with warmth and respect, their admiration obvious. They genuinely liked him, which spoke highly of his character.

Once they'd made it through the men who bowed and smiled at her, Ravyn looked at Carac and said, "I just learned a great deal about you."

"Oh?" he asked, brows raised.

"I have seen men who attempt to gain the respect you have with yours. It appears to come easily to you."

"Perhaps because I began as just a lowly squire and earned what I have now. I was exactly where they are," he explained. "Nor do I ask them to do anything I, myself, would not do."

She eyed him skeptically. "Really?"

"Aye," he said with a nod.

"It is just that you talk to Lord John as if you are of equal rank."

Carac's silence was intriguing. Did he have a secret? Ravyn inwardly laughed. Everyone had secrets, but it appeared as if she'd somehow found Carac's.

"This is my first time meeting Lord John," she said when he remained silent. "All anyone can talk about in the village is how his honor is now in question. I might have gone to Lord Bryce had he not been defeated today."

"It was not a fair fight."

Ravyn nearly tripped over her feet at his words. She had been hoping for just such an admission, but she hadn't expected to get it so soon. "How do you mean?"

"Never mind." Carac halted and faced her. "Now it is my turn to apologize. I should not have spoken so candidly."

"Do you owe your allegiance to Randall?"

Carac's gaze narrowed. "Nay."

"Then you have done nothing wrong."

His brow furrowed as his head tilted slightly. "I beg to differ. My reputation is built on honor. I always do what I say I will. I have amassed my army because my men know I will treat them fairly. I am sought after by lords from many countries to fight for them because they know I will not let them down. In all my years, I have learned many secrets and have never shared a single one."

"I do believe you are one in a million, Sir Carac."

His chest expanded as he drew in a breath. "I doubt that."

"Why do you do this? For coin? Because you like war?"

He looked away and rested a hand on the hilt of his sword. "The money is good, I will not lie. I keep a small portion and divvy the rest up among my men. They are paid well and fed regularly." His gaze slid back to her. "War is a way of life. There will always be someone trying to gain the upper hand on someone else. Do I like battle? Nay. But I am good at it. At least that is what got me my army. Nowadays, I merely have to arrive on a battlefield and, most times, my opponent surrenders before a drop of blood has been spilled."

"And today?" she asked. "I heard in the village that none of your men were even injured, much less killed."

Carac shook his head, his lips compressing. "I have no explanation for today."

She wanted to believe that he didn't have a hand in it, but until she saw the witch and found out if magic were involved, she couldn't determine anything with any certainty.

"What will become of Lord Randall?" she asked.

"I wish I knew. John told me that Lady Sybbyl is with him."

Ravyn's attention snagged on the name. "Lady Sybbyl?"

"Another guest at the keep."

"And she went alone to see Randall?"

Carac's lips twisted. "Your face looks as confused as I'm sure mine did when I learned the news."

"It is just...." She trailed off, at a loss for words.

"Odd?" Carac supplied with a small laugh. "It certainly is."

5

Northern Isles of Scotland
Blackglade

The sea was calm, the water barely rippling at the surface. The salt hung heavily in the air as the softest whisper of a breeze brushed against her skin.

Malene drew in a deep breath as she stood at the top of her tower and gazed out at the cloudless sky that met the dark waters of the sea on the horizon.

The pillars around her were curved inward now. She looked down at her palms and the faint blue light that radiated from each. The power within her was growing rapidly. She could feel it, though she had no control over it. At least not yet.

She let her hands drop to her sides. As the Lady of the Varroki, she was meant to lead those who were now her people. She hadn't asked for—nor wanted—this role. The magic had chosen her. It was a destiny she couldn't run from.

To think she had been living her life unknowing what awaited her. Then Armir found her.

Fierce, stern Armir. He was never far. Even now, she felt him standing behind her, waiting and watching. Her silent sentry.

He kept his thoughts to himself, only sharing with her when she forced the issue. Not that she could blame him. She kept many things from him, as well. Like her desire to be anywhere but Blackglade, to be anyone *but* the Lady.

She didn't want the power or the obligation. All she yearned for was a husband who loved her and children to fill her home. A simple dream.

But one that would never be hers.

In truth, Armir should be leader of the Varroki. The band of witches who hid on a northern island off the coast of Scotland was immensely powerful. Their ancestors were both Vikings and Celts—two formidable tribes.

Both steeped in magic.

The Varroki and their calling to keeping witches in line was all Armir cared about. If only the Lady of the Varroki could be a Lord.

If only the power within her had chosen Armir.

If only...

She felt Armir move closer, stopping behind her and just over her right shoulder. So close, she could feel his warmth. For an instant, she wanted to lean back against him and pretend that she wasn't shouldering a great responsibility that she wanted no part of.

He wouldn't refuse her. He might even put his hands on her to hold her—though it was forbidden.

But he *had* touched her. In fact, he'd carried her twice that she knew of from the top of the tower to her chambers when the power rushed through her so fast that she passed out.

"Dark clouds are on the horizon," he said.

She moved her gaze until she spotted them. "There is always a storm."

"You did not sleep last night."

There was little about her life that Armir didn't know. The only thing she could really keep from him was her thoughts as well as her dreams—and nightmares.

"It is why you came up here before dawn," he finished.

She had been standing atop the tower for hours. Some of it was because what she'd seen in her dreams was disturbing, but it was also time where she could forget the role she had in things and just be herself.

"Do you wish to tell me what troubles you so?" Armir asked.

Malene turned to him. Every time she saw him, she was arrested by his handsomeness. With his full bottom lip, prominent cheekbones, and square jaw, he was more than gorgeous. He was striking.

Eyes of the palest green watched her with the intensity of a hawk. His golden blond hair was long and held back at the top of his head in a queue and bound every three inches with a leather strip. The sides of his head were shaved to show off his tattoos.

She had the urge to run her fingers along one, but she kept her hands to herself. Armir was there to make sure she continued to do her duty as Lady.

"The First Witch went to great lengths to ensure that her bones were scattered to the wind. For thousands of years, not a single fragment was found," Malene said. "Until Braith located the Blood Skull."

Armir's lips thinned for a moment. "I admit, the Blood

Skull is a powerful weapon, but we know it chose its Warden. The Coven cannot get their hands on it now. I believe that even if they had, it would not have worked for them. It was meant for Braith."

Malene pulled a strand of flaxen hair from her lashes. "No one should have found the skull."

"That cannot be undone now. What is it that worries you so?"

She shot him a hard look. "The Coven. It is always the Coven. Their strength is increasing, Armir. I can sense it like a great blanket falling over the world, blocking out all light."

"They often gain power, but it does not last long. The past has proven that. *We* ensure that."

How she wished he was right, but she knew this time would be different. "Instead of waiting for witches to find them, the Coven is locating the women themselves and forcing them to join the Coven or die."

Armir's gaze briefly looked to the sea. "I am aware."

"What if they find out about us? What if they learn of the warlocks?"

Armir's eyes narrowed. "They will be in for a rude awakening if they try to force any Varroki to join them. Male or female."

It was true, the Varroki were powerful. So formidable, in fact, that they had singlehandedly kept the Coven in check for untold generations. But things had changed. And not in favor of the Varroki.

"And now that the Coven knows that the tales of the First Witch are true? If they can find her skull, then they can find the rest of her."

Armir took a step back as if her words had struck him. "Are you saying that you believe the Coven is attempting to resurrect the First Witch?"

"No witch since has been as powerful. She knew it was a possibility. It is why she ordered her bones be separated then distributed and hidden upon her death—so that no one could bring her back."

A gust of wind swirled around Malene, yanking the skirts of her gown around her legs and tugging her hair from her braids. Armir wasn't taking her announcement well, but when she dreamed of the First Witch being brought back to life, neither had she.

"Are you sure?" Armir asked.

She shook her head. "I have no proof other than a dream and a sick feeling. But you have to admit, it sounds exactly like something the Coven would do."

"Aye," he ground out, his face lined with exasperation.

She walked to the other side of the tower to the stairs that led down to her chambers. But she stopped when she reached the steps and gazed down at the cottages and buildings far below her.

Malene waited until Armir was beside her once more before she said, "I am not Varroki."

"You are now."

"But I was not born here," she added. "I have no idea why I was chosen as Lady. I look upon these people and wonder how they can accept me."

One side of Armir's lips lifted in a slight curve of a smile. "Because the magic decided."

"Regardless, I am responsible for these people. What happens to them, happens to me. The Varroki have been a formidable force against rogue witches and the Coven for generations, but we have fewer and fewer warriors like Jarin now."

"You speak of the alliance you wish to have with the Hunters Jarin discovered."

She turned her head to Armir. "Those Hunters are stalking the Coven just as we are. Can you see a reason why we should not join forces?"

"Our warriors have always worked alone."

"Yet Jarin, Leoma, and Braith functioned well together. They triumphed, in fact."

Armir conceded with a nod. "I know well what happened. Jarin is one of our best warriors, and he was impressed with what he learned of the Hunters."

"I wish to meet the witch who is recruiting these Hunters."

Pale green eyes widened. "You cannot bring the witch here." When Malene didn't reply, a deep frown formed on his brow. "The Lady does not leave Blackglade."

She smiled because there was no use arguing with him. But she also didn't need Armir's permission. While it was true the other Ladies hadn't left the tower or even the city, there was nothing saying that she couldn't.

And that's what she was counting on.

In the five years since being brought to Blackglade, she'd read through the extensive library in her chambers. She learned about every Lady before her—how each was chosen, as well as how they died.

Most were more than happy at their position, but there were others, like her, who strained against the bonds that the power brought them.

But there was another who fell in love with her commander. The two had run away together. Unfortunately, there was no happy ending for the couple. Both were killed by Varroki warriors. The commander for leaving his post and daring to touch the Lady, and the Lady for refusing the mantle of her position.

It was why Armir went to such lengths to make sure he

kept his distance from her at all times. But what few understood was how lonely her position was.

Malene could leave the tower and walk among the streets of the city, but she was held in such reverence that she wouldn't be able to have a real conversation with anyone. Which was why she remained at the tower.

With only Armir as company.

It was no wonder that she'd come to long for his touch, to think of him as more than her commander. But she also knew nothing would ever come of it. Armir was too invested in his position and what the Varroki stood for.

There was nothing—not even love—that would make Armir forget his vows to his people.

Not that she loved him. But loneliness could do strange things to a person. Add that to the isolation and not even so much as a simple touch on her arm, and it was enough to drive someone to insanity.

She had no idea how the other Ladies had done it. However, it explained why few held the position for more than seven years. All died...one way or another.

"Your thoughts take you very far away," Armir said.

She wondered what he would do if she told him that she often thought of jumping from the tower into the sea below. How would he react if she told him that she longed with all her heart for a simple life with a family?

His pale orbs studied her, patiently waiting for a response. Then she realized that he might very well have such yearnings himself.

"Do you have a woman?" she asked.

One blond brow rose in puzzlement. "Nay. My position forbids it."

How could she have forgotten that? "Do you want a wife? Someone to share your life with, I mean?"

His green gaze slid away. "A commander cannot have such thoughts. My life is dedicated to you."

"You mean whoever is Lady," she corrected. "Is it any wonder the Varroki population is declining? The warriors live in solitude, never taking a mate or having children, and then there is the commander. I imagine there are other positions that have the same stipulation."

He gave a nod without looking at her.

"That has to change," she stated before brushing past him to the stairs.

6

W hat was it that kept drawing Carac's attention to Ravyn? She was, without a doubt, an exquisite woman, but it was something else that he couldn't quite put his finger on.

Even after nearly an hour talking with Ravyn as he walked her around the keep earlier hadn't given him a clue. And now, as he held her crossbow inspecting the craftsmanship, he had a suspicion that there was much more to the lady than she allowed to be revealed.

Sounds from the bailey pulled his attention away from the weapon that was as unique as its owner. He set the crossbow near the saddle and gave Ravyn's mare a pat on the neck before walking to the entrance of the stables.

Carac stood in the doorway and watched as Sybbyl rode straight to the steps of the keep where John awaited her, a triumphant smile on her face. John helped her dismount, his hands lingering on Sybbyl's waist.

Carac shifted so that he could see them better and caught Sybbyl lean close and whisper something into John's ear.

Whatever it was made him exceedingly happy as they walked into the keep.

Carac stared at the spot long after they'd departed. While it wasn't odd for those who hired him to keep him in the dark about some of their plans, there was something in the way John and Sybbyl acted that rubbed Carac raw.

Not to mention what had occurred on the battlefield.

"Carac."

He turned at the whisper to find Simon striding into the stable through a back door. The tight way Simon's features were held indicated bad news.

Carac met his friend in the middle of the stable, but Simon continued to pace, his agitation apparent. As was his anger. He waited until Simon eventually halted, his gaze on the ground as he shook his head.

"That bad?" Carac said.

Simon swallowed loudly and raked a hand through his dark locks. "In my years as a knight, I have seen a great many atrocities, but today will forever be etched upon my mind."

For Simon to say such a thing, Carac knew whatever he'd witnessed had to be truly appalling. "Is Lord Randall alive?"

"Barely." Simon lifted his head and took a deep breath before turning his dark eyes to Carac. "You were right to be concerned."

"I think you better start from the beginning."

"The few men who survived this morning's attack abandoned Randall, not that I can blame them. I heard many of them whisper that magic was involved."

Carac frowned. This wasn't the first he'd heard the word. More and more, he heard whispers of magic being used. He never understood why people immediately thought it was supernatural when they saw something they couldn't explain. Although, he had to admit, he might have said the same thing if he were in the place of those other men on the battlefield.

"I had that same look," Simon stated.

Carac's worry grew as his friend's gaze moved away from him as if Simon were caught in the things he had seen at Bryce's castle. "And?" Carac urged.

Simon shook himself and cleared his throat. "It was easy enough to get through the castle gates. Lady Sybbyl brought a large force of John's men with her, but they did not seem to care who came or went."

"John's men?" Carac asked.

"Aye. She ordered them about as if she were their commander, not John."

"If she were John's intended or wife, I might see that happening..."

Simon shrugged as if to say *who knows*. "Once inside the gates, I was able to move about easily. At first, the mood was subdued. Defeat was written on everyone's faces. Then Sybbyl had Randall dragged from his castle and tossed into the middle of the bailey."

Carac crossed his arms over his chest as he listened. "If anyone went to Bryce Castle, it should have been John. Or me. Not a woman."

"Sybbyl either does not seem aware of the rules or does not care. It was evident by the way she treated Randall. He asked that the people inside the castle be allowed to leave unharmed. Sybbyl refused."

Carac's arms dropped to his sides in shock. "What?"

"She told him to get on his knees and beg her. He did. Without hesitation. Her laugh, Carac, it was the most evil thing I have ever heard."

Carac leaned against a pillar and digested Simon's words.

Simon licked his lips. "Sybbyl then asked for the Staff of the Eternal."

"What is that?" Carac demanded.

His friend shrugged. "Apparently, Randall knew, because he said he could not hand it over. Sybbyl responded by killing four of his men."

"She did?" Carac asked. "How?"

Simon hesitated, his eyes on the ground for a long moment. When his gaze lifted to Carac once more, his voice wobbled as he said, "She held her hands out, one over the other. As she drew them apart, a bright blue flame formed. She then pointed to four of the knights, and they were consumed by fire. I still hear their screams of agony."

Carac could only stand mute as he tried to comprehend what it was he heard.

"Someone doused one of the men with water, but it did nothing to extinguish the flames. Women were screaming and rushing about, trying to get away, while knights ran them over in their haste to leave. Then the gates slammed closed. By themselves."

Carac rubbed his temple as his head began to ache with what he knew was truth and what Simon was sharing. If it had been anyone other than his closest friend, Carac wouldn't have believed a single word.

But the reality was etched on Simon's face.

Simon turned to the side and put his hands on his hips. "Sybbyl randomly chose people after that. The smell of burning flesh filled my nostrils as shrieks of fear and cries of pain filled my ears. Even the animals began to scream. Randall begged Sybbyl to stop, but she seemed to be enjoying it. The delight as she picked person after person to die made me sick to my stomach."

Carac didn't want to hear any more, but he didn't have a

choice. He needed this information, though he wasn't quite sure what he could do against a woman who could use blue fire. He wasn't even sure what she was.

"Witch," Simon said. "Some brave soul asked Sybbyl what she was, and she said she was a witch from the Coven. Then she returned her gaze to Randall. She gave him one last chance to hand over the staff or everyone would die."

"He gave it to her," Carac guessed.

Simon dropped his arms to his sides and faced Carac. "He told her where it was. It needs to be dug from the ground. I believe that is the only reason she did not kill him right then."

"Where is Randall now?"

"In his dungeon."

It was Carac's turn to pace as he rolled the information in his head over and over again. Witch. Magic. Could it be real? He halted and swung his gaze to Simon, who was watching him.

"I know what I saw," Simon said. "I know what I heard."

"Aye. I do not doubt you, old friend. Yet this news is incomprehensible."

Simon shrugged one chainmail-clad shoulder. "I believed that as well until a few hours ago."

"What did Sybbyl do with the others in the bailey?"

"They're alive. For now, but I do not believe she did it out of mercy."

Carac snorted loudly. "Most likely she intends to use them to get Randall to do whatever she wants."

"I agree."

Carac glanced at the door. His own men were mixed in with John's. While he wasn't sure who knew about Sybbyl being a witch and who didn't, he wasn't ready to bring his men in on this. Right now, he had to determine who he could trust —if anyone.

"I have seen any number of maneuvers on the battlefield and in life," he said. "I learned how to counter nearly all of them. But this is something that no amount of hours spent training with a weapon can help me defend against."

"Then what do we do?" Simon asked.

Carac shot a reassuring smile to his friend. "We tread very carefully until I decide if we leave or not."

Simon's brow furrowed in confusion. "Leave?"

"I received a missive from Braith today. He said he has something important to discuss with me."

"If Braith says it is important, then you should go."

Carac blew out a harsh breath. "That was my intention until you returned with this news."

"We cannot leave, Carac. These people are defenseless against Sybbyl."

"So are we, old friend. I daresay, none of our shields will stand a chance against her."

Simon's lips twisted ruefully. "She killed children today. Innocents, who just happened to be in her line of fire."

"You did not mention the children before."

Simon shrugged and turned away, but Carac knew that Simon had made his decision to fight Sybbyl and John the moment he saw a child murdered. It brought up memories Simon struggled with every day.

"The past still has a hold of you," Carac said as he came to stand beside his friend.

Simon swallowed, nodding. "I thought it was buried until...."

"I know." Carac put a hand on his friend's shoulder for comfort. Even though it had been ten years since mercenaries riding through his village had trampled Simon's son, his heart had never fully healed from it. Or his wife taking her own life.

Simon sniffed and lifted his head. "There has to be some way to fight Sybbyl. Everything can be killed."

"That it can, but before we attempt to lop off her head, we need to learn more. Sybbyl might not be the only witch here."

"What do you mean?"

"A woman arrived today. She is hiding something, I'm sure of it."

Simon raised a brow. "All women hide things."

Carac strode to the stall were Ravyn's horse was munching on hay. He pointed at the crossbow next to the saddle hanging on the stable wall. "She also carries a dagger with her."

"Sybbyl has no weapons," Simon pointed out.

"Perhaps Ravyn is not as skilled with magic."

Simon inspected the crossbow closely, lifting it to peer at it from all angles. "It was made with a skilled hand. It is much smaller than those our men use, which means that this one was made specifically for a woman. There are also additions to it I have never seen before. The markings etched on the handle look Celtic."

Carac had missed those. He took the weapon from Simon to see for himself. The symbols were small and meticulously carved with a steady hand. There was something about them that brought about a sense of calm, though he couldn't begin to understand why.

"What do you know of the new arrival?" Simon asked.

Carac replaced the weapon. "Her name is Lady Ravyn. She claims to be with her maid on the way to her uncle."

"You do not believe her?"

"I know she is hiding something, but *what*, I cannot be sure as yet."

Simon ran a hand along the crossbow. "I am interested in meeting anyone with such a weapon. Can she use it?"

"She claims she can."

"To travel alone with just her maid is dangerous."

Carac nodded slowly. "Aye. However, she gives the impression that she can take care of herself."

"So we need to determine if Lady Ravyn is here to help Sybbyl or not. It could merely be a coincidence that she arrived today."

Carac lifted one shoulder in a shrug. "It could be something as simple. She said she would have gone to Lord Bryce's, but she heard in the village what had happened with the battle."

"She is cautious," Simon said. "Good."

"Or a skilled liar."

Simon met his gaze, staring for a long moment. "Now who is letting the past hold them?"

"It was a hard lesson I had to learn twice, but learn it I did."

"That is all well and good, but what about Lady Sybbyl?"

Carac stopped short of rolling his eyes. "We need to keep our distance. I do not want her discovering that we know what happened at Bryce Castle. I am dining with them this evening. Hopefully, I can discover something then."

"What about Braith?"

Damn. Carac had forgotten about his friend's request. "I will send him a message letting him know that I will come as soon as I am able."

"Carac, you need to be careful with Sybbyl."

"I need to be on guard around Sybbyl, John, John's men, and Lady Ravyn. At this point, I trust no one but you."

Simon ran a hand over his jaw. "At least your men are stationed outside the castle walls."

"They spar and mingle with John's men as they did this afternoon."

"That was after the battle. I can put them on drills tomorrow."

Carac gave a nod of agreement. "Post extra guards, as well. I will return to camp tonight."

"If you do not, I will be back looking for you."

Carac laughed, but it was forced. He had never been in such a situation before, and in truth, he had no idea what he was doing.

But, somehow, he knew he might find some answers with Ravyn.

Or did he just want to be around her?

7

Impatience burned with a blaze as consuming as the sun. When Ravyn spotted the woman riding ahead of six men into the bailey, she knew it was the witch. If only Ravyn could see her face, but the hood of the cloak was pulled up, preventing even a glimpse of the witch's hair.

"Is it the witch?" Margery asked from her spot beside her.

Ravyn shrugged, trying not to let her frustration get the best of her. "I cannot tell."

"You will at supper once you get near her."

"Aye." That's usually how it happened unless a Hunter saw the witch in action. There was just something about a witch that Ravyn could detect if she were close enough.

Margery swung her head toward Ravyn. "It would have been better to know before you sit at the same table with her."

"I will not launch myself at her, if that is what you're worried about." Ravyn remained at the window in an attempt to see more of the woman.

"It is not too late for us to leave. You can beg off this

evening by saying you are exhausted from travel. I can bring food to you. Then, we can leave at first light."

Ravyn knew Margery was trying to give her an out, and she loved her friend all the more for it. "I have come this far. I will not leave now."

"Is there nothing I can say to change your mind?"

She put her back to the window. "Nothing."

"After what we learned in the village about the battle, we can deduce that a witch is definitely helping Lord John. And I suspect it is for something other than kindness. Whether the woman who just came through the gates is the witch, I do not know yet. But I will find her. No witch in the Coven does anything without a reason. She most likely wants something, and I will ferret out what that is."

"Carefully," Margery urged.

Ravyn gave her a flat look. "I am the best Hunter for a reason. You do not have to keep telling me to be careful."

"Of course, I do. Never have you gotten so close to a witch who could be the one that killed your family."

"I have always hunted her. The Fates finally decided to let me find her."

Margery raised both brows as she held out her hands. "Exactly. After all these years, you might have the one responsible. Without a doubt, you are the best Hunter we have, but when it comes to your family, you are blinded by your vendetta."

"I have no interest in dying." She smiled at Margery. "I do not want to just take down this witch. I want the entire Coven. I know that fight will be long and difficult. I will not do anything stupid."

Margery rolled her eyes. "Being here without more Hunters is not exactly what I would call smart."

Ravyn laughed and glanced out the window. Her gaze

caught the tall figure of Carac. His eyes were shrewd as he scanned the bailey, his blond head moving slowly from one side to the other before he made his way toward the castle doors.

"He is handsome," Margery said.

"Without a doubt."

Margery's head jerked to her. "I hear a note of something in your voice."

"He does not trust me."

"And that upsets you?" she asked with a chuckle.

Ravyn pressed her lips together. "I hate to admit it, but it does."

"Then tell him the truth. Tell him all of it."

She shot Margery a sardonic look. "Have you gone daft?"

"He could help us."

"Or he could be working with the witch and Lord John."

Margery shrugged, her lips twisting. "Even if we know for a fact that Sir Carac is not part of the witch's plan, you will still tell him nothing."

"I could," she retorted, angry that Margery knew her so well.

"The only reason I know what I do is because I'm a Hunter. You consider anyone not associated with the abbey an outsider. You shut yourself off from them, pretending to be whatever character you make up for that particular scenario. And you never let anyone get to know the real you."

Ravyn gawked at her. "I do what I must to keep my identity a secret. The Coven knows about us Hunters now, though it was no fault of Leoma's. They would have discovered it eventually, but now that they know, I will do what I must to continue taking them out."

"Killing them." Margery blew out a breath. "Just say it."

"Aye. I kill them."

Margery looked to the side for a long moment before returning her gaze to Ravyn. "All I am suggesting is that you trust someone other than those from the abbey. You never know when you might need someone else."

Her words sounded too much like a prediction of what was to come, and Ravyn didn't like it. She decided to change the subject. "What did you learn with the other servants?"

"Very little," Margery replied in exasperation. "They are tight-lipped for sure, but I will end up discovering more from observing them. I can tell you that each of them grew nervous as soon as I asked about the other lady."

"I do not suppose you got her name, did you?"

Margery grinned. "Give me some credit. She is Lady Sybbyl."

"Sybbyl," Ravyn repeated, hoping it might jar some memory from the murder of her family, but all she remembered was the screams of her family, her father begging for them to be spared, the witch's blond hair, and her laughter.

"Have you thought about what will happen if this witch is not the one who murdered your family?"

Ravyn swallowed and walked to the chair before the hearth. A chill ran through her, seeping into her bones so that not even the heat of the blaze could warm her. "The witch I hunt has blond hair that shines like spun gold. From the descriptions we were given of Sybbyl, she has such hair. Yet, if it turns out that Sybbyl is not the one, I will still kill her. It is what we do to those of the Coven."

"Aye, it is what we do," Margery said as she came to stand near the hearth.

Ravyn pulled her gaze from the flames and looked at her friend. "Now that Braith is the Warden of the Blood Skull, we have an advantage over the Coven, but I do not believe it will last long."

"Meaning?" Margery asked with a frown.

"The skull is from the First Witch. From everything Leoma learned from the Varroki warlock, Jarin, and what Braith imparted from what the skull told him, there is a very good chance the Coven is looking for her bones."

Margery rubbed her hands together as she shook her head. "The tales of the First Witch state that upon her death, she commanded her bones to be scattered across various countries. Surely, no one would be daft enough to have another of her bones in England."

"What if it was not meant to be here?" Ravyn asked. "But what if it ended up here over the centuries?"

"I suppose anything is possible. Why do you ask?"

Ravyn leaned her elbow on the arm of the chair and propped her chin in her hand. "I have been thinking about it since Leoma and Braith returned with the Blood Skull."

"I did overhear Edra telling Radnar that she felt the skull was the start of something."

Ravyn slid her gaze to Margery. "From what Braith told us, the Coven was actively looking for the Blood Skull for many years. It might behoove us to think that they are looking for all the bones."

"In that case, any witch we hunt, we need to determine what they are doing."

She nodded, smiling. "Exactly."

Margery pulled her out of the chair. "It is time for supper."

Ravyn straightened her gown and removed the dagger at her waist. She laid it on the table before smoothing her hands over her hair. After a reassuring smile from Margery, she walked from her chamber down the corridor to the stairs.

She paused on the landing to look below. Her gaze landed on Carac first before moving to the woman he spoke with.

Her long, golden blond hair was pulled back in a loose braid that fell to her hips.

"There you are," John said as he walked to the base of the stairs.

Ravyn smiled and ascended the steps, all too aware of Carac's and Sybbyl's gaze on her. But she kept her eyes locked on John.

Flirtation came naturally to Ravyn, and for whatever reason, men of all ages responded to her. Since John obviously had a connection to the witch, Ravyn wanted to drive a wedge in it where she could. It might not last long, but something was better than nothing.

John held out his hand for her when she reached the last step, and she accepted with a smile that held just a hint of interest.

He led her to Carac and Sybbyl, both of which had yet to stop staring at her. Ravyn smiled at Carac, amazed to find it was genuine and not forced in any way. Now was not the time for her to be interested in a man.

"Lady Ravyn, let me introduce you to Lady Sybbyl," John said.

Ravyn lowered herself into a small curtsey and bowed her head before meeting Sybbyl's blue eyes. She had to keep the smugness from her face when anger and jealousy flashed in Sybbyl's gaze.

With one introduction, the two were immediate adversaries. But it went deeper than that, because now that Ravyn was close enough, she could tell that the woman was a witch. It was the way she held herself, and the look in her eyes.

"I hope you two beautiful ladies are hungry," John said, unaware of the tension. "We have a feast to dine on."

John escorted Ravyn to the table while Carac attended to Sybbyl. To Ravyn's surprise, they did not go to the dais at the back of the great hall. Instead, they sat at one of the many other tables.

John released her once Ravyn was in her seat then said, "It is not often that I have two such stunning women as guests. I decided it would only be us four dining this evening."

Sybbyl's lips thinned into a forced smile as she glared.

Ravyn shot him a wide grin and said, "What a lovely idea. Thank you."

Carac sat across from Ravyn, a crooked smile on his lips as he watched her, letting her know he knew exactly what she had done.

With John beside her and Sybbyl across from him, it was a cozy, if awkward, meal. John was either an imbecile or uncaring that Sybbyl was livid with him, and Ravyn kept him talking about his lands and family so that he rarely looked away from her as they ate.

Every once in a while, Ravyn would look up and see Carac staring at her. He did attempt to keep Sybbyl occupied, but the witch was having none of it. Sybbyl repeatedly turned the conversation in whatever direction she desired.

Ravyn was somehow always able to figure out what a man wanted or needed to hear, as well as what to ask him about to make her appear interested. In fact, she could keep a man occupied for hours with simple conversation, a seductive smile, and direct eye contact.

But she grew tired of the game with John and decided to take a more direct approach. Maybe it was because Sybbyl could be her family's killer. Or perhaps it was because Carac was covertly studying her, and she couldn't keep her mind focused on John because of it.

Ravyn took a drink of wine before she bit into a piece of cheese. She grinned when John's gaze dropped to her lips. Men were so predictable.

"How long have you known Lord Randall?" she asked.

John shrugged, all the while grinning like a besotted fool. "All my life. Our families have had a strained relationship for generations."

"It is sad what happened today." Ravyn looked down at her trencher, but her attention was on Sybbyl.

"These things happen."

She wanted to roll her eyes at John's retort. "What will become of Lord Bryce? I mean, you have his lands now, but he is still nobility."

"He has no heir," Sybbyl stated icily. Then her blue eyes shifted to John. "Is that not right?"

John cleared his throat and stared at the table, his fingers nervously brushing against his goblet. "Aye. His son and wife died."

"Surely, there is other family?" Ravyn decided to play dumb to see how much information she could get.

Sybbyl stared at John for what felt like hours before he glanced at Ravyn, his lips trembling in a smile. "Randall is the last. Which means that I will get his title."

Ravyn was not happy with this news. "From what I hear, Lord Randall could sire an heir with a new wife."

"He will not," Sybbyl announced in a tone that brooked no argument.

Ravyn looked into the witch's blue eyes and wished she had her crossbow or even her dagger so she could kill her right then and there.

8

Carac didn't think he had ever sat through a more interesting meal. Granted, he wouldn't have called it enjoyable, but it was fascinating watching Ravyn.

As soon as she arrived, Sybbyl had taken immediate offense. It didn't help that John seemed entranced by Ravyn's beauty and engaging smile. By the way Sybbyl stared daggers at him, Carac imagined that what awaited John later that night would be anything but pleasant.

But Ravyn was utterly captivating. She easily maneuvered the conversation into whatever territory she wanted without John even realizing it. Carac attempted to talk to Sybbyl, but it didn't last since she couldn't stop glaring at John, and Carac was more interested in listening to Ravyn anyway.

In his observations, he noted that while Sybbyl didn't attempt to hide her disdain, Ravyn went out of her way to all but ignore Sybbyl. The times when Sybbyl did speak, Carac caught a slight stiffening of Ravyn's body.

But the most interesting thing occurred when Ravyn spoke about Randall. Carac learned without asking a question or uttering a single word that Ravyn was definitely *not* working with Sybbyl and John.

Whose side she was on was another matter entirely.

Yet what he'd discerned was a good start. He'd uncovered more than he hoped for, actually. For starters, Sybbyl was the one running things, and John was scared of her. And with one sentence, Ravyn exposed Sybbyl and John's plan to take Randall's title as well as his lands.

The silence that fell after Sybbyl's statement that Randall would not father a child was strained. Ravyn lifted her dark eyes to his. Their gazes clashed and held. Then, her lips curved ever so slightly.

"Do you flirt with every man near you?"

Carac frowned at Sybbyl's question, immediately offended. But Ravyn calmly slid her gaze to the side and locked eyes with the witch.

"Are the barbs in your words because you feel threatened by me?" Ravyn asked softly.

Carac leaned an arm on the table and let his gaze move from Ravyn to Sybbyl and back again. The underlying tone in their words was a different kind of battle that he had never witnessed before. And it was fascinating.

He knew all about blood and steel, but this battlefield was a different kind altogether. One he wasn't sure where to stand to avoid getting bloodied. Because their weapons were ones of words and looks that could char a man where he stood.

For John's part, he kept his eyes on his food and didn't attempt to interfere. Which was probably for the best.

"Threatened?" Sybbyl asked with raised brows. "By you?"

Ravyn eyed Sybbyl, the smile never leaving her lips. "I have always appreciated directness."

"Then let me be direct," Sybbyl said as she got to her feet. "If you want John, then take him."

Ravyn drew in a breath and slowly released it. "I have always found that a strong man is more useful than one who can be...managed."

"Then you obviously have no idea what it means to be a woman."

"On the contrary," Ravyn replied, her gaze turning fierce. "Strong women need strong men."

Sybbyl made a sound in the back of her throat. "Then you are a fool."

After a glance at John, Sybbyl turned and walked away. Only a moment later, John rose and mumbled something before hurrying after her.

Carac expected Ravyn to make her excuses and leave, but instead, she poured more wine into her goblet and looked at him as she drank.

"I apologize for that exchange," she said once she'd set down her glass.

He smiled and shook his head. "I, for one, am not. It was interesting. A lot was said with few words."

"I would have preferred to say what each of us really meant, but it is a game we women play," she replied with a shrug.

"Why play it?"

The corners of her eyes crinkled as she smiled. "You men spar with weapons while women use words."

"Some also use weapons."

She laughed and tore off a piece of bread to pop into her mouth. "You still doubt that I can use it?"

He lifted one shoulder. "I would like to see for myself."

Her smile dropped a little.

He very much wanted the smile back. What had he said that disturbed her so? "I hope you do not mind, but I had a closer look at the crossbow. What are the markings on it?"

"They are symbols for strength, wisdom, courage, and patience."

"You put them on there?"

She grinned. "I did."

"Why those four?"

Her gaze slid away as if she were deciding whether to confide in him. Finally, she looked at him once more. "When I was only four, my family was murdered. My father, my three brothers, my two sisters, and my mother. I was the youngest, and Mum pushed me behind her to hide me. Somehow, her plan worked."

"My lady," Carac said, shocked. "I am sorry such an event occurred."

She swallowed and pushed her trencher away. "The feeling of such helplessness as my family screamed in pain haunts me to this day. It is why I learned to use the crossbow. The symbols are for me. Strength to remind me that I must continue on, wisdom to help guide me in all decisions, courage to face what I seek, and patience to wait however long I must."

"What do you seek?" He suspected it was a who, but he held off asking that.

Ravyn smiled brightly, but it didn't hold the light of earlier. "A lady cannot give up all her secrets."

"I suspect you hold a great many."

She blinked, her face frozen. "Why do you say that?"

"I am a knight, my lady. I look at others on a battlefield, but many times I can size up my opponent during a simple conversation."

Ravyn licked her lips and put her hands in her lap. "Everyone holds secrets, Sir Carac. Some are little, some big. Some have only one, and others have so many that they almost suffocate."

"Which are you?" he asked.

She looked at her lap briefly. "I am not sure you really want to know."

"I do, actually."

"I would like to take a walk. Will you accompany me?"

Surprised by the invitation, Carac nodded. They rose and walked toward the stairs that led to the battlements. "Would you like your cloak? The weather is chilly."

She shook her head and continued onward. Carac walked beside her out onto the battlements. He clasped his hands behind his back while she looked pensively over the land as they strolled leisurely.

"How long has John been your liege lord?" she asked after a long while.

Carac was a little surprised by the question. "He is not. I amassed my knights over the years until I had the army you see before you."

"Impressive," she said as she stopped and looked at the fires burning from the camp two hills away. "So you hire your sword out."

"I do, but I am also fair. Many times, just the arrival of my army makes my opponents lay down their arms and surrender."

Her head swiveled to him, and she smiled. "Very impressive. So, you would say you are a fair man."

"Aye. I try to be. I will forgive many things and offer mercy when I am able, but I cannot abide betrayal in any form."

She wrapped her arms around herself and shivered against the cold night air. Her eyes were bright in the moonlight, her gaze sharp. "What happened this morning at the battle?"

"Direct," he murmured.

Ravyn shrugged, her lips twisting. "It is one of my faults."

"Or a virtue, depending on how you look at it."

"If you would rather not answer, I understand."

He placed his hands on the cold stones and blew out a breath, watching it billow around him. He gave a shake of his head and looked at his camp in the distance. "In truth, I have no answer. My men are highly trained, but they did not have to even get close before Randall's men fell dead."

"What do you think was the cause?"

While Carac believed Simon, he couldn't just blurt out that magic was involved or that Sybbyl was a witch. Then there was the fact that he didn't know who to trust. His instincts told him that Ravyn was trustworthy, but he didn't want to take any chances.

He shrugged. "I know not."

After a moment, Ravyn turned to him and moved closer so their bodies were nearly touching. "Be wary, Sir Carac. Not everyone is as they seem. You appear to be a good man. Take your army and leave before it is too late."

"I accepted a contract with John. I am here for a fortnight." Damn, but it was hard to talk to her when she was so close.

"A pity you cannot get away from this place."

Now that caused him alarm. "Why?"

"I like you, Sir Carac. If you cannot leave, then do not trust anyone."

She began to turn away, and he grabbed her arm to stop her. "Explain yourself."

"You would not believe me if I told you."

He studied her a long moment. "You have been direct all evening. Why stop now?"

"Secrets." She put her hand on his cheek before dropping her arm.

"Lady Ravyn, why would you warn me and then not explain what the warning is?"

"Is it not enough that I did caution you?"

If he were talking to a man, he would think he intended to attack someone at the castle, but Ravyn was a lady, which meant that he had to think differently.

"You can trust me," he told her.

She smiled sadly. "I barely know you."

Carac had to admit that she had a point. He released her arm, and she took a step back. There was so much he wanted to ask her, but she didn't appear to want to divulge anything more.

"Thank you for the walk," she said as she looked toward the camp. "There is no one listening out here."

Just before she walked away, she met his gaze. In no uncertain terms, she told him that others could be listening inside the castle.

Carac remained for a few minutes, going through his conversation with Ravyn. Then he made his way down to the stables and saddled his horse.

He mounted and rode into the bailey. The hairs on the back of his neck stood on end. He looked over his shoulder and saw a figure in a window watching him. As he was turning back, he saw a second figure in another window—both women. Which was Sybbyl, and which was Ravyn?

Carac rode toward the gate, nodding to the guards who opened them. He urged his stallion into a gallop over the rolling landscape to the camp.

His squire, Rob, was there to greet him and take the stallion. Carac made his way to his tent. Once inside, he found Simon waiting for him.

"Well?" Simon asked.

"Sybbyl is the one controlling John, as we thought. Also, she detests Lady Ravyn."

Simon's brows rose at the news. "Was it obvious?"

"They exchanged words," he said with a shake of his head. "I've never seen the like before."

"Did you get anything else?" Simon asked.

"John intends to take Randall's title. Oh, and Ravyn warned us to be careful. She also let me know that others are listening to conversations within the castle."

Simon slowly nodded in approval. "I really need to meet her."

Carac smiled as he recalled the fire in Ravyn's eyes when she and Sybbyl exchanged words. Secrets or not, Ravyn was most intriguing.

9

I t was the witch. After all the years of planning and training and hunting, Ravyn was sure she had found the one responsible for killing her family.

But she wasn't positive.

That horrific night was a blur of screams and blood—and the witch's laughter. No matter how many times she tried, Ravyn couldn't pull up anything more than the fact that the witch had golden hair.

Sybbyl certainly fit that profile. Even if she wasn't the one who murdered Ravyn's family, Sybbyl was a witch. And no doubt part of the Coven.

Ravyn didn't get any sleep that night as she thought over coming face-to-face with Sybbyl, but that was nothing compared to hearing the witch's cold contempt for Lord Randall. Not to mention the plan she and John had concocted.

Ravyn was a superb Hunter, but the one thing she hadn't learned to do was read people. At least not well enough to claim to have mastered it. She wanted to believe that Carac was not part of John's plan, but she couldn't be sure.

On their walk, he had pressed her for answers. She wanted to give them to him, but she'd held back. Carac was smart. If he weren't in league with John and Sybbyl, then he would figure it out on his own.

If he was...well, she had said nothing that could let anyone think she was a Hunter. Because Ravyn had no doubt the Coven kept their eyes open for anyone they even thought might be one.

"I'm ready."

Ravyn turned her head to Margery, who was fastening her cloak. She gave the woman a nod, and they walked from the chamber together. Few were moving about so early in the morning, allowing them to walk the castle without running into anyone.

They made it to the stables without incident. After saddling both of their horses and checking weapons, they mounted and rode toward the closed gate.

Ravyn nodded at the guards. "Good morning. May we pass?"

"It is early, my lady," one stated.

She held his gaze and smiled. "Very observant of you. I am an early riser, and as such, I like to get on the road before others. I have a long way to go, so please, open the gates."

They hesitated, and just when Ravyn thought she might have to use a firmer tone, the guard motioned for the others to let them pass.

As soon as the gates were open, Ravyn nudged her mare into a gallop with Margery on her heels. Neither spoke for the next few leagues until Margery pulled even with her.

"No one is following."

Ravyn drew back on the reins to slow her horse to a walk. "Good."

"I thought they were going to keep us there."

"I think they nearly did."

Margery grinned. "That would have been a dreadful mistake."

"Extremely," Ravyn replied with a smile.

They looked at each other and laughed. Ravyn moved her mount off the road into the tree line. She kept watch as Margery changed from the gown to her Hunter attire.

When Margery finished, Ravyn quickly did the same. While she liked wearing gowns, she preferred to be in the leather breeches that would give her full movement of her body in a fight.

With her cloak fastened and hood covering her braided hair, Ravyn walked to where Margery held the horses and took the reins of her mare. "Ready?"

"Nay, but we do not have a choice."

Ravyn put a hand on Margery's arm. "We do. At least, *you* do. I asked you to remain and watch my back, but I know your heart is not here. Return to the abbey. I will be fine."

"I am not going anywhere but with you," Margery replied. She covered her lower face with the black scarf before she put her foot in the stirrup and swung her leg over her mare. "I decided yesterday that this will be my last mission. I thought that this was what I wanted to do, and I know I am skilled enough with weapons to achieve it…"

"But your heart is not in it," Ravyn repeated. "I know."

Margery looked away and sighed. "There are many other ways I can help, and I intend to do that."

"I know you will. Are you sure you wish to stay?"

"I am here already, and we both know you need someone to curb you every now and again."

Ravyn grinned, even though her heart was heavy. She mounted and adjusted her cloak behind her before using a black piece of material to cover the lower half of her face.

She said nothing more to Margery as she clicked to the mare and headed across the countryside to Lord Randall's castle. Ravyn knew Sybbyl was doing something there, and she was going to find out what it was.

They rode swiftly, keeping far from roads where they were likely to run into others. Ravyn wanted to get a feel for Bryce Castle and the occupants before she faced off against Sybbyl.

Ravyn also kept a wide berth from any of Carac's army. She had no wish to run into him or his men. It was usually fairly easy to keep out of another's way. Most saw only what they wanted, never noticing that she stood in the shadows completely covered except for her eyes.

But this wasn't her typical mission—not that *any* of them were normal. Each assignment held its own problems and setbacks. However, this undertaking was personal.

While Ravyn knew that by allowing her feelings into it, she was putting herself at a distinct disadvantage, she couldn't stop it. There were many things she learned to control or work to her advantage, but her emotions when it came to her family wasn't one of them.

If only the hardest part of the assignment were her feelings. Close behind was Carac. She wanted to dislike him, but she didn't. In the little time she'd spent with him, she discovered that he was intelligent and cool-headed. He didn't make rash decisions or seem reckless.

Yet, try as she might, she couldn't quite determine which side he was on. And that bothered her. Because she was unsure of his allegiance, she had to steer clear of him. The fact that he appeared as interested in Lord Randall as Sybbyl and John troubled her.

She slowed her mare and dismounted once they neared the edge of the forest, dropping the reins to the ground. The horses were trained to await them or come with a certain whistle. Ravyn glanced at Margery as she grabbed her crossbow and specialized attachment with several arrows so she could fire in quick succession. Margery gave her a nod before they set out.

They moved through the trees like ghosts, leaving only silence in their wake. Ravyn lost track of the hours she'd spent learning how to disappear in a crowded market or coming up alongside someone without them knowing she was there. But it didn't compare to the time she devoted to moving through a forest, crowds, or other places while chasing someone.

Ravyn suddenly halted, her senses picking up that they weren't alone. She pressed herself against a tree and listened while Margery did the same about thirty yards to her left.

Ravyn waited for a flight of birds or other startled animals to show her where the intruder was. But there was nothing. The forest remained calm, but her instincts were telling her that someone was out there.

And her gut was never wrong.

She turned her head to look at Margery, whose questioning gaze was locked on her. Ravyn gave a small shake of her head. Margery jerked her chin toward their destination, indicating that she thought they should go.

Ravyn motioned her forward, but she remained behind, watching. Nothing so much as shifted with Margery's departure.

Ravyn tightly gripped her crossbow, her gaze scanning the area all around her. The hairs on the back of her neck stood on end. She was being watched. Was it a witch?

If it were someone from the Coven, they wouldn't wait to attack. The witches would have gone after her and Margery as soon as they spotted them. Patience wasn't a virtue of the Coven. The witches were actively looking for Hunters, waiting to take one of them out.

She wasn't going to give them the chance.

Witches had all sorts of abilities with their magic. There were also other creatures who were drawn to magic—things that she preferred to stay away from at all costs.

Then there were the Varroki. Presumably, they were allies of the Hunters, but Ravyn had yet to meet one herself. She would hold off forming an opinion until that day came. It still boggled her mind that there were warlocks. Never did she believe that men could have magic.

She looked over her shoulder to check on Margery's progress and found that her friend had reached the edge of the forest safely. Now, it was her turn. Ravyn took a deep breath and pivoted from behind the tree.

For several heartbeats, she didn't move another inch as she waited for an attack. When none came, she slowly made her way to Margery. At the tree line, she looked across the expanse of land with trees dotting the terrain of rolling hills surrounding the castle.

"There are knights everywhere," Margery whispered.

Ravyn looked for Carac's blond hair, but she didn't see him. A part of her was disappointed. She liked him. And she'd enjoyed the way he looked at her.

The desire she'd spotted in his green gaze had made her blood rush with need. It was too bad she didn't have more time to get to know him. She suspected there were many layers to Carac, and she would've enjoyed peeling back each one to discover the real man beneath them all.

Suddenly, she frowned. While many of the knights stationed around the castle were from Carac's army, there were many more who were John's.

"We will have to wait until nightfall," she whispered.

Margery nodded, her lips pursed. "If they're smart, they'll double the guards then."

"They will still be easy enough to get through."

"Unless Sybbyl is expecting us."

That was a possibility, and Ravyn would take that into consideration when they approached the castle. She had hoped they would get in and out of the castle before Sybbyl suspected anything, but that wasn't going to happen.

She glanced at Margery, knowing that her friend only remained to help her. The last thing Ravyn wanted was for Margery to get pulled into a battle with a witch, but there might not be any other way around it.

There was still the niggling feeling that they were being watched. It was one of the few times Ravyn wished she had some magic to locate who it was so she could dispatch them. Surely, if someone had seen them, the culprits would have attempted to detain them.

She and Margery were good at hiding, but so must be whoever observed them because she had yet to find any trace of them. That disturbed Ravyn greatly.

A witch would have no need for such tactics.

Unless the witch were trying to draw out a Hunter.

As far as Ravyn knew, Sybbyl was the only witch there, but she couldn't continue thinking along that path. It would get her and Margery killed. She needed to prepare for other witches—which was easier said than done.

It was going to be a long day. They couldn't remain where they were and leave their horses unattended. The mounts needed to be hidden so no one would stumble upon the mares and start looking around for her and Margery.

Margery shifted and looked back through the forest. "I know where to hide the horses."

She pulled her gaze from the castle to nod at Margery. Then she went back to counting the knights—both Carac's and John's. Off to her right, she could just make out the tops of the tents from Carac's camp. Was he there? Or was he inside the castle?

And while she didn't know why, it was important to her that he not be involved with Sybbyl and John's plot.

10

Carac wasn't sure what pushed him to search the forest surrounding the castle. The entire night, he had thought about what John and Sybbyl said to Ravyn.

While Ravyn had kept her expression at ease, there had been a wealth of goading from Sybbyl that didn't quite add up. It was almost as if Sybbyl were pushing Ravyn toward something. But either Ravyn was smart enough to realize it and not give in, or she was oblivious to Sybbyl.

Either way, it gave him pause. That, added to Simon's declaration of Sybbyl being a witch, and the last thing Carac could do was rest easy.

What little sleep he had was filled with dreams of Sybbyl killing everyone. Or him stripping Ravyn of her clothes and making love to her.

He alternated waking up in a cold sweat or with a cock so hard that he ached. Not even pleasuring himself eased the yearning for the ebony-haired beauty.

Before dawn, he and Simon were searching the woods looking for...he didn't know what, but that didn't matter. He knew he had to be there. It was the logical place for an attack to be waged. Or for someone to spy.

It wasn't long before he spotted two figures moving swiftly through the forest. They were slim, their legs encased in leather with tall boots. The cloaks moved with them, never tangling or getting in the way.

He and Simon ducked out of view behind a fallen log as the duo drew closer. Carac struggled to get a look at one of their faces, but their hoods were pulled forward, and something covered the lower halves of their faces.

There was something about the way the taller one moved that he recognized. If only he could place *how* he knew it. Carac realized that the two were headed toward the edge of the woods, so he shifted closer to get a better look at them.

He was glad he had forgone his armor. Otherwise, he never would have been able to move without being heard. As it was, he must have spooked the pair, because the tall one drew up and flattened against a tree—mere feet from him. Seconds later, the second did, as well.

Carac froze from his position on his knees. He looked through the leaves of a bush to stare at the cloaked figure. When his gaze lowered to the crossbow, he frowned when he recognized it.

Then the person's head turned, and he saw the brown eyes he had gazed into hours earlier. He felt as if he'd been kicked in the balls by his stallion.

Of all the people he'd thought he might find in the woods, Lady Ravyn wasn't one of them—if that was her name at all.

The way her gaze kept sweeping the trees, she knew she was being watched. She looked right at him, but Carac was too well hidden for her to see him.

He didn't understand why her face was covered, or why she was out there at all. When she finally moved away from the tree and followed her companion to the edge of the forest, he wished he were near enough to hear their conversation.

A few moments later, the shorter of the two retraced her steps, disappearing into the trees. Carac spotted Simon trailing her at a distance while keeping hidden.

It was just as well because he wasn't going to leave Ravyn. Carac wanted to know what she was about. A part of him wanted to stand up and demand that she tell him everything. But he also knew that she was the type of person who would give him anything but the truth if challenged that way.

He'd never known such a woman. Despite his anger, his blood burned for her, the lust hotly rushing through him.

His gaze lowered to her shapely leg as she bent and the cloak fell away. His cock hardened instantly, his balls tightening as he stared, transfixed.

First witches, and now a lady running around in trousers. Carac didn't know what to make of it, but he knew if he remained near Ravyn, he might find out.

After a bit, she stood and finally pulled her gaze away from the castle to look behind her. Once more, her eyes scanned the trees. She felt his stare.

She moved with skill and grace, her training obvious. But who would teach a woman—nay, *two* women—such things? Now he knew that the crossbow Ravyn carried wasn't just for show.

His legs began to cramp, but he didn't move and take the chance of alerting her to his presence. Nearly an hour passed before the second woman returned. She made her way to Ravyn and handed her a waterskin and a small bag before taking up position farther away.

Carac searched for Simon, but his friend took longer to return so as not to be seen. Neither had food or water, but it wouldn't be the first time they'd gone hours without.

Just as Carac prepared to remain however long Ravyn did, he heard his name being shouted. He grimaced when a patrol riding from his camp toward Bryce Castle diverted to the forest.

More of his men were coming from behind with his and Simon's horses in tow. He watched as Ravyn and her friend hurried away. Carac rose from his hiding place and waited for his men to find him.

"We've been sent to find you, Sir Carac," one of the men said.

Carac raised a brow as Simon joined him. "By who?"

"Lord John," came the reply. "He's at your tent."

Simon sighed loudly as their horses were brought to them. Carac mounted, his gaze moving in the direction where Ravyn had disappeared. No doubt she was long gone. He hated that he wouldn't be able to see what she was up to, but with her interest in Bryce Castle, if he stuck around long enough, he just might find out.

He spun his horse and nudged it into a gallop as the group left the forest—and Ravyn—behind. Carac rode hard to his tent, and just as his men had told him, John was waiting inside. Along with Sybbyl.

Carac entered with Simon on his heels. Carac's gaze briefly landed on Sybbyl before moving to John. "My lord. What can I do for you?"

John stood with his hands clasped behind his back, a deep frown marring his brow. "Lady Ravyn and her servant departed this morning."

"She did state that she would only be there for one night," Carac said.

Sybbyl walked around his bed, her eyes lingering on it before fastening on him. "It was the way she left."

"On her horse?" Carac didn't know why he felt the need to defend Ravyn or be so sardonic to Sybbyl. It just came out.

A smile briefly pulled at John's lips before he cleared his throat when Sybbyl glared at him. "Lady Ravyn left at dawn without a word to us."

Carac crossed his arms over his chest. "While I admit that could border on impolite, I do not understand the fuss."

"We are...concerned...about her," Sybbyl said.

It was a load of shite, but Carac didn't call her on it. Yet. "Because she travels alone?"

"Not exactly," John said. He let his arms drop to his sides as he shrugged. "Sybbyl believes that Ravyn might not have been entirely truthful with us."

Carac ignored the witch entirely. "I did not get any such feeling from her. Besides, what reason would Lady Ravyn have for being deceitful? She stayed one night and asked for nothing."

Silence filled the tent after his question, which was his intention. He wanted to force both John and Sybbyl to admit to something. And they couldn't blame Ravyn for anything without revealing their complicity.

Sybbyl came to stand between him and John. It irritated Carac to such a degree that he had to restrain himself from physically shoving her out of the way.

"I do not believe she is who she says she is," Sybbyl stated.

Carac still refused to look at her. He shrugged and told John, "She did nothing untoward to anyone at the castle."

"I want her found and returned to me."

Sybbyl's demand sent Carac's fury to the boiling point. The witch wasn't married to John, nor had she hired Carac, so he didn't have to listen to her demands.

"Did you hear me?" Sybbyl asked, taking a step closer to him.

"Carac," John said as he came up beside Sybbyl. "I am asking you to find Lady Ravyn and her servant."

While he had no intention of doing as they asked, Carac wouldn't outright tell John or Sybbyl that. If he did, they might go to someone else. This way, Carac could confront Ravyn and warn her. Of what, he didn't yet know.

But it didn't bode well that Sybbyl and John wanted her brought back.

"Is that all?" Carac asked in a flat tone.

John glanced at Sybbyl. "There is one more thing. I want you at Bryce Castle."

"Why?" he demanded.

John swallowed, his eyes dropping to the ground for a moment. "To keep watch over things when I am not there. I want the transition to go smoothly."

Carac wanted to ask if Randall were still alive because as long as he was, John couldn't do anything. But Carac remained silent as Sybbyl continued to stew in her anger.

John cleared his throat. "One more thing. You will take Lady Sybbyl's orders as if they are mine. At all times."

At this, Carac wanted to balk. He lowered his gaze to the witch to find her smirking. "I cannot find Lady Ravyn and be at the castle at the same time."

Sybbyl lifted her chin, her blue eyes glacial as she glared. "I have no doubt that you will think of something."

She stormed past him with John following. Carac dropped his arms and turned to watch them leave. Only then did Simon give a shake of his head.

"Bloody hell," Simon said.

"You do not know the half of it."

"I think it was wise not to tell them about the pair we saw in the forest. I know you will not believe me, but the one I followed was a woman."

Carac looked at his friend and twisted his lips. "And the other was Ravyn."

Simon's eyes widened. "Are you sure?"

"I would know her eyes anywhere."

"What are you going to do?"

Carac thought about Ravyn's interest in Bryce Castle, as well as Sybbyl's and John's. "I am headed to the castle."

"What of the women? Is Sybbyl right? Is Ravyn lying?"

Carac lifted one shoulder in a shrug. "You saw Ravyn's crossbow. Given the way she held it, she knows how to use it."

"Aye, and I saw the way the two moved. They are skilled."

Carac nodded. "I agree."

"Do you think they might know Sybbyl is a witch?"

Though Carac still hadn't seen Sybbyl do anything...witchy, he had no cause to doubt his friend. And Simon's question was plausible. "They might. Sybbyl did not like Ravyn. I thought it was merely because John could not keep his eyes off Ravyn, but I think it might go deeper than that."

"I'd like to talk to Ravyn," Simon said.

"Me, as well." Carac actually wanted to do much more than talk. He yearned to ravage her lips in a kiss that stole her breath and made her soften against him.

Simon shifted to face him. "Carac, be careful around Sybbyl. You did not see what I witnessed yesterday."

"You think she would harm me?"

"In a heartbeat."

Carac swallowed as he thought over his friend's words. "I will be more controlled in the future."

"All of us need to be wary of her. See for yourself when we go to the castle. Those that witnessed her slaughter will not meet her gaze or even look at her."

Carac ran a hand through his hair. "Send six men to look

for Ravyn and her partner. Tell them nothing more than that the women need to be found and returned to John for their safety."

"You are actually going to do it?" Simon asked with a frown.

He grinned. "After what I saw today, I would like to see anyone take Ravyn or her friend against their will. No one will find them."

Simon smiled and ducked from the tent to carry out the order. That gave Carac a moment alone to think about things. Simon's warnings about Sybbyl should be heeded, but Carac also needed to see things for himself. It was time he went to Bryce Castle and learned the fate of Lord Bryce for himself.

11

Blackglade

How could one woman make him lose patience so quickly? Armir drew in a deep breath and slowly released it, trying to rein in his growing ire as Malene stared at him.

He couldn't look into her large, soft gray eyes for long. She wasn't the first Lady of the Varroki he had served, but she was the first who had the blue radiance in both hands.

From the moment he saw Malene, he'd recognized the fierceness within her. Her quiet strength.

She had known nothing of magic. Even now, he wondered why she had been chosen as Lady, but the longer she ruled the Varroki, the more he understood.

She wasn't rash or reckless. She was brave and steadfast. While she fought the confines of her role, she worried over the people who weren't hers.

"Admit I am right," Malene said, a small smile curving her lips.

Armir briefly looked away. The constant nearness to her had been eating at him for years. Her innocence was as breathtaking as her beauty. But the power of the magic growing inside her was glorious.

It magnified her loveliness so that anyone near was utterly mesmerized by her. And he was no exception. Her talk of changing the various positions of the Varroki to allow them to take a spouse brought mixed feelings.

He agreed with her. It was actually something he had been thinking about for a few years. His mistake had come when, for the briefest of moments, he'd allowed himself to imagine taking her to his bed. And that simply couldn't happen.

"Armir."

He shuttered his thoughts and made himself look into her eyes. Malene stood wearing a gown of soft green with an intricate ringed girdle resting on her shapely hips before falling down the front of her skirt.

Her flaxen hair was plaited into several tiny braids on the right side of her head while the rest of her mane hung down her back. Her heart-shaped face was utter perfection from her smooth skin to her large eyes to her high cheekbones to her plump lips.

"You are correct," he finally admitted. "You have the power to change our laws."

Her smile was effervescent and made him catch his breath. "Tell me why no other Lady has altered any of the laws?"

"Probably because they did not bother to read through the library."

Malene gave him a flat look. "What you really mean to say is that most did not know how to read."

"Neither did you."

"Until I made you teach me."

He had been immensely impressed by her first order to him. It showed that she wanted to know what was before her to face whatever came. And she had done that and much, much more. "Aye."

She touched the book she'd opened on the table between them that outlined her role as Lady of the Varroki. "As of today, a new law goes into effect removing celibacy from all positions."

"Even yours?"

Gray eyes held his gaze for a long, silent moment. "All positions," she repeated.

"As you wish," he said with a bow of his head. Once more an image of him taking her to his bed filled his mind before he shoved it aside. "I shall notify everyone that you have added a new law."

"Do it quickly. There is somewhere I wish to be."

Armir frowned. Surely, she wasn't thinking of visiting the witch who'd begun the Hunters. But he could tell by the determined set of Malene's chin that it was exactly what she meant.

"There is no need for your concern," Malene said. "You will be with me."

He wasn't sure if the idea of going with her was a good one or not. It was his duty to protect and guide her, but he was all too aware of the precarious state of his thoughts the more time he was alone with her.

Yet, he would not allow anyone else to go with her. He bowed once more before turning on his heel and striding from the chamber. As he made his way down the stairs to the bottom of the tower, he let his mind sift through her changes and how they would help the Varroki in many ways. But after a great many generations of such customs, change wouldn't come easily.

It didn't take long for him to spread the word about the new laws. There was concern until he shared why Malene changed their traditions. Once the Varroki learned that their Lady was concerned about their race dying out, they accepted the new decree with a degree of enthusiasm he hadn't expected.

Although, Armir was curious as to how Jarin and the rest of the warriors would take the news. They were trained from a young age to be alone. They fought alone, lived alone. And died alone.

Malene's new edict was exactly what the Varroki needed. He'd hoped he would at least like her. He'd never expected to admire or be in awe of her. Yet that's exactly what had occurred. It'd happened so slowly, he hadn't been cognizant of it until that moment.

While fully aware that Malene didn't wish to be Lady, she accepted the role with dignity and grace. He would protect her with his life. She was the best thing to have happened to the Varroki in thousands of years.

And if need be, he would watch over the man she chose to stand beside her.

That thought soured Armir's thoughts, which was why he stopped it. After seeing to the guards around the island, he returned to the top of the tower.

He knocked twice and entered to find Malene bent over the law book as she finished writing her new edict. She straightened and beamed at him.

"This is the first time since I arrived at Blackglade that I feel as if I've done something good," she said.

He frowned at her words. "You've done many good things."

"Is that right? Name one."

"Look at your hands," he said with a jerk of his chin. "All Ladies harness the blue radiance in one palm. It has been eons since any have held it in both."

Her smile slipped as she fisted her hands. "I did not learn magic. It chose me, for reasons I have yet to determine. It grows within me without any encouragement on my part."

"In the five years of studying magic and the Varroki, you still do not understand."

She widened her eyes and cocked her head. "Please explain, then."

"While I could not explain why the magic chose you at first, I am beginning to finally understand. You might strain against the confines, but you have learned a great many things. It is not only your mind that has grown but your magic, as well. It continues to develop because you allow it to. You do not hold your magic back out of fear, or grasp for it to lord it over others."

A deep furrow formed on her brow. "I think I would know if I were helping the magic grow."

"When you were a child, did you feel your bones expand? Your skin stretch?"

"Nay."

"It is the same with magic," he told her.

Her gaze dropped to the floor as she slowly nodded. "That does make sense."

He hoped with her new laws that she would stop looking back at the life she left behind. There was a good future for her here, and maybe she might allow herself to see it if she didn't feel pressed into the position.

Armir hadn't wanted to force her to Blackglade, but he'd been prepared to do just that. Once a Lady was chosen, they had to take their place, or the magic shielding Blackglade from the Coven and the outside world would fade.

But he hadn't had to toss her over his shoulder. Instead, he'd coaxed and persuaded until he swayed her into agreeing to return with him. Every day of their journey to Blackglade, he continued to convince her that it was the right thing to do for the people.

Malene cared nothing about her position or the power it granted her. When he realized that, he'd had his first shred of hope that she would last longer than most of the other Ladies. And in many aspects, she had.

The longest a previous Lady had ruled was ten years. And that simply wouldn't be long enough. It had taken Malene five just to reach where she was. If she could make it past the doomed seven-year mark, there was a real chance she could do wondrous things for the Varroki.

Malene walked around the table to him. "Do you approve of what I have done?"

He was taken aback by her question. "My feelings do not matter."

"They do to me. You are my only friend here."

"You could have others."

She glanced away but chose not to reply.

Armir looked down at the faint blue light that glowed from her palms. "I do approve. It is a step we should have taken a hundred years ago. There will be some who will cling to the old ways."

"I suspected that. And respect it. Will you be one of them?"

"I have not thought about it." It was a lie. The fact was, he didn't wish to speak of it until he'd had time to mull over what this new edict would mean for him. Until then, he would keep his decisions to himself.

Her gray eyes stared hard. "You should. Everyone deserves happiness."

"And if I am happy?"

"That's all that matters," she replied with a soft smile. She licked her lips. "Ready?"

"You are intent on this meeting, then?"

Malene gave a nod. "Very."

"We do not have an exact location for the Hunters, and the magic it takes to get there—"

"Is painful," she said over him with a nod. "I know."

Armir rarely used his magic to make huge jumps in travel because the effects were debilitating, but they didn't have the luxury of time to make a traditional journey.

To his shock, Malene held out her hand. When he hesitated, she raised a brow. "Afraid to touch me? I changed that, as well."

"Your law allowing celibate positions to now marry will go over much easier than me touching you."

She held his gaze. "Who is to know but us?"

While she had a point, Armir knew he would be willingly crossing a line if he took her hand. Already, he'd toed it by carrying her into her chamber twice, but he gave himself permission to do that since it was to protect her.

This was something entirely different.

"We must be touching to do this magic together," Malene said. "Unless you would rather we go separately."

"Nay," he said hastily. So much could go wrong.

"Then you must not trust me to do the magic necessary for such travel."

"I did not say that."

Through it all, her hand awaited his. He drew in a deep breath and wrapped his fingers around hers.

"I have never done this type of magic," she confessed.

As they faced each other, their gazes locked, Armir could almost forget their positions. If they lived other lives elsewhere, he would have pursed Malene, wooing her until she succumbed to him.

He took her other hand, pulling her closer. The excitement of freely touching her was explosive, and his efforts to tamp down those feelings were futile. "Then we do it together."

After her nod of agreement, Armir's gaze lowered to her mouth. His blood heated as her lips parted and her chest rose swiftly. They spoke in unison, reciting the traveling spell together. It wasn't long before the tower grew hazy as their thoughts centered on the forest Jarin had told them about.

The strength of Malene's magic slid along his body, seductively wrapping around him. His magic swelled in response to hers so that the clasp of their fingers tightened. Their gazes locked, the spell pushing their bodies closer and closer until they were merely breaths apart.

In a flash of light, the tower was gone, replaced by tall trees and bright sunlight. Whatever pleasure Armir had felt was gone as his skull felt as if it were being yanked apart.

Malene bent over and gagged. He moved behind her, holding her as she emptied her stomach, while each movement only made his headache worse.

When she finished, he guided her to a tree. As he lowered her to the ground, his feet slipped on the dead leaves, and they slid together into a heap. He held her against him to break the fall, and once on the ground, neither moved.

He squeezed his eyes shut to stop the world from spinning while waiting for the pain in his head to recede. Malene was draped over his chest. Her breathing was shallow, and she had a death grip on his arm.

He should give her words of reassurance and let her know

that this would ease in a moment, but he couldn't get anything past his lips.

When the silence continued, he dared to crack open an eye, only to be blinded by the sunlight. He saw that Malene had fallen asleep.

He closed his eyes and held her tighter.

12

"That was close," Margery said.

Ravyn watched the group of knights from a distance. She could neither hear what they said nor see them clearly before they rode from the forest. "Aye."

"They were looking for Carac."

"I heard." Everyone probably heard with the way the men were shouting.

Margery made her way down the tree she had climbed and landed beside Ravyn. "In these woods."

Ravyn swung her head to her friend. "Your point?"

"You said someone was watching us. It could have been Carac."

"I would have seen him."

Margery gave her a look that suggested she didn't believe a word Ravyn said.

"If it was Carac, why did he not approach us?" Ravyn demanded.

Margery yanked down Ravyn's face scarf. "Perhaps because he was not sure of our intentions since we were covered."

"Carac is a knight. He would not sit by and watch. He would have attacked."

"Then you would have had no choice but to shoot him."

Ravyn hated that Margery was right. Not that Ravyn would've shot Carac—not to kill, anyway. Wound, perhaps.

Margery rolled her eyes. "You like him," she accused.

"I do not know him."

"Ravyn."

"What?" she asked in frustration. "So I think he is handsome. That means nothing."

Margery crossed her arms over her chest. "You are attracted to him."

Ravyn tried to lie, but it died on her tongue.

"I knew it," Margery said with a shake of her head.

"That will not stop me if he is in league with John and Sybbyl."

Margery dropped her arms and looked at the castle. "Perhaps we need to determine which side Sir Carac is on."

"I intend to."

Her friend's russet gaze swung back to her. "I mean, tell him who you are and why we are here. See how he reacts."

"You want me to show our hand to a potential enemy?" Ravyn asked in shock.

"You forget, while you were flirting with John and Carac at supper, I was with the servants, listening to them as well as observing you. It was the way Carac made sure never to get too close to Sybbyl that caught my attention."

Ravyn glanced at where Carac's knights had disappeared. "I saw that as well, but that could mean anything."

"We could stop Sybbyl quicker if he were on our side."

"You are assuming that he will join us. Have you thought about what will happen if he is with John and Sybbyl?"

Margery gave a firm nod. "You will have to kill him."

"You make it sound as if I enjoy taking lives."

"Nay. I merely stated the obvious."

Ravyn snorted in irritation. "Perhaps you should be the one to kill Carac."

"If you will not, then I will do what is necessary."

"Margery, I kill witches," Ravyn said, letting the frustration heat her words. "I kill Coven witches because of the horror they bring, the destruction they leave in their wake. I only take the lives of others if I am fighting for my own. I take no pleasure in it. Ever."

Remorse filled Margery's face. "I did not mean to suggest otherwise. Forgive me."

Ravyn waved away her words. "You are right. Hunting is not for you."

"Perhaps, but I do want to end the Coven. I will do my part. Whatever that may be."

They clasped hands, sharing a grin.

The rest of the day was spent mostly in solitude, each woman taking up positions to view the castle and the movements of the knights.

That also meant that Ravyn was left alone with her thoughts. No matter how hard she tried, she found herself thinking of Carac again and again. What was it about him that drew her? She had been around other handsome men, but his magnetism was more than that.

It could be his confidence in life and war or the way he treated his knights like family. Maybe it was the way he looked at her as if he were trying to decipher her thoughts, as if he were interested in every word she said. There was also the possibility that it had something to do with the roguish smile he'd flashed her when she told him she could use the crossbow.

Her gaze dropped to the weapon in her hands. Carac had taken a close look at it, close enough to see the inscription of

Celtic symbols. If that had been him in the forest earlier, then he'd seen the weapon.

Which meant he knew it was she.

He'd remained hidden to see what she would do. It was so obvious that she nearly groaned out loud. If she saw Carac again—which she didn't intend to do—she would be able to discern very quickly if he was the one watching her.

But the question remained. Why hadn't he called out to her, stopped her, or any number of other things? Why had he simply watched? Was it because he was curious? Or was it something else? Like he was in league with Sybbyl?

Ravyn was grateful when dusk finally settled over the land. She was able to pull her thoughts away from her conflicted feelings about Carac and focus on getting into the castle and finding Lord Bryce and whatever it was Sybbyl hunted for.

When it was dark enough, she and Margery made their way to the keep. They took different routes. Margery chose to get in through the back, but Ravyn opted for the side of the fortress.

The stone wall surrounding the stronghold soared above her. Upon first glance, it appeared slick with no way to get over it without a ladder or rope, but that didn't stop Ravyn. She had scaled such obstacles before.

Making it to the castle proved easy. The guards patrolling the battlements were looking for riders or someone approaching the gates. No one peered down the wall.

Ravyn slung the strap of her crossbow over her head and then slipped her arm through before she got a good grip on the stones and began her climb. She went slowly to ensure that she didn't lose either her foothold or the few handholds she found. Her arms began to shake halfway up, but there was no time to stop and rest. The only option she had was to make it to the top.

When she finally reached the battlements, she had to hold her place as two guards stood just feet from her, talking. She closed her eyes, focusing her strength on her fingers and the grip they had, as well as her footholds. It felt like forever before the guards moved on.

But when it came time for her to get over the top, she couldn't move. She'd used so much energy on the climb and holding her position that she feared she wouldn't be able to make it over.

Then she thought about Sybbyl. The mere notion that she could be the one who'd murdered Ravyn's family gave her the boost she needed to finish her climb.

Ravyn squatted in the shadows and shook out her arms as she looked one way and then the other, taking note of where the guards were stationed. She kept to the shadows as she took a quick look at the castle and the bailey. The few guards she saw meandering about below were off duty, their attention on women and drink. The other knights had their concentration outward, leaving her to make her way unseen to the door leading from the battlements.

Ravyn never left the shadows. Once inside, it was easy to hear anyone coming and duck out of the way. The castle was eerily quiet except for two voices. As soon as she recognized one as Sybbyl's, she headed in that direction.

"I told you never to doubt me," the witch said.

John laughed before belching loudly. "I do not."

"Oh, you did, *my lord*. You did not think Randall would give me the staff. Perhaps I should discipline you again after that incident with Ravyn."

Ravyn frowned. *Staff?* She inched closer and looked around the corner to peer down into the great hall. Sybbyl and John were sitting alone, no guards near. It would be the perfect time to kill the witch, but Ravyn hesitated. She needed to know what staff Sybbyl was after.

John drank deeply from his goblet and leaned back in his chair. "I learned my lesson. I admit, I thought Randall would put up more of a fight."

"He saw what I can do," Sybbyl stated arrogantly.

John leaned toward her and put his hand behind her head to draw her close. "You make me ache with need," he said before kissing her.

Ravyn rolled her eyes at the scene. The two made her sick to her stomach. But then again, anyone who joined with the Coven made her nauseous.

"I love the authority you command," John said between kisses. "It makes me hard. No other woman has done that to me."

Sybbyl shoved him back into his chair before she pulled up her skirts and straddled him. "I can feel how much you want me," she purred.

"Please, let me inside you. I need to feel you."

"Is that your idea of begging?" she asked, raising her chin.

As soon as John laid Sybbyl on the table, spread her legs, and knelt between them, Ravyn turned away. The sound of the chair being shoved back and then Sybbyl's moans reached her.

Ravyn was beyond irritated. She wanted more information, not to hear the two having sex. But she wasn't going to stand around and listen to them. She would explore on her own.

It took only a little while before she found the master chamber, but Lord Randall wasn't there. She did a quick search of the room to see what she could find, only to come up empty-handed. Not that she'd expected to find anything.

She sighed because she knew there was only one other place for Lord Bryce. The dungeon. She backtracked and used another set of stairs that took her to the lower levels. Halfway down, the sound of approaching footsteps caused her to race back up the steps to hide.

Finally, she made it to the kitchens, where the servants were too busy to notice her. She stole a piece of bread and a block of cheese that she hastily ate while making her way through the castle. After that, she found another set of stairs that took her to the dungeon.

Ravyn listened for anyone before she put her foot on the first step when someone grabbed her from the side and yanked her into the shadows.

Instinct immediately kicked in, and she fought them, but strong hands held her. Just as she was about to slam her head forward into her assailant's face, she heard her name from a voice she honestly never thought to hear again.

Carac.

"What the bloody hell are you doing?" he demanded.

That one sentence confirmed her theory about him in the forest. There were many replies she could give him, but she lifted her face to his, meeting his green gaze.

He pulled down her scarf as they stared at each other in the faint light of the torch several feet away. He shook his head, his expression a cross between relief and exasperation.

"This is the last place you should be," he told her. "Sybbyl has ordered that you be found and brought to her."

At this, Ravyn smiled. "I'd be more than happy to go. I planned to confront her anyway."

Carac shook his head again and wrapped his long fingers around her arm before hauling her after him. Ravyn allowed him to lead her. She could have gotten away. She didn't know *why* she went with him, only that she wanted to.

When they entered a small chamber, she found Margery already there with another man. Ravyn removed her crossbow and set it on the table in the center of the room before she faced Carac.

His gaze raked her from head to foot and back again. Then he glanced at the other man. "This is Simon, my best friend and my right hand."

"Sir Simon," Ravyn said. She then slid her gaze to Margery, who gave her a small nod. "This is Margery, my friend and equal. Margery, this is Sir Carac."

Everyone looked at the other, then Ravyn faced Carac. "Why did you stop me?"

"Why?" he asked, taken aback.

Ravyn felt Margery's gaze, and their earlier conversation came back to her. The chamber grew quiet as she and Carac stared at one another, each waiting for the other to bend first.

It went against everything Ravyn was, but she knew someone would have to give up some information in order to move things along. She didn't want to spend hours in the room when she could be stopping Sybbyl.

Ravyn inhaled deeply before slowly releasing the breath. "I am not a lady. It was a lie. I am after...someone."

"The witch," Simon stated.

Her head whipped to him. "You know?"

Simon gave a single nod. "I saw Sybbyl here yesterday. She killed so many."

"You are after Sybbyl?" Carac asked, confusion in his gaze.

When Ravyn didn't reply, Margery released a loud sigh and said, "We are Hunters. Specifically, we hunt witches who are part of the Coven."

"I will help you," Simon said. "Sybbyl cannot be allowed to kill any more."

Carac threw up his hands, palms out. "Wait. Everyone, just wait."

"I told you what I saw," Simon stated.

Ravyn watched a muscle in Carac's jaw jump before he dropped his arms to his sides and said, "I know, old friend. However, witches are not supposed to be real."

"Says who?" Ravyn asked.

Carac opened his mouth, but nothing came out. Finally, he shrugged. "I have no idea."

"Well, I know they exist," Ravyn said. "I have killed several, and if we do not stop Sybbyl, more innocents will die."

Carac held her gaze for a long moment. "Tell me more."

His soft demand sent a thrill through Ravyn. The idea— the *hope*—that he might side with them left her breathless with excitement.

13

I n all his life, Carac had never thought to ask someone to give him information on witches. As if it were as common as battle tactics.

Yet, here he was, doing just that.

He glanced at Simon to find his friend focused on Ravyn. Margery kept her gaze on the door and her hand on the hilt of her sword. It was easy for Carac to notice how both Ravyn and Margery stood like any battle-hardened warrior would.

How had he missed it before? That was an easy answer. They had been women, so he hadn't allowed himself to consider it. Not even when he saw Ravyn's crossbow.

Now that he was aware of the difference in her, he had a hard time looking at anything—or anyone—but Ravyn. He had been attracted to her from the beginning, but now that he saw who she truly was, he ached for her. It went bone deep, sinking through skin and muscle to latch on to his very soul.

This...yearning...wasn't something he was accustomed to. Lust, aye, but not the persistent, unrelenting craving to pull

Ravyn close and breathe in her scent, to feel her warmth and discover her curves.

Watching her move in the forest with such elegance and skill had set his blood afire. But it was staring into her dark eyes now, taking in the magnificent warrior woman she was, that made it nearly impossible to breathe.

Her seductive brown gaze studied him silently, unaware of his inner torment. "Are you sure you want to know?"

"I do not," he admitted. "However, I see no other option. You, Margery, and even Simon know what to expect. I need to, as well, if I am to help you."

Ravyn's full lips pressed together briefly. "Knowing and experiencing what a witch can do are two different things."

"I am aware of that, but I have to begin somewhere. Unless you want to invite Sybbyl for a demonstration."

Ravyn's eyes lit with a fire that burned with retribution. "That will happen soon enough, and you will not get in my way when it does. She is mine."

"We can help kill her," Simon said.

Carac crossed his arms over his chest, curious at Ravyn's heated words. "We are the best at what we do."

"It will not matter how skilled either of you is," Margery stated.

Carac glanced at Margery before his gaze returned to Ravyn. "Why?"

"Witches can only be killed by certain types of wood or metal, and it is different for each witch. Or," Ravyn continued, "by weapons like mine and Margery's. Instruments that have magic added to them."

Carac rubbed a hand over his mouth before dropping his arms to his sides. Shite. Of all the things he'd thought they might say, that wasn't one of them. "I think, perhaps, you should start at the beginning."

"I will stand guard," Margery said. She walked to Ravyn and paused. "I do not like the idea of Sybbyl or one of John's knights coming upon us."

Simon started toward her, but Margery held up her hand. "You should remain to hear the story. Besides, no one will see me."

"Let her go," Ravyn urged Carac and Simon.

Carac relented and nodded to Simon, who leaned a shoulder against the wall and waited impatiently for the story to begin, his gaze darting to the door.

Ravyn watched Margery slip out of the chamber before she met Carac's gaze. "Once, a very, very long time ago in the north, the Vikings learned of a woman who could do magic. The Norse have always revered anyone with special abilities, but this woman went above and beyond what any others could do. She was the First Witch. Her name was lost through the centuries, but after her, more and more women developed similar skills, though none could match her in power."

Carac knew very little about the Norse, and with just a few sentences, he found himself completely immersed in Ravyn's tale.

She drew in a deep breath. "Some of the stories say that the First Witch was good, some say she did bad things with her magic. No one really knows because it was so long ago. Before the First Witch died, she commanded that her bones be scattered across various lands upon her death. For eons, legends about the First Witch were told among other witches. The story shifted and altered until it eventually faded with time. But the few things that remained the same were that she was the first, and that she feared someone bringing her back to life—which is why she insisted that her bones be hidden.

"After her death, and the scattering of her bones, life went on. Witches moved from the north into all lands. As with most everything, some used their abilities for good, while others chose the darkness and made the decision to benefit from their magic with power, immortality, and many other things."

Simon blew out a breath and mumbled, "Shite."

Carac had to agree. It was difficult enough for him to accept magic, but add in immortality, and he was pushing his limits.

Ravyn glanced at the floor before continuing. "I do not know exactly when the Coven was formed, but that group of witches has been a problem for hundreds of years. Documents show they were always a significant force, but a few decades ago, they began to search out other witches."

"For what purpose?" Carac asked.

"To force them to join them. Any witches who refused were killed."

Carac frowned, unsettled by such drastic actions. "Those kinds of measures are used when a party intends to dominate another."

Ravyn nodded slowly. "Exactly. One witch named Edra lived quietly in a village while keeping her abilities secret. She fell in love with a man named Radnar. One day, the Coven came looking for her and gave her an ultimatum: join them or die. She knew if she refused the Coven outright, they *would* kill her. So she ran from everything she knew and loved—including Radnar—because she feared they would take their anger out on those she cared about.

"For seven years, Edra kept ahead of the Coven, always on the run. Then, one day, she had enough. She decided to take a stand and fight against the three witches who had been after her. Edra fought them, unknowing that Radnar happened to be in the area and witnessed everything.

"Edra, with Radnar's help, defeated the witches. Since he

now knew her secret, she told him everything. Time had not diminished their love, nor could they remain separated any longer. They decided to face the Coven together. On their journey, Edra spotted a homeless, starving girl and offered her —Leoma—a home. Leoma went with Edra and Radnar, and she was the first of many who found shelter and comfort with the couple.

"Edra converted the ruins of an abbey into a home and took in anyone running from the Coven, as well as any orphaned child who needed help. Knights came and joined Radnar, and together they taught all who wished to pick up a weapon how to fight witches. And so, we became Hunters."

Carac was well aware that Ravyn didn't mention whether or not she was an orphan. There was a story there, and he longed to know everything there was to know about this warrior woman who made him burn with need.

"All of you can fight?" Simon asked.

Ravyn laid a hand on her crossbow. "Everyone at the abbey has duties. Those of us who wanted to hunt the witches learned how. We trained with all weapons, but if we favored one over another, that is what we chose."

Carac widened his stance. "These knights who trained you, they knew what you were leaning to fight against?"

"Aye," she replied. "Some came for only a short while, teaching everything they knew before moving on. Others decided to stay and chose the abbey as their final destination. However, more than just knights trained us. Men from other places found us and shared their knowledge in weapons, battle, and espionage, as well."

"You never feared that someone had been sent by the Coven?" Carac asked.

Ravyn shrugged. "Of course, we did. But Edra's magic ensured that the abbey was hidden from everyone unless you knew how to get in. Also, each person was required to walk beneath an arch to reach the abbey. Edra spelled that gateway to reveal anyone or anything hidden that might mean us harm. Besides, up until recently, the Coven had no idea we were hunting them."

Simon pushed away from the wall. "What changed?"

"Leoma was on a mission, hunting a witch. A lord was after the same woman for killing his ward and had no idea what she was."

Carac frowned as he cocked his head. Surely, Ravyn couldn't be speaking of Braith. His friend's ward had been murdered, but Carac hadn't heard of Braith going after the person responsible.

Ravyn continued. "The man foolishly tried to fight the witch on his own. Leoma ended up saving his life, and the two decided to team up."

"The man's name," Carac demanded.

Ravyn paused for a moment. "Braith."

Simon's head jerked to Carac. "Did you not receive a missive from Braith?"

"Aye," Carac answered.

"Braith did say that he knew of others he wished to ask to join in our fight against the Coven," Ravyn replied.

Carac let that news sink in as he got back to the story. "So, Braith and Leoma fought the witch."

"They fought several. The Coven killed Braith's ward to get him to follow the witch because they needed him."

Carac squeezed his eyes closed briefly as he shook his head. "Why? Did he know of witches beforehand?"

"Nay. They wanted him to find the Blood Skull."

"I do not like the sound of that," Simon said tersely.

Ravyn's lips flattened. "The Blood Skull is from the First

Witch. And the only one who could retrieve it was a descendant of the person who hid the skull."

"Braith," Carac said.

Ravyn nodded. "When he took the Blood Skull, he became its Warden. In his hands, the relic is protected and protects him in return. In fact, it brought him back to life."

Carac was going to need a drink after this. "Can you not use the Blood Skull to end the Coven?"

"That is what we wish to do. Unfortunately, it is not that simple." Ravyn licked her lips and shifted her feet. "When Leoma and Braith fought the Coven, the witches learned about us. Now, they are after us. We were always at a disadvantage before, reacting to where we learned a witch had struck a village or an innocent. We would then track and kill them. Now, they are drawing us out, all the while continuing on with whatever quest they're on."

"Which is?" Carac asked.

Ravyn swallowed heavily. "We do not know for sure, but we suspect that the Coven's goal is to find all the bones of the First Witch and bring her back."

"Even if they do, you said that Braith has the Blood Skull," Simon pointed out.

She shrugged. "I would like to think that the Coven cannot succeed, but it is a chance that none of us at the abbey are willing to take."

Carac nodded in agreement. "How many witches are in the Coven?"

"We have no idea. There were four Coven elders. Braith and the Blood Skull eliminated two. If we locate a witch, we now follow them to see if they are after something before we kill them."

"How many of you have stopped a witch since Leoma and Braith?" Carac asked.

Ravyn glanced away. "There are only a few Hunters. That is why Braith wanted to bring in more men he thought might join us in this war—so we can track more witches at once."

"I see," Simon stated.

Carac thought of the staff that Simon had mentioned earlier. "Anything a witch is after is of interest, aye?"

"It is," Ravyn agreed.

"There is an item here. A Staff of the Eternal, or so we heard it called. That is what Sybbyl wants."

Simon's face twisted in disgust. "She killed dozens to get Randall to give it to her."

"Sybbyl would not remain here if she had the staff," Ravyn said, her eyes alight with anticipation. "There is still a chance I can stop her."

"*We*," Margery corrected from outside the chamber.

Simon nodded. "Aye. We."

"Neither of you has weapons that can kill Sybbyl," Ravyn pointed out.

Carac shared a grin with Simon. "Perhaps not, but there are other ways we can aid you."

"I need to talk to Randall," Ravyn said.

Carac lifted one side of his mouth in a grin. "I can bring you to him."

"Then do. I have no wish to wait another moment," she urged.

Carac pivoted and led the way out of the chamber. He couldn't believe that he was going to war against witches, but it was the first time in a long while that he felt there was something worth fighting for.

Not to mention, he would be standing alongside Ravyn while doing it.

14

The brush of their fingers as Ravyn walked beside Carac to where Lord Randall was being held sent a charged rush of something roaring through her, a feeling so strong that she almost tripped over her feet.

Lust scorched her, sending her up in flames so hot that she was singed from the inside out.

And all from the barest of touches.

What would it be like if she kissed Carac? Touched him?

Took him into her body?

She grew flushed, sweat trickling at her brow with the direction of her thoughts. No one at the abbey had ever urged her to use her body. Ravyn had done that on her own. She had never been ashamed of her curiosity or the pleasure that she found.

But this...whatever *this* was...took her by surprise. She knew desire, had felt attraction, and had given in to temptation. The draw she felt to Carac was something more—something much, much deeper.

She wanted to explore what it was, to see where it could lead. Yet, the fact that she was near a witch made her pause.

Coven witches never hesitated to use others against the one they wanted to hurt. Sybbyl already suspected Ravyn. Given a chance, the witch would turn her attention on Carac...and he would pay with his life.

The four walked through the damp, gloomy dungeon together. Above Ravyn, the ceiling was one arch after another, holding up the weight of the castle above. Behind her and Carac, Simon and Margery kept pace. No one spoke.

Ravyn had always hated dungeons. They were never a good place, and while she understood the need for them, she also knew the horrors some were subjected to within the bowels of such places.

She found it odd that there were no guards anywhere. Then again, with Sybbyl here, the witch wasn't worried about Randall getting free or anyone helping him.

They walked down rows of empty cells, each bleaker than the last, even with their doors open. At the very end of the corridor stood a closed, metal door.

As they approached, she saw the figure in the back of the cell. His arms were chained to the wall. He was pitched forward, as if his legs had finally given out.

The fine clothes of Baron Randall Bryce were soiled and ripped. The very posture of the man spoke of someone who had been broken both mentally and physically. This wasn't the first time Ravyn had seen such a sight, but it didn't make it any easier to witness.

She halted before the door and wrapped a hand around a metal bar. The soft vibration she felt made her release it instantly and step back.

Carac frowned at her. She shook her head and whispered, "Do not touch it."

"Magic," Margery replied.

Ravyn swung her head back to the man within. "Lord Randall, I come as a friend."

He didn't so much as twitch. Ravyn didn't know if he was asleep, pretending not to hear her, or if he was dead. She slung the strap of her crossbow over her shoulder and tried again.

"What happened to your people is not your fault. Even if you had given Sybbyl what she asked for the first time, she would have taken those lives. It is what a witch such as she does."

The soft rattle of the chains filled the air as Randall slowly lifted his head of matted black hair. Ravyn inwardly winced when she saw the blood on his face from his broken nose and cracked lip. One eye was swollen shut, but she glimpsed the look of a shattered man in his good eye—and she hated Sybbyl all the more.

"Who beat him?" Margery demanded.

Simon said, "I suppose it was Sybbyl."

Ravyn shook her head. "The things a witch does to a person most often cannot be seen. This was the work of men."

"John's knights," Carac said, anger in every syllable.

Margery turned on her heel and ran back the way they'd come as quietly as a ghost.

Ravyn moved as close as she could to the bars. "Lord Randall, you are not alone. I will help you."

"Run," he rasped. "Run far from this place."

"I cannot. I *will* not."

His face crumpled. "The Devil has come to Bryce Castle."

"Sybbyl is evil, but she can be stopped. I need to find that which she seeks."

Lord Bryce jerked against his chains. "Run!"

Margery returned then with a loaf of bread. She chucked it

through the metal bars, and it rolled to Bryce's feet, but he wasn't able to lean down and get it.

"Please," Ravyn begged him. "Tell me where the staff is."

Carac turned to Simon and said, "Find the key."

Ravyn didn't take her eyes off Randall as Simon hurried away. She worried that he was too broken to understand what she wanted from him—or too scared to tell her anything.

"It may be too late," Carac whispered to her.

But she wasn't going to give up that easily. She nodded to Carac before she said to Randall, "You knew the staff was here."

His head dropped forward as he moaned in pain.

"You knew it was here," she continued, "because your family has been guarding it. You tried to keep it hidden from Sybbyl by pretending you did not know what it was. Let us help you."

"You cannot," Randall mumbled.

Carac jumped in before Ravyn could speak. "We can. It is I, Carac, my lord. You have my word that we will keep the staff out of Sybbyl's grasp."

"Sir Carac?" Randall said as he lifted his head enough to look at them.

Carac gave a nod. "Aye, my lord. We can help you."

"I am beyond saving," Randall replied.

"The staff is not," Ravyn added. "You have no idea what will happen if Sybbyl gets it."

Randall made a sound at the back of his throat. "I know the Staff of the Eternal was never supposed to be unearthed. I know that it can be wielded to bring destruction to thousands."

"We have no wish to use it," Ravyn said. "I know of a place where it can be hidden once more."

Carac's head suddenly whipped around. He jerked his gaze to Ravyn. "Hide."

She didn't need to be told twice. Both she and Margery went in opposite directions. The only place for them to hide was within open cells, and Ravyn wasn't too proud to admit that it made her skin crawl to be inside one.

Flattening herself against the damp stones, she waited in the shadows, her heart slamming against her ribs as she heard footsteps approaching.

"Carac?"

Ravyn recognized the voice but couldn't place it immediately.

"What are you doing here?"

John. Ravyn should've known he would venture down here. No doubt Sybbyl was with him. If only Ravyn hadn't touched the bars. Most likely, that was what drew the couple to the dungeons.

"You wished me at the castle," Carac replied.

"Not in the dungeon," Sybbyl said.

Her voice was close. Ravyn fisted her hands and readied to leap out and begin her assault. With a little more coaxing, Randall would reveal where the staff was located, which meant there was no more need for Sybbyl.

Carac grunted. "You did not say that before."

"I am saying it now," Sybbyl snapped. "I have guests coming to visit Lord Randall soon, and they have no wish to see you or anyone else."

Ravyn frowned, unease stirring her gut. The only ones who would be coming at Sybbyl's behest were more witches. The elders, even.

Ravyn's plan to kill the witch would either have to begin now, or she would need to wait. Frankly, as much as she enjoyed ridding the world of evil, she wasn't so keen on going head-to-head with an elder.

When Leoma had done it, she hadn't known who Eleanor was. Now, the Hunters had names and descriptions of the remaining elders. And while any witch was a formidable opponent, none compared to an elder.

There was a reason there were only four elders. It took powerful magic and years of wielding it in order to achieve such a rank. The elders were all intelligent, treacherous, devious women who ruled the Coven like their own kingdom.

"When was the last time Lord Randall ate?" Carac demanded.

John's voice sounded nearly in the chamber with Ravyn when he spoke. "That is a good question."

"What does it matter?" Sybbyl exclaimed. "It is not as if he will live through this."

"If you continue saying such things, you will give him no incentive to help you," Carac stated.

Sybbyl muttered something under her breath. "I suppose you threw that bread to him."

"Aye," Carac answered.

"I knew someone was down here."

Ravyn dropped her head against the wall behind her. She shouldn't have touched the door. Sybbyl would never have come if Ravyn had kept her hands to herself.

"We should feed him," John told Sybbyl. "He has yet to give us the exact location."

Sybbyl made a noise that sounded like a loud half-snort, half-laugh. "By all means, feed him. Not that it will make a difference once my friends arrive. If Randall wishes to save himself pain, he will tell me what I want to know before then. Otherwise, his suffering will last for months."

There was a click and then a loud creak as the cell door

swung open. Ravyn turned her head to listen, but the earthen floor made it difficult to determine much movement.

Minutes passed in silence. Ravyn was still toying with the idea of attacking Sybbyl. Margery would be waiting for a sign, and it would limit the number of people who could get hurt.

If Ravyn managed to kill Sybbyl, she would still have to deal with the arrival of the other witches. Even if she found the staff and got out in time, those left behind would pay for what she had done.

Enough innocents had felt the wrath of the Coven. Ravyn couldn't, in good conscience, do such a thing. She'd become a Hunter to rid the world of Coven witches, but also to protect those who couldn't defend themselves.

If she ran away instead of facing the other witches, she would be going back on everything she stood for. Her other options were to kill Sybbyl and face the arriving witches—be they elders or not.

Or, she could wait.

The smart move would be for her to be patient and discover who was coming to Bryce Castle. Information was what the abbey needed, especially if this Staff of the Eternal were part of the First Witch. As much as it pained Ravyn, she must hold off on her attack.

"Satisfied?" Sybbyl asked sarcastically.

There was a pause, and then Carac said, "He needs water."

"I have some," Simon said as he walked through the dungeon.

Ravyn hated not being able to see. She listened as Carac and Simon gave Randall food and water, but it ended quickly as Sybbyl ordered them out.

The slamming of the metal door echoed through the dungeon like an ominous hammer—or blade—being dropped. Ravyn listened as John droned on about his army, but the voices didn't move away.

In fact, they remained very near to Ravyn.

Sybbyl shushed John. A moment later, John asked her, "What are you looking for?"

Ravyn couldn't remove her crossbow for fear of making a noise. She silently withdrew the dagger at her hip and waited for Sybbyl to walk into the cell.

Several tense moments went by before Sybbyl huffed loudly and said, "Everyone out. Now."

Ravyn listened as John, Sybbyl, Simon, and Carac left the dungeons. Getting out unseen now would be a challenge, but it also gave her a chance to talk to Randall once more.

15

Worry knotted painfully in Carac's gut. No matter how many times he tried to return to the dungeon, his way was continually blocked either by men or locked doors. But Ravyn was still down there.

And he couldn't just leave her.

Simon was also trying to find a way to rescue Ravyn and Margery, but Carac wasn't optimistic. The entire time Carac had spoken with Sybbyl and John, he noted how the witch's gaze kept going to the various empty cells.

As if she knew that Ravyn was there.

There was a part of him that wanted to see Sybbyl do magic so he would witness the proof himself. While he believed Simon, and Ravyn's story was believable, he needed to see it for himself.

At the moment, however, his focus was on Ravyn. If he didn't find a way to get her out of the dungeon, it was only a matter of time before Sybbyl found her. And the thought of that infuriated him.

His strides were long after he dismounted and handed his

horse to Rob before heading to his tent. He had all but been kicked out of Bryce Castle. Which did nothing to lessen his growing ire. Or worry.

Carac might think of Ravyn as a warrior woman, but she was first and foremost, a female. It had been ingrained in him from birth to protect women, and that's what he was desperately trying to do.

Shoving aside the flap, Carac stepped into his tent and immediately drew up short at the sight of a crossbow on the table. *Ravyn*. His gaze swung to his bed to find a cloaked figure. She raised her hands and shoved back the hood of her overgarment.

Without thinking, he made his way to her, stopping short of grabbing her and pulling her up and into his arms. "How did you get out?"

"It was not easy," she confessed while glancing at the entry to the tent.

"No one will bother us the rest of the night," he assured her.

"Not even Simon?"

"He announces himself before entering."

Ravyn nodded and relaxed.

Carac glanced around for something to do. He spotted the jug of water and hurried to it. After pouring two goblets, he turned and held one out to her.

Ravyn glanced at the drink before rising to her feet. She closed the distance between them and grasped the goblet from his hand. "Thank you."

"Have you eaten?"

She took a drink, waiting until she swallowed before shaking her head. "There was no time."

"And Margery?"

"Outside your tent. We do not intend to remain long. I

just wanted you to know we are safe."

He set aside his water. "Sybbyl is looking for you. I even sent men searching. You cannot go out there."

"Of course, I can," Ravyn replied with a smile. "We are good at remaining hidden."

"Perhaps. Yet I doubt you will rest easy. No one will search for you here." As soon as the words were out, Carac knew that he would do anything to keep Ravyn in his tent.

With him.

"And Margery?" she asked.

While he wanted time alone with Ravyn, he couldn't very well tell her that. "She can remain here with you. She could also sleep in Simon's tent."

"Carac," Simon called from outside.

He looked at Ravyn to await her nod. Once she'd agreed, Carac bade Simon enter. His friend's gaze immediately landed on Ravyn. He gave her a welcoming smile.

"Ravyn, I wanted to let you know that I have given Margery my tent. No one bothers me. Ever," Simon stated. "You both can sleep there undisturbed the rest of the night."

Carac swung his head to Ravyn to find her lips curving into a grateful smile. The thoughts that filled his head of kissing her, removing every inch of leather from her body, and laying her on his bed rolled away like smoke.

"That is very kind," Ravyn told Simon. "I cannot thank you enough."

Simon bowed slightly. "We are fighting this war together. Carac can show you the way."

With that, Simon turned on his heel and departed.

"Margery wanted me to tell you about us," Ravyn said. "She thought you might help."

Carac raised a brow. "You did not agree with her?"

"I am more wary of others."

"That is probably wise. I can have food brought to you and Margery."

She smiled. "We would appreciate that."

"And where shall I have it sent?" Surely, he wasn't the only one who felt the attraction between them. Ravyn had to feel *something*.

"Simon's tent."

Carac barely held his disappointment back.

"For Margery," Ravyn finished.

He couldn't hold back his grin. "And you?"

"I wish to take your offer. Of sleeping here. With you."

All the blood rushed to his cock at her words. Did the woman have any idea what she did to him? How nothing but her words had him ready to drop to his knees and beg to touch her?

She softly set her goblet beside his, her eyes lowered to the ground for a brief moment. "Does my forwardness shock you?"

"Actually, I quite like it."

"Really?" she asked, stepping closer.

He nodded, moving so that their bodies brushed together, and he rested his hands on her hips. "Indeed."

"Would you like to hear more?"

"Aye." The word came out like a hoarse whisper. With the desire coursing through him with such speed and heat, he was surprised he could speak at all.

Her brown gaze swept over his face as she put her hands on his chest. She flattened her palms against him and moved her touch upward to his neck and then his jaw.

The feel of her hands was like a brand, even through his clothes. If this were what she did to him now, he was likely to go up in flames when he finally got her naked. Just the thought of her bared before him made his mouth go dry.

"I have wanted to touch you since I first saw you," she confessed. "You stood so imposing, so strong, that my body was drawn to you of its own accord."

His hands slid around to her back where he splayed his palm against her and pulled her closer. Blood rushed through his body, pounding in his ears.

It felt as if he had craved Ravyn for an eternity. Holding her made him feel alive. As if he had just now woken from an eternity of sleep. That, somehow, her touch pulled away the veil that shrouded the world, allowing him to finally see it clearly.

See her.

Everything was alive and vibrant. But all he saw was her. Inky black hair, seductive eyes, and a smile that pulled him ever closer.

His hunger grew with every beat of his heart. The longer he went without tasting her lips, the more he yearned for her.

His gaze dropped to her mouth as she rose up on her tiptoes. Her lids slid shut as her lips parted in invitation. He stared at her upturned face a moment more before he closed his eyes and lowered his head.

Time stood still as their lips pressed together. They held still a heartbeat before he went in for another kiss, moving his mouth over hers. When she tilted her head to the side and ran her tongue over his lips, he moaned loudly and moved his hand down to her shapely bottom before he pressed her against his arousal.

The kiss deepened, their hunger propelling them forward. He couldn't get close enough, couldn't kiss her long enough. The more he sought, the more she willingly gave.

And the more he craved.

He was drowning in her taste, in all that was Ravyn—and

he did it happily. She was beautiful, strong, courageous, and resourceful. And she was in his arms.

The need to shout it to the Heavens had him breaking the kiss to draw in a breath. He smoothed his hands down either side of her face and took in her loveliness. From her kiss-swollen lips to her heavy-lidded eyes that made his balls tighten with uncontrollable need.

To his surprise, she took a few steps back out of his arms. He thought she had changed her mind until she unclasped her cloak and tossed it to the side. He stared, transfixed, as she began removing various weapons.

With each piece that fell to the ground, he grew hotter and hotter for her. She paused and smiled at him before bending over and taking off one tall boot then the other. His mouth went dry when she unhooked the tight vest that molded to her upper body and beneath her breasts and let it fall from her shoulders.

His heart began to pound uncontrollably when she stood in only her dark red shirt and leather trousers. Never did he think a woman would look good in men's attire, but Ravyn had proven him wrong.

She was decadent. Supremely sensual.

Utterly erotic.

He waited with baited breath as she unfastened the pants and pushed them down her legs to step out of them. Leaving her in nothing but the shirt that skimmed the tops of her thighs.

Instead of taking it off, she reached up and removed the strip of leather holding her braid. She shook out her long, midnight tresses and let her beautiful locks fall around her.

Her hands grasped the hem of the shirt, but he quickly stopped her. "Nay. Not yet."

She cocked her head to the side. "You do not wish to see me?"

"Very much so. But this sight of you is...sublime."

Her answering smile made him itch to have his hands on her again.

He shrugged out of his padded jerkin, letting it fall to his feet. Next, he unbuckled the belt holding his sword and set it aside. Ravyn's eyes sparkled as they watched him.

His gaze dropped down to her long, bare, shapely legs and he found that he couldn't concentrate. If he had met her years ago, Carac would never have left his castle and hidden who he really was from others.

He would've taken her as his wife and made love to her every day, filling her belly with babies. His home would have been a place he wanted to be instead of something he didn't wish to see.

Carac bent and removed the dagger from his boot, setting it on the table next to her crossbow. Then he unbuckled the scabbard at his waist with the double knives hidden at his back.

When Ravyn smiled at the sight of them, he couldn't help but grin back. She understood the need for hidden weapons, those that an enemy couldn't see. The kind that had saved his life—and most likely hers—on many occasions.

He pulled his tunic from his trousers before he tugged off his boots and tossed them aside. It was everything he could do to remain where he was and not reach for her.

As if sensing his need, she backed up until she reached the bed. She tucked one leg beneath her and slowly lowered herself until she sat, one hand on the blanket to hold herself up.

Carac couldn't wait to lay her back and have her hair spread around her and her legs wide as he thrust inside. Deep. Hard.

He could think of nothing but her. She filled his thoughts and his senses. Like the witches she hunted, he was completely spellbound by her. And he had to admit, he quite liked it.

"I would see more," she urged in a seductive voice that made his cock jump.

By all that was holy, he was going to enjoy making her his. And not just for the night. He might never let her go.

16

S he was absolutely, undeniably captivated. Ravyn couldn't look away from Carac's gaze. Hunger burned brightly in his green depths, brazen and shameless.

A lock of blond hair slipped over his forehead. He walked to her, removing his tunic as he did. Ravyn's mouth fell open when she saw the hard body bared to her. Muscles honed and firm, molded to form a splendid specimen.

The various scars that covered him proved the many battles he had been involved in—and survived. Her mouth watered, and her hands clenched, aching to run along the muscles of his stomach and chest.

She longed to feel his strong arms around her. She yearned to have the weight of him on top of her. She craved to feel his arousal slide into her.

"Woman, you are bringing me to the edge," Carac rasped.

She lifted her gaze to his and saw a muscle ticking in his jaw. Ravyn rose up onto her knees and laid her palms on his chest. The pure heat of him made her shiver in anticipation of the pleasure she knew would come.

It was there in his ravenous gaze, in the way his hands clenched and unclenched, in the rapid rise and fall of his chest. It was in the very air around them, charged with lust and need.

A sigh she couldn't hold back escaped her lips as she smoothed her hands over the hard sinew and ran them up to his thick shoulders and corded neck. Power. It radiated from him, as formidable as the sun.

It was part of what drew her to him. He wielded it as expertly as a sword, but he did it with grace and elegance. His power was not just in his body, it was also in his mind.

Carac was a true warrior, the kind of man who would always fight for innocents and the on the side of good. How had she not recognized that as soon as she saw him? Not that it mattered. She saw him now, truly saw him.

And she was awed by the man before her.

He lifted a hand and gently set his fingers on her cheek before slowly sliding them down to her jaw. She couldn't take her eyes off his face as his gaze followed his hand over to her mouth. With her breathing shallow and her heart slamming against her ribs, he stared at her as if she were the most precious thing to him, as if he would protect her for all eternity.

His head lowered until their lips were breaths apart. But he didn't kiss her. He rubbed his jaw against one side of her face and then the other. All the while, his other hand wound around her back and skimmed down her butt before clutching a handful and pressing her against him.

She gasped at the feel of his arousal. His eyes met hers, a small, satisfied smile appearing before he pressed his lips to hers.

Ravyn dug her fingers into his back at the first touch of his tongue against hers. His taste was wild and erotic, fierce and carnal. Their kiss grew frenzied, the fires of their desire consuming them.

And they willingly stepped into the blaze.

A shiver raced over her when she realized that Carac was gradually lifting her tunic. His callused palm grazed her hip, then her waist. She moaned when his thumb caressed the underside of her breast.

He persisted, tantalizing her with his touch, but never actually touching her. It was too much. Ravyn tore her lips from his and tried to jerk off her tunic. But he stopped her. She looked into his green eyes, silently questioning him.

"Do you know how long I have dreamed of removing your clothes and baring your body to me?" he asked in a low, decadent whisper that made her sex clench.

"Nay."

"From the first moment I saw you." His gaze lowered to the tunic that was bunched at her waist. "I thought of how I would remove your gown slowly. Then I saw you today. The sight of your curves so boldly and beautifully exposed has made me think of little else."

She was taken aback by his words and the desire she heard in them. Her breasts swelled, her nipples puckered, eagerly awaiting his touch.

"I am yours," she declared.

He briefly looked at her with a crooked grin that sent her heart tripping over itself. But his attention returned to her tunic. With both hands on her waist now, he smoothed his palms along the indent and then down to her hips before moving up again.

This time, he didn't stop. This time, he pushed the fabric higher. She raised her arms over her head, her eyes on his face as he slowly moved the tunic to expose her breasts and then higher until he threw it aside, forgotten.

"By the Heavens," he whispered and held his hands a few inches from her.

No one had ever treated her with such care or looked at her with such yearning before. It took her breath away.

His gaze locked on her right forearm where a Celtic raven was tattooed, its wings spread. She held still as he lifted her arm and ran his thumb over the design. Then his head swung to her other arm as he lifted it to see the Nordic rune.

"The raven is considered to be one of the wisest and oldest of animals, and for the Celts, it played an important role in protection, magic, and prophecy," she explained.

His green eyes met hers. "And this one?"

She looked at the tattoo. "It is a Nordic rune. To the Vikings, it symbolizes courage."

"Beautiful," he murmured, stroking both tats.

Finally, he returned his hands to her hips. Then his gaze lifted to her face. There were no words, but none were needed. The passion between them was palpable, the desire tangible. There was no escaping it, no avoiding it.

And neither wanted to.

Carac moved swiftly, one arm going around her as he lifted her and put her on her back. He then loomed over her, his face tight with need, his eyes dark with desire as he situated himself between her legs.

Her lips parted on a silent moan when he cupped a breast and held it as he bent and wrapped his mouth around her turgid peak. He teased her nipple until she was rocking her hips against him and gripping his arm tightly.

He didn't relent. She arched her back when he moved to her other breast to repeat the same delicious torment. The need tightened within her so that she barely noticed that he still wore his trousers.

She raked her nails down his back when he rose over her to

rock his hard cock against her exposed womanhood. The rush of pleasure was so great that she groaned for more.

But she should have realized that Carac was far from done with her. He kissed her chest, her breasts, and down her stomach. It wasn't until he pressed his lips against her hipbones that she bit her lip in anticipation.

He settled between her legs, his warm breath fanning her swollen flesh. A cry tore from her at the first touch of his tongue against her sex.

She tangled her hands in the blanket when he found her clit and ruthlessly brought her to the edge of oblivion. He expertly and easily worked her body with his tongue and mouth until she was mindless with desire.

Then he slid a finger inside her. Ravyn was caught in a web of rapture so moving, so stirring that she felt transcendent. She was ensnared by need, imprisoned by desire in a way where she could do nothing but lose herself in the ecstasy.

She was so caught up in the rapturous feelings rushing through her that the orgasm caught her by surprise. The strength of it was ferocious, sending her spiraling into bliss so intense that it momentarily blinded her.

The sight of Ravyn's body locked in pleasure was just what Carac wanted to see. He looked up into her face to find her mouth open on a silent scream, her eyes closed, and her arms straining as she gripped the blanket.

But it was her body clamping around his finger that nearly made him spill his seed right then. He wanted—nay, he *needed* —to be inside her. To merge their bodies and tangle their limbs.

He wanted her screaming. For him. For the pleasure he gave her.

Carac pulled his finger from her and braced his hands on either side of her. The sight of Ravyn flushed with gratification caused his balls to tighten.

Her eyes slowly opened as she loosened her hold on the blanket. Their gazes met, and she sat up, wrapping her arms around his neck as she kissed him.

As their tongues dueled, he lowered himself down upon her. But she quickly took over and rolled him onto his back. He tried to keep her against him, but Ravyn ended the kiss and sat up. With her eyes on his face, she placed her palms on his chest and leaned forward so that her hair fell like a curtain around him.

Just when he thought he would get to kiss her again, she smiled and nipped at his earlobe. Before he could react, her hand was around his aching cock.

Carac jerked at the feel of her. Then she moved her fist up and down his length. For a man already on the verge of a climax, it was too much. He grabbed her arm to halt her before she pushed him over the edge.

Her knowing smile said she knew exactly what she had done. But there was no remorse in her dark depths...only the promise of more to come.

The same promise he had given her.

The longer he was with Ravyn, the more of a match he realized they were. His thoughts halted when she rose up on her knees and held herself over his arousal.

He leisurely caressed his hands up her thighs to her hips as she lowered herself upon him. The first touch of her tight, wet body around him had him tightening his grip. Once she was fully seated, he waited for her to begin moving.

Her low moan made sweat break out over his body. He

cupped her breasts, tweaking her nipples as she slowly increased her tempo.

To say that she was magnificent atop him was an understatement. Her visceral, raw passion mixed with her allure was a heady combination that he happily found himself ensnared in.

He sat up and moved her onto her back before pulling out of her. Then he flipped her onto her stomach and raised her hips. He stilled as his gaze took in the tattoo of a snake eating its own tail that covered her entire back. He wanted to know what it meant, but that was for later. Now, he needed her.

He thrust into her. The soft cry of approval that fell from her lips propelled him onward. He gripped her hips and began to drive into her. She pushed her hips back against him, creating friction between their bodies and fanning the flames of their need.

She rose up on her hands, and he leaned over her so they were cheek to cheek. Sweat glistened on their bodies, causing her hair to stick to both of them. She reached around and tangled her fingers in his hair as he continued to move in and out of her.

With their breathing ragged, and desire pushing them, he was soon pounding into her, thrusting hard, deep, and fast as her cries urged him onward.

Driven by a force as old as time, their bodies came together again and again. Passion consumed them as pleasure inched them ever closer to the pinnacle.

Then, Ravyn cried out, her body bucking beneath his. He straightened and kept plunging into her tight body, intent on prolonging her bliss. But the feeling of her clamping around his cock sent him careening off the cliff. He held her tightly and thrust once more as his seed spilled from him and her body milked him.

She reached around and touched his leg in the silence. Carac pulled her against him as they fell to their sides. He held her too tightly, but he couldn't stop himself. He knew he had something special in his arms, and he wasn't about to let her go.

To his satisfaction, she brought his hand to her lips and kissed it before snuggling against him. After a few moments, he pulled the blanket over them and heard her sigh.

It made him smile. Then again, almost everything Ravyn did made him grin. He wasn't sure what the next days would hold, but he knew he would be standing beside her through it all.

And he didn't intend for this to be their last—or only—time together. If he had his way—and he usually got his way—she would be in his bed and in his arms every night.

Anyone who tried to get in the way of that would be struck down. Because he'd finally found something that he would fight the world for. Ravyn.

17

Malene opened her eyes and stared in confusion at the tree limbs above her. She watched leaves sweetly swaying on the branches, the wind softly rustling them to make a magical harmony.

It was then she realized her head was rising and falling, matching the sounds of deep breathing that reached her ears. Her gaze shifted lower, and she spotted tall, brown boots she knew well attached to legs that stretched out.

Armir. The entire episode of them jumping to the forest to locate the Hunters filled her head. How he held her as she was sick from the magic, how he had staggered to hold them both up, how he'd never let go of her.

She took a deep breath, her heart skipping a beat when she felt an arm tighten around her waist.

Not only was she lying on Armir's chest, but he held her against him. It was the most provocative, sensual embrace she had ever experienced. And she was loath to break it.

This was the most relaxed she had ever seen him. More

than anything, she wanted to look at his face. But to move would most likely wake him.

She didn't know how long they lay together before she realized that he was awake. It was a subtle shift in his breathing. Neither said a word or moved. They remained locked together in silence, simply enjoying their surroundings and each other.

At least, she was.

For all Malene knew, Armir was trying to figure out how to get away from her. That thought made the peace she'd found scatter like birds.

She closed her eyes and committed the moment to memory before she took a deep breath, acting as if she were waking. She wanted to cry out when Armir's arm slid from her. After one more heartbeat, she opened her eyes. Without waiting for Armir to do or say something that might wound her, she sat up and looked around.

Then she turned and faced him. He, too, sat up. Their gazes met, clashed. No matter how much she looked, she couldn't discern what he was thinking. That's how it always was with Armir.

"How do you feel?" he asked, his pale green orbs studying her.

"Horrible. You?"

"Not much better." He let out a sigh and leaned to the side, resting on his hand. "I believe we slept for several hours."

She looked at the sun coming up through the trees. "Actually, I think it could have been all night."

A deep frown furrowed his brow. "I have never been struck down for so much time after doing magic before."

Malene hid her hands as she climbed to her feet. She might not have had anything to do with it, but she didn't wish to talk about it either way. Turning away from Armir, she wiped her skirts and tried to stop thinking about being in his arms.

It was probably a good thing that she had been unconscious. Otherwise, she might have done something incredibly foolish.

"Malene."

His voice coming from close behind her made her jerk slightly in surprise. "Are you well?" she asked.

"Aye," he answered in a clipped tone. "I am more concerned about you."

She whirled to face him and raised her hands, palms out so blue light shone around them. "Me? Look at this. I can handle the magic."

Instead of retorting angrily, he merely raised a blond brow. "Is that why both of us were on our arses the remainder of yesterday and last night?"

She dropped her hands to her sides. "Do not worry about me."

"You are the Lady of the Varroki. It is my duty to be concerned."

He had said those same words many times, but for some reason, this time, they irked her. "Because you do not want to have to explain to everyone that I died? Or is it because you have no wish to find the next Lady and train her?"

Seconds passed as he stared at her without a clue as to his thoughts. Nothing showed on either his face or in his posture. Then he said in a soft voice, "Both."

Just as she figured.

"And neither," he added. "The truth is, you are the strongest Lady the Varroki has seen in ages. I believe that you can do untold things. Without a doubt, you are powerful, but that does not mean you are immortal."

She pulled a leaf stuck to the material on his arm. "I know that."

"You do not, and I do not blame you for it. These past five years, you have felt the magic within you growing, but you have yet to test it against anyone. It is easy to grow arrogant, to think that nothing can harm you. I knew it was a risk for you to leave Blackglade."

"If you were so against it, why did you agree?" she asked, thoroughly perplexed.

He moved closer and reached up. His hand came away with a twig that was tangled in her hair. "Because I know once you have made a decision, nothing will stop you. I knew if I fought to change your mind, that you might very well leave on your own. I would rather stand beside you against whatever we encounter."

"You are a powerful warlock yourself."

He lifted one shoulder in a shrug. "I have only encountered the Coven thrice in all my years, and each time, they left a lasting impression."

"Meaning?"

Armir looked away. "Which way should we go?"

The fact that he wouldn't answer her made Malene's curiosity grow. In all the times they had spoken of the Coven, she hadn't realized that Armir had encountered them, let alone three times.

If he didn't want to talk about what the Coven did, then she wouldn't press. "The abbey could be anywhere."

"It is hidden by magic."

"Then we need to make our presence known."

His head snapped to her, pale green orbs narrowed in warning. "You will also alert any Coven members nearby."

"Do you prefer that we walk around for the next days or weeks searching?"

Armir's lips flattened. "As you wish."

Malene might have suggested letting the Hunters know she was there, but she didn't know what to do. Most everything she did came on instinct. Sometimes, she made a fool of herself, but most times, her intuition was accurate.

She placed her palms together and closed her eyes. Then she opened herself up to the magic within her. She felt it amassing. Behind her eyelids, she could see the blue light growing brighter, building with her magic.

Malene then focused her thoughts on the Hunters. Once her magic was great enough, she sent out a silent call that another witch—hopefully only those at the abbey —would hear.

Once the signal had been sent, she dropped her hands and opened her eyes. The blue lights of her palms were still glowing brightly, bathing Armir in their radiance.

His gaze was on her, a peculiar expression on his face. She blinked, and it was gone. As if it had never been. But she knew what she'd seen. What it was, however, was another matter entirely.

"I suppose we will know shortly who took notice of my summons," she said, needing to fill the silence.

"Aye."

Most of her time was spent alone with Armir in the tower, but only now was she aware of their current circumstances. In Blackglade, her situation was normal. But she was out in the world again. Alone with a virile, handsome man.

Things might be more worrisome if he were attracted to her, but Malene knew that wasn't the case. It saddened her, but then again, maybe she was drawn to Armir because he was the only man she saw on a regular basis.

She wasn't going to wait around to be found. Without a word to Armir, she walked past him to explore while she could. Who knew how quickly she would have to return to Blackglade.

Not that it wasn't pretty. Its wildness appealed to her more than she liked to admit. Remote, stormy, and, some might say, feral, Blackglade was as beautiful as it was harsh.

Still. It had been five years since she had seen anything other than the sea from her tower. Malene wasn't going to let this opportunity pass. Besides, if the Coven were going to be defeated, then she and the Hunters needed to meet.

A union of the two groups would be necessary to eradicate the Coven. And that's exactly what she planned. To remove any and all trace of the Coven. It was time someone took drastic action. For too many centuries, the Varroki had battled the witches of the Coven off and on. And the Coven had grown strong.

Maybe too strong for the Varroki.

Especially when the number of Varroki was diminished.

Armir moved up alongside her. "You have changed much."

She glanced at him, laughing softly. "It has been five years. Of course, I've changed."

"I mean in the last few weeks."

His words concerned her. "A good change?"

"I would say so," he replied. "You have more confidence. It's almost as if you know your path now."

She jerked her head to him. One of Armir's purposes was to keep her on her path. If he thought she didn't need him, then he might leave. And she wasn't prepared for that.

"It is a good thing," he said before she could form a response.

She faced forward once more. "It means you have done a fine job."

"It means you are the right person to lead our people. Even though you still long to have another life."

Her steps slowed. "It has been years since I have said anything about that."

"Do you think I do not see you staring out over the sea? Do you think I do not see the yearning in your eyes?"

At this, she halted and faced him. "You have said nothing of it."

"There was no reason."

"Because I could not go anywhere."

He held her gaze, his silence answer enough.

It was then that Malene became aware they were being watched. She glanced at Armir to see that he was looking around because he felt it, too.

There was a rustle of leaves, and then a woman wearing a white cloak appeared from behind a tree. Blond hair fell on either side of her face. Beside her was a man with long, dark brown hair graying at the temples.

Malene faced them as Armir drew closer to her.

"Be at ease," the woman said. "I am Edra. I believe you are seeking me."

Malene smiled at the witch. "I am. I am Malene, Lady of the Varroki. And this is Armir, my second in command."

"A pleasure," Edra said. She glanced at the man beside her. "This is my husband, Radnar. Come. We will bring you to the abbey."

"You trust us?" Armir asked skeptically.

Edra was already turning away, but she stopped and looked at Armir. "Leoma spoke highly of Jarin upon her return. Both she and Braith said he was instrumental in helping to defeat the Coven. Jarin shared his culture with Leoma, and she, in turn, told us. I have been expecting you."

"We have common enemies," Radnar added. "It is our hope that we can join forces against the Coven."

Malene nodded. "That is why we have come."

"Then let us begin. The Coven does not know where we are, and we would like to keep it that way," Radar said.

Malene looked at Armir to find him staring at her. He gave her a slight nod. With that, she followed Edra, while Armir remained right beside her.

And she was coming to realize that she liked him there.

18

It was a grand thing to be woken with a hard body against her and tantalizing lips on her neck. Ravyn moaned when she felt Carac's arousal.

"I need you again," he rasped near her ear.

His fingers wound in the strands of her hair and pulled her head back, exposing more of her neck. She loved his dominant nature. It called to her on a level she hadn't known she wanted —or desired.

He moved her onto her back and situated himself to push inside her when Simon said his name outside the tent.

Carac stilled, and Ravyn's eyes flew open. Without a word, both quickly rose and began to dress. Once her pants and tunic were on, Carac bid his friend to enter after pulling on his own trousers.

Simon ducked beneath the flap and gave her a quick nod, but he kept his eyes on Carac. "We need to get to Bryce Castle immediately."

Ravyn pulled on her boots and reached for her vest as she

eyed the men. She wanted to demand to know what was going on, but she kept quiet and listened.

Carac found a tunic and yanked it over his head. He began reaching for his weapons and securing them to his person. "What happened?"

"Five leagues away, a family was slaughtered," Simon stated.

Ravyn paused, her heart leaping in her chest. She knew what Simon would say next, but it didn't make it any easier to hear.

"It is being said that witches did it."

Carac's gaze moved to her, their eyes meeting. Without looking at Simon, he asked, "Did they catch those responsible?"

"Nay."

Ravyn found her cloak and fastened it before slipping the dagger into her boot. Every instinct she had urged her to go after the witches to avenge the innocents that were killed. This wasn't the first time witches had struck families since hers, but each time grew harder and harder to bear.

With barely any movement of the tent flap, Margery entered and walked straight to Ravyn. "Are you all right?"

Ravyn felt Carac's gaze on her. "Fine."

"What do you want to do?"

Ravyn walked to the table and found her crossbow and a small quiver of arrows. Her hand shook slightly when she reached for the weapon, but once she had her fingers around it, she calmed.

Ravyn turned her head to Margery. "I want to kill every last Coven member."

"I am ready," Margery said with a lift of her chin.

Carac took a step toward them. "It is not that simple."

"Aye, it is," Margery argued.

Ravyn put a hand on her friend's arm. "Carac is right. Sybbyl suspects that we are Hunters. This could be a diversion."

Simon crossed his arms over his chest. "That was my thought, as well. That is why I said we needed to get to the keep."

"In case Sybbyl tries to locate the staff while everyone's attention is elsewhere," Carac said.

Ravyn knew going to the castle was the right thing to do, but she thought of the now-dead family. What if there was a child—like her—crushed under the weight of a family member and waiting to be rescued? What if even one of them was alive? What if she could kill a witch? That would be one less Coven member to fight later.

"Ravyn."

She jerked at the sound of her name. When she looked up, all three were staring at her. "Aye?"

Margery eyed her with a worried frown. "I can go check out the story about the family."

"Nay. We remain together," Ravyn said.

Simon dropped his arms. "Dawn is approaching, and the men are already waking."

"Then we go now," Carac said and looked at her.

Ravyn nodded in agreement.

Margery gave her one last look before following Simon out of the tent. Ravyn slung her crossbow over her shoulder and waited for Carac to put on his boots and jerkin. His eyes watched her as if waiting for her to say something.

Finally, he stood. "Margery seemed particularly worried about you."

"She frets."

He raised a blond brow, his skepticism obvious. "And your distraction?"

"Deciding which witches to hunt."

His lips twisted ruefully. "I will not push you if you do not wish to share."

She watched as he went to the opening to look outside before he motioned her ahead of him. She raised her hood and hurried out. To her surprise, her mare stood saddled next to his horse. She glanced at Carac to ask how, but he was already speaking.

"Simon followed Margery to where she put the horses. He retrieved them last night."

Ravyn climbed onto her mare and glanced around. "You trust your men?"

"I used to." He mounted and turned his stallion toward her. "Then I met Sybbyl. Now, I trust only Simon, you, and Margery."

Ravyn didn't get a chance to reply as he nudged his horse into a gallop. With a press of her knees, her mare quickly leapt after them.

The sky was turning gray as the darkness gave way to the ball of light slowly rising on the horizon. She inwardly grimaced each time one of the shadows hiding them pulled away as if burned by the sun.

She spotted the castle in time to see the last part of the sun reveal itself. Carac reined his mount to a stop before they reached the fortress.

She drew up alongside him as his head turned to her. Then he asked, "Do you think you can get us in without being seen?"

"Aye. What about Simon and Margery?"

"They will go in another way."

It was smart to split up. Maybe she would've heard that if she hadn't been thinking about the murdered family. She followed Carac as he turned his horse to a copse of trees. Once there, he dismounted.

Ravyn looked at the castle. Now, Carac would be the one to follow her. She quickly ran over the terrain, keeping as low as possible and trusting that he could keep up. She wasn't disappointed. The only time she paused was when they got close enough to see the sentries along the battlements. Then it was a matter of waiting for the guards to turn before they sprinted the rest of the way to the stronghold.

Ravyn glanced up at the wall, her hands flat against the stones.

"Surely, you do not think to climb it," Carac stated.

She looked at him and grinned. "How do you think I got in the first time? But there is another way."

"I was hoping you would say that."

Ravyn hurried to the postern door and pulled it open before slipping inside. Carac quickly followed and pressed close behind her.

"How the hell did you do that?"

"I broke the lock when Margery and I used it last eve to escape."

He grunted, which caused her to smile. Then they were on the move again, working their way inside the castle through the servant's entrance. Sybbyl's massacre of so many within the castle meant that there were few to avoid. The few servants that remained were busy with the morning meal.

That made it relatively easy for her and Carac to get past them and use the back stairs to make their way to the dungeons and Randall. They were turning a corner when she spotted one of John's knights.

Carac grabbed her and pulled her into a small, narrow chamber before they were seen. Another knight joined the first, and it soon became apparent that she and Carac weren't going anywhere anytime soon.

Ravyn blew out a breath and leaned her head against the wall. No windows or other exits made it impossible to leave another way. "I suppose we will be here awhile."

"It looks that way," Carac agreed with a frown. "And nowhere to hide if anyone looks in here."

She slid down the wall until she sat on the floor and set her weapon beside her. The ride over, she had thought of little else but Carac's parting words to her in his tent. He'd known she was hiding something, but he hadn't pressed her about it.

"I am an orphan," she said into the silence.

From his spot by the door, he swung his head to her. After a long stare, he moved to the wall opposite her and sat. "I suspected that when you told me how Edra took in children."

"She is the one who found me. I was being beaten for stealing a loaf of bread." Ravyn hadn't thought about that day in years. "I begged for food for days, but everyone ignored me. Pretended I was not there. The hunger became so bad that I had no other choice."

His green eyes filled with anger. "You were a child. How could anyone not share food with you?"

"It would mean taking me in, and I was not their responsibility."

"And your family?"

She lowered her gaze to the floor and swallowed past the lump in her throat. "I remember very little of my early life. I know I was loved and cared for."

He frowned but didn't speak.

Ravyn looked at him and shrugged. "It is almost as if my life started the night my world was ripped apart. I do not recall how it began. What I do remember is being yanked from my bed. The fear was palpable, like a living, breathing entity.

"My father went outside along with my two eldest brothers. When the door opened, I caught a glimpse of long, golden blond hair. The night was as silent as death. Then I heard her laughter. It sent chills down my spine, and even at such a young age, I realized evil was upon us." She put her hand over the Nordic rune tattoo on her left wrist. "I have no recollection of why we left our home, only that the next thing I remember, we were standing outside. I was barefoot, and the frigid ground hurt my feet, but I said nothing. My mother hid me behind her. I gripped her skirts tightly and buried my face in the material.

"I heard someone speaking, but I could not make out the words—or maybe I had no wish to. Then the screams began. My sisters, my brothers, and my father. They were all yelling, terrified and in pain. My mother sobbed and begged for it to end, and all the while, I heard the maniacal laughter and felt heat from fires so hot that I can feel them on my cheeks even now. Each time one of the screams faded, the woman laughed harder, delighting in the pain and death. Then, there was only my mother left."

Ravyn paused and drew in a shaky breath. "She kept one hand by her side, gripping her skirts where my hand was. There was no need for her to tell me to keep hidden. I knew. She had stopped begging at this point. She stood still as stone while fire crackled all around us. There was a long stretch of silence. I can only imagine that my mother and the witch had some kind of stare down. In a split second, the witch took my mother's life. When she died, she fell backward, on top of me, but it prevented the witch from finding me."

"How long did you stay there?" Carac asked.

Ravyn looked down at her hands. "At first, I was terrified

to move. I had no idea if the woman was still there, and I had no wish to leave my family. I remained there as the smell of burning bodies filled the air. It could have been days, I know not. When I did finally think to leave, I had to work hours to move from beneath my mother. That's when I got a look at what was left of my family. All six of my siblings and my father had been burned, along with everything else. My mother had been...decapitated."

A muscle twitched in Carac's jaw. "And no one would take you in?"

"They were frightened the woman would return. I had no idea it was a witch who killed my family until Edra found me. She stopped the beating I was being given and brought me to the abbey. She gave me a home, food, and a new family. There, I learned about witches. Edra had been hunting the one who murdered my family. Otherwise, I probably would have starved to death."

Carac nodded slowly. "The news Simon brought of a witch killing the family brought back all of the memories."

"It did. As soon as I decided to become a Hunter, I knew I wanted to find the woman who took my family from me. There is a chance that Sybbyl could be that witch."

19

If he'd thought Ravyn was a warrior before, Carac knew for certain now after hearing what happened to her and her family. It was no wonder she worked so tirelessly to hunt down witches.

"If Sybbyl is the witch you search for and you kill her, what will you do then?" Carac asked.

Ravyn stretched her legs out before her and crossed her ankles. "The fight with the Coven is just beginning. Ridding the world of the witch who slaughtered my family is one of the goals I hope to achieve, but there are many other evil witches out there."

"Have you thought about asking witches to join you?"

"Of course, but most are hiding from the Coven because once the Coven finds them, they either join the group or die."

"I have not seen any women with tattoos as you have. What does the one on your back mean?"

Ravyn grinned. "The Ouroboros. It is the symbol that Edra and Radnar chose for our group. Some see the snake and believe it to be evil. When in fact, the symbol signifies infinity."

"It is stunning."

"Each of us chooses where we have it. Some are small, some are not."

Carac glanced at the door. "How many Hunters are there?"

"Not nearly enough. There is only a handful of us."

It was no wonder Braith had reached out to him. Knights may not be trained like Ravyn and the other Hunters, but they were well versed in war. With the right weapons, they could do a lot of damage if working with the Hunters.

"What made you become a knight?"

Ravyn's question pulled him from his thoughts. He stared at her a long moment. They had shared their bodies and souls during the night, and while they hadn't spoken, there was no denying that a bond had formed between them.

She'd shared the story of her traumatic childhood. Perhaps it was time he did the same. It had become such a practice to keep his identity secret that it was second nature.

"My training began early," he told her. "My father wanted a son who could defend his lands and people with him."

Ravyn's eyes widened a fraction before her brow furrowed. "Lands?"

"The only one who knows my true name is Simon. I am Duke Carac de Vere."

"Why would you let others believe you are something other than a lord?" she asked incredulously.

Carac's mind drifted to the past, a time he longed to forget. "My father was deeply in love with my mother. I was only five summers when she died in childbirth. My father was distraught. He turned to drink, drowning himself in it to dull the pain.

"It became so bad that my uncle began helping around the castle since I was too young. But I looked after my younger brother. Things continued like that for years. My father grew weaker, the alcohol slowly killing him while I grew stronger. My uncle always swore he would turn things over to me when the time came, but I was in no hurry to take control. I was focused on my training and my brother. Then, one winter, my father fell from the battlements in a drunken stupor. He broke his back, but that was not what killed him. He froze to death."

Ravyn's face was contorted with distress. "That is horrible. I am sorry."

Carac shrugged, the pain of his father's passing long gone. "Things happen. I learned a lot watching my da succumb to his grief. There were days he was sober and spent time with my brother and me. I prefer to remember him like that than the man who so loved his dead wife that nothing else mattered. Not even his sons."

"You have good memories of him. That is what counts."

"Aye." Carac drew in a breath. "It was both a blessing and a curse when my father died. His pain was over, but mine had only just begun."

Ravyn cocked her head to the side. "How so?"

"My uncle had become used to my brother and me being on the training field. Although I left the day-to-day running of the lands to my uncle, I was well aware of what was going on through the years. I knew the people he cheated, the money he stole, but I said nothing."

"Why not? What he did was wrong."

Carac rubbed the back of his neck. "I made reparations behind his back to those he cheated. As for the stealing, it was a pittance. By running the castle, I was allowed to do what I wanted. I thought it was the better bargain. Turns out, I was wrong.

"The thefts grew larger until I had no choice but to confront him. My uncle promised it would stop, and I forgave him. I took over most of the duties then, but I allowed him to remain with the agreement that he would do nothing to compromise the family or the castle and its people."

"Did he do as promised?" Ravyn asked.

Carac swallowed as he shook his head. "My uncle became friendly with a neighboring lord who wanted to align our families. He had a marriageable daughter, and there was my brother and I to choose from. I refused since I had no wish for a wife at the time. My brother was still young and enjoying his freedom. Both of our parents were gone, so I did not want to force him into something he did not want."

Ravyn nodded in agreement. "I would not have either."

"Apparently, the lord offered my uncle a chest of gold if he could get one of us to marry his daughter. While I was dealing with matters at the castle, my uncle took my brother hunting. At least, that is what I was told. In truth, he took my brother to the lord. My brother fought to get free from my uncle, and in the ensuing struggle, my brother was killed."

Ravyn's lips parted, her eyes filled with remorse. "Oh, Carac."

"To say I was filled with rage is an understatement. I banished my uncle from the castle before I killed him with my bare hands. After I buried my brother, I hired a steward to run the castle and fully devoted myself to my training. The day I got my spurs, I had no one but Simon to celebrate with. I could not return to the castle and continue on with marriage and children and such. So, I hired myself out to lords. Simon was always with me, and we quickly developed a reputation. Soon, other knights joined up with us after each victory on the battlefield. Before I knew it, I had an army at my disposal."

Ravyn blinked, her dark eyes watching him closely. "Do

you intend to remain in this life forever? To one day die on the battlefield? Or will you return to your home and take up the mantle you were born to?"

It was a question he had been asking himself for some months now. There had been no reason for him to go back to the castle alone. At least, there hadn't been. Yet he could see himself on the battlements with Ravyn by his side.

"My duty is to my family. I know it is what both my father and brother would want," he answered.

She lifted her brows. "What stops you?"

"I have seen much of England and even Scotland. I have traveled to France, Aragon, Italy, and the Holy Roman Empire. The things I have seen and experienced have been amazing, despite the fact that I was taking the lives of others in the process."

A smile curved her lips. "I want to hear about every place you have seen."

"I will share the stories willingly."

Her head leaned back on the stones. "I cannot imagine seeing all of those places. No wonder you hesitate to go home."

"It is more than that. If I return unmarried, then every father, brother, and uncle around with a marriage-aged woman will be after me. I prefer to make my own decisions."

She laughed softly and shook her head. "Oh, poor you, having women paraded before you to choose from."

He grinned as he looked briefly at the floor. "You make it sound as though it could be enjoyable. But I would rather find the woman I want as my wife another way."

"Really? How so?" she asked with a grin.

"Being put in tough situations so I can see what she is made of is a good start. Sharing a cold night together with only the heat of our bodies is even better."

Her eyes blazed with passion, a look he was coming to know well. "That does sound reasonable. I believe the woman would be able to get a sense of what you are made of, as well. She would need to know that you could command in the bedchamber as well as, or better even than, on the battlefield."

Carac's balls tightened, need coiling through him. "Oh?"

"A woman wants to be pleasured, just as a man does. If you see to her needs, then she will be sure to see to yours."

By the stars, he was on fire for her!

Ravyn's eyes turned seductive as she tilted her head to the side. "Would you want a meek woman? One who turned to you for everything?"

"I thought that was what I wanted, but I have come to see that a woman with a warrior spirit is more to my liking. A lady who would stand beside me in all things."

"*All* things?" she asked, brow raised.

He gave a single nod of his head. "All."

"What about your wandering spirit? Would you grow tired of remaining in one place?"

That was a concern, but it was becoming less of one. "I have seen enough of the world. It is time I return to my holdings. What about the woman with her incredible warrior spirit? Would she be content?"

"There will always be a villain in one form or another to fight. As long as she can do that, she would be happy."

Carac wasn't sure, but they could have just agreed to spend the rest of their lives together. And it pleased him immensely. Neither had come out and said that the woman was she, and he would want to have such a conversation. He needed to have it because he wanted her to know that he was falling for her.

In rapid fashion.

It was odd, this feeling growing inside him. He was enamored with her because she was so different from other women he had encountered. Her beauty made his heart catch, but it was her spirit that stole his breath.

She was perfect for him. In every way. He hadn't even known she was what he had been looking for until she came into his life, but now that she was there, he wasn't going to let her go.

Silence stretched as their previous conversation hung between them. Ravyn's lips parted as if she were about to speak, but their heads jerked toward the door at the sound of Sybbyl's voice.

They got to their feet and moved closer in order to make out what the witch was saying, but it helped little. Though they could hear Sybbyl's distinctive voice, they couldn't make out the words.

Then the witch walked away. Ravyn began to pace the chamber. He didn't need to ask what she was thinking. Ravyn wanted a piece of Sybbyl—whether she was the witch who killed Ravyn's family or not. It mattered little.

Sybbyl was of the Coven.

And they all needed to be stopped.

Carac stepped in front of Ravyn and put his hands on her to halt her. "We will get her."

"Not stuck in here," Ravyn snapped. "We have to find the staff. For all we know, the other witches are here. Or worse, they've already found the relic."

He held her gaze and gave her arms a squeeze. "Then we leave."

"How?" she bit out, a frown upon her brow.

Carac grinned and dropped his arms to his sides. "We get past the guards."

"Aye. Without alerting Sybbyl or John."

"Do you trust me?" he asked.

She drew in a deep breath and slowly released it. "I do."

He motioned her against the wall while he moved to stand behind the door. Then he slammed the bottom of his foot against it.

The guards' voices halted. A moment later, footsteps approached. Ravyn smiled as she swung her crossbow from her shoulder. As soon as the door opened, she fired the weapon, the arrow puncturing the man's heart.

Carac waited until both guards were inside the chamber before he pushed the door closed and kicked the second guard in the back of the knee. The man went down. Carac then stabbed him through the ribs with two quick jabs.

With both guards dead, he went to the door and peeked out to find the corridor empty. He turned and met Ravyn's gaze. They shared a smile before hurrying out to find Bryce.

20

The excitement and hope that surged after having gotten out of the chamber evaporated like smoke. Ravyn stared at the empty cell where Randall had been. She had come so close to getting him to reveal the location of the staff the previous night, but he had been stubborn. Then he grew obstinate and refused to speak at all.

Ravyn had had no choice but to give him some time and try again. Yet, apparently, that decision had been the wrong one. Now, he was gone, and she couldn't get the location of the staff, which meant that the Coven would beat her to the artifact.

"I failed," she said.

Carac shook his head. "This is merely a setback. We can still win."

Her head swung to him. "You say that because you have not fought the Coven."

"And you keep telling me that. I understand that the witches cannot be killed with anything but your and Margery's weapons, but I know battle. Simon knows war. We are four against them."

She nodded, realizing that he was right. "I am happy to have you fighting beside me, but you have yet to see what they can do. Each has different magic. They can strike at you from several feet away."

"Then we use that against them."

Ravyn rubbed her temple where her head was beginning to throb. Normally, she was good at coming up with a new plan when something went awry, but whether it was Carac or Sybbyl or the fact that it was the staff they were after, she couldn't seem to clear her head.

She blew out a long breath. "How?"

"First, we find them. I suspect they are digging somewhere in the castle. If I had to guess, I would say below the dungeon."

Carac could be onto something. She nodded, liking things so far. "Sybbyl will be on the lookout for Margery and me, which means she will have a lot of guards."

"We should be able to find them easily enough. Then, we sit back and wait for them to locate the staff."

At this, Ravyn shook her head. "The Coven cannot get their hands on it."

"The odds of us preventing that at this point are moot. You need another plan, one that gives us the advantage."

"How, if Sybbyl has the staff?"

Carac put his hand on the hilt of his sword. "You are looking at this as either getting the relic or not. You need to assume that the staff will land in their hands, as inconceivable as that is."

It was unthinkable, but he had a point. If she stopped thinking about getting to the staff first, then that opened up several possibilities to take it from the Coven. Not that it would be easy.

"You realize that you will be going up against several witches?"

Carac shot her a lopsided grin. "Of course."

She wouldn't list all the ways she had seen witches kill, but it would be better if Carac were prepared for what might happen. Instead, he was going on what Simon had told him and the little she had shared.

"I know the risks," Carac told her, as if reading her thoughts.

"Not really. Witches strike quickly and from seemingly nowhere."

"Then we need a place that works to our advantage," he replied.

She threw up her hands. "And where might that be?"

"Right here."

Ravyn gawked at him. "In the dungeon?"

"The castle," he corrected.

She looked around the dungeon, trying to think of other places in the keep. She didn't want to fight the knights as well as the witches. Sybbyl and the others of the Coven would be plenty.

Carac took her hand and pulled her after him back to the entrance to the dungeon. She liked the feeling of his long fingers intertwined with hers. It gave her a sense of security, much as his presence did.

For the first time, she didn't feel as if she were facing this fight alone. Margery was a good friend, but she didn't make decisions. She always preferred for Ravyn to decide everything. It was one reason Margery didn't go hunting on her own.

Ravyn looked at the back of Carac's blond head and smiled. A moment ago, she had been distraught about the

Coven finding the Staff of the Eternal. Now, her thoughts were on confronting the witches and gaining the artifact.

Because she wouldn't stop until she had it.

———

Sybbyl watched the knights tearing down the wall. Behind it lay the Staff of the Eternal. As soon as she learned that the Blood Skull had been lost to the Coven, Sybbyl had become more determined than ever to find another bone from the First Witch.

The information hadn't been easy to obtain. In fact, it had cost her greatly—but in the end, it was worth it. The witches who were servants to the elders had a wealth of information.

They rarely spoke about anything they learned since the elders were quick to take a life if anyone did, but Sybbyl's objective to become one of the elders had her watching everyone.

She picked up small things here and there, and it was one of those little tidbits that'd brought her to Angmar's servant. The young witch was often the brunt of Angmar's wrath. All Sybbyl did was wait until she saw the young one with a new bruise, her anger visible.

Then, Sybbyl merely said the right words as she healed the girl, giving comfort where there had been none. The lass was eager for a friend—or for *anyone* to treat her decently. It took less than a week for Sybbyl to pry the information from her— the next location where a bone of the First Witch was suspected to be.

There were two potentials, and Sybbyl had chosen Bryce Castle after watching John for a single day. He was so easy to manipulate, but then again, most men were. It didn't matter that he preferred the company of other men. With the right amount of magic, he was soon eating out of her hand.

She looked down at Randall, who was on his knees beside her, his head hanging dejectedly. John was on her left, and knights surrounded them.

Once she brought the staff to the elders, they would give her the reward she sought. All the years of scraping by to grow her magic while competing against others in the Coven were about to be forgotten.

She deserved to be an elder. She had the power, the intelligence, and the wherewithal to get what others couldn't. If the Coven's plans were to come to fruition, then they needed her.

Sybbyl was so confident in what was to come that she sent word to the remaining elders of what she had discovered. Matilda and Angmar should arrive any moment. And she couldn't wait to show them the staff.

Wooing John to join her and defeating Randall had been incredibly effortless. The only hiccup was the arrival of Ravyn, who Sybbyl believed to be a Hunter. The fact that Ravyn and her servant had yet to be found all but confirmed it.

Not that Sybbyl was worried. She was more than capable of taking care of a couple of Hunters.

The grunts of the men, and the sound of rock smashing against rock filled the area. With each piece of wall removed, she was that much closer to finding the staff.

Thoroughly defeated, Randall couldn't even look at what was happening. His gaze was on the ground. When the Coven found all the bones to the First Witch, this is what awaited the world.

Everyone without magic would be slain. Those who were left would have a choice to join the Coven—or die. In the end, the only ones on the Earth would be those with magic.

Because while the Coven was strictly made up of women, she knew for a fact that warlocks existed.

She'd met one when she was very young. He hadn't known she saw him, but there was no denying it. The very thought of a world where everyone held magic made Sybbyl giddy. No longer would she be the outcast because she had been born different.

Everything she wanted was within reach, and she had done it on her own, just as she had done everything in her life.

"Faster," she ordered the men tearing down the wall.

They increased their movements as John rubbed his hands together beside her. "Will you let me hold it?"

"Nay."

His head swiveled to her, his gaze serious. "I will beg. Just as you like," he whispered.

She smiled and patted his face. "We shall see. Now, head to the great hall. I want you there to greet the elders if they arrive before the staff is found."

"You want me to go?" he asked, taking a step back.

Sybbyl laughed. "Are you scared, John?"

"Terrified," he admitted while nodding.

"Good. Show them that. They will enjoy it."

"Will they...kill me?"

"Most likely not."

His face went pale, which made her laugh again. Ah, but it was a good day. Tonight would be even better!

She gave him a little shove to get him moving. Even then, he dragged his feet walking away from her. He even looked back over his shoulder, but she ignored him. John was like a puppy. He was loyal but a nuisance. He needed strict discipline at all times.

In fact, he had come a long way since the first time she'd brought him to her bed. He was eager to learn, and keen to please her. It was really too bad that he would have to be killed along with all the others without magic.

Then again, she would find herself a warlock. All would work out.

Minutes passed as she watched the workers. A part of her wanted to use her magic to blast through the wall, but she didn't want to take the chance of breaking the staff. Besides, the Bryce family had gone to a lot of trouble all those generations ago to hide the artifact. They would have put precautions in place for anyone—especially witches—to come looking for it.

"You will not get it."

The whisper made her frown. She looked down at Randall. "Finally found your backbone, have you? Well, I hate to disappoint, but I *will* have it."

"You will hold it," he said and raised his head to look at her. His hazel eyes burned with an emotion she couldn't quite name. "But it will not be yours."

She faced the lord and glared at him. "What have you not told me?"

"Nothing," he replied with a grin. "I merely speak of what is to come."

"I have worked to acquire this staff. I even summoned Coven elders to show it to them. We are very close to finding it...thanks to you. It will be in my hands soon."

His smile never wavered. "Are you sure?"

"I will hand it to the elders, of course, but then I intended to join their ranks."

Bryce chuckled. "High aspirations, I see."

"The highest."

"It will not be the Coven who wields the staff."

Everything he'd said before was irritating but nothing

more than an annoyance. This was something entirely different.

And it alarmed her.

"What are you talking about?" she demanded.

He looked at the wall being dismantled. "Did you ever wonder why the First Witch went to such trouble to disperse her bones? She knew what was coming. Already, the Coven has lost the Blood Skull."

How did he know about that? "That was a fluke."

He cut his gaze to her. "Was it? Ask your elder with the burns. The Blood Skull chooses its Warden. Do you think the staff will be any different?"

There was a shout from the men as the last of the stones tumbled down, exposing a wall of earth. And an archway.

21

Just as Carac had thought, it was easy to find Sybbyl and John in chambers below the dungeon. He wasn't overjoyed by the number of knights surrounding them, however. The men working to tear down the wall had removed their armor to allow better movement.

The witch was so worried about uncovering the staff that she didn't bother to post guards down the narrow corridor. She might not think it the best place for a battle, but he knew it was perfect.

The only thing he would have to worry about was knights coming up behind them. But their attackers would have to get in line to fight them. The perfect way to ensure that neither he nor Ravyn were overrun.

If only Carac knew where Simon and Margery were.

He felt Ravyn move up behind him and peer around his shoulder just as Sybbyl commanded John to return to the great hall. Both he and Ravyn quickly backtracked. Ravyn hid in a dark corner. He found another and immediately did the same.

John passed both of them without looking up. Carac

suspected that it wouldn't be long before either John or Sybbyl sent for him. Once he couldn't be found, then others would begin looking for him.

He hoped that they would be out of the castle with the staff before then. But that would only happen if everything went according to plan. And nothing ever went as planned.

Once John's footsteps faded away, Carac hurried to where Ravyn had hidden only to find the space empty. His lips pressed together as he strode to the entrance of the chamber where Sybbyl and the knights were.

Sure enough, Ravyn was watching them. There was no way he could see for them to get out of the castle without a skirmish. His mind drifted to his men. No matter how this upcoming battle turned, he would not leave his men to the will of a witch. Whether they sided with him or not, they had a right to make up their own minds.

He came up behind Ravyn, who glanced his way. Carac flattened his back against the wall as Sybbyl began talking to Randall. Listening to their exchange with interest, Carac was happy to hear Randall stand up to the witch—even if it was too little, too late.

Not that Carac blamed the man. He would have done the same in the lord's position. Most people would have after innocent lives were threatened.

As Carac listened to Sybbyl's confidence in the Coven gaining the staff, he wondered what kind of power could come from such an artifact. Ravyn hadn't mentioned what the relic could do, and there was a chance that she didn't know.

That in itself worried Carac. Witches could already kill easily. With the staff, the Coven could do untold damage across the country. Even the world.

He peered over Ravyn's shoulder and waited until everyone's back was to him, then he hurried to the other side of the doorway. No sooner had he gotten there than a shout went up, followed by the sound of tumbling rocks.

The dust finally cleared, which allowed Carac to see the men moving away from the opening. He spotted what appeared to be an arched doorway that looked thousands of years old.

Though he'd heard both Ravyn and Simon talk about what witches could do, he had yet to see anything. So when Sybbyl spoke a few words in a language he didn't understand, he was surprised to see the heavy rocks holding up the wall sliding to the side to make a path for her.

He glanced at Ravyn, but she didn't seem interested in the show of magic. If he were going to fight those of the Coven, he needed to get used to such displays—and be prepared for them.

But how did one get ready to fight a witch? They already had the advantage with their powers. It seemed a foregone conclusion that they would win in any conflict against those without.

Sybbyl walked to the arch and halted before it. His gaze narrowed to try and determine what it was she stared at on one of the stones. It wasn't until she reached up to trace the faded carving that he realized what it was.

With a snap of her fingers, the torches in the chamber flared. The ensuing light was so bright that the knights within turned their heads away and raised their arms for protection. Even he and Ravyn jerked back from the flash, but Carac didn't take his gaze from Sybbyl.

It was the only reason he saw that there were many more carvings covering the entire doorway. The witch looked at them twice before she turned her head to one of the knights and motioned him to her.

He grudgingly did as she commanded while the others took a tentative step back.

"Enter," she commanded the man.

The knight withdrew his sword and grabbed a torch before he walked under the arch, his armor clinking. Carac and Ravyn exchanged a glance, each curious as to what was through the doorway.

Seconds turned to long, silent minutes. Carac was beginning to think that there was nothing to be found on the other side when, all of a sudden, there was a startled, fearful shout that was cut off mid-yell.

Then a torch rolled from the darkness to the entrance, still lit.

Undeterred, Sybbyl's gaze landed on another knight, one without armor. "Your turn."

The knight hesitated before turning to his sword leaning against the wall. He grabbed it and made his way to the torch. After bending to retrieve it, he straightened and met the witch's gaze.

Sybbyl raised a brow. "What are you waiting for?"

He turned and faced the doorway and stared into the blackness for a long moment. Finally, he took a step. Little by little, the darkness swallowed his body and the light of the torch.

Carac counted the seconds. The second knight lasted longer than the first, but, unfortunately, the sound of his strangled cry—cut off just like the first—reached them.

Sybbyl whirled around, her gaze moving over each knight. "Who is my next volunteer? Surely, there is someone brave enough to go inside."

Carac grinned as not one of the men stepped forward. Finally, Sybbyl pointed to a man and crooked her finger at him. The man was also without armor. He visibly shook the closer he got to the doorway. Sweat rolled down the sides of his face. He opted not to draw his sword. As it was, his hands trembled so badly, he could barely hold the torch.

Then he wouldn't move. Sybbyl had to shove him through the doorway. The knight stumbled into the dark and tripped so that he landed on his knees. For a moment, Carac didn't think he would get up, but the knight finally climbed to his feet and withdrew his sword.

He vanished into the darkness. It was only a few moments later that a terrified scream drifted from the entrance. It went on awhile before it abruptly ended.

The silence that followed was so eerie that it made the hairs on the back of Carac's neck stand on end. While he and Ravyn watched the entire episode, the remaining knights had all been slowly inching backwards.

The first few reached the doorway where he and Ravyn stood. The knights turned and rushed away without a second look at either of them.

More and more of the knights made their escape. But not all of them. Sybbyl turned and saw them. She raised her hand, her face twisted in anger.

"Run," Ravyn hissed.

He looked at her to find her moving back away from the doorway. Just as Carac was about to do the same, he felt something grab hold of him. A look down confirmed that there was nothing touching him, but there was no denying what he felt.

"Nay!" a knight who was slowly being dragged back into the chamber with Sybbyl screamed.

Carac tried to grab hold of something on the wall, but he came up empty. All the while, the knights were returned to Sybbyl.

And then it was Carac's turn. He briefly met Ravyn's gaze

before he was physically pulled into the chamber by Sybbyl's magic. He dug in his heels, but it did no good.

The witch's eyes widened when she spotted him. She lowered her arm, which halted his progress. "Spying on me?"

"I heard yells and came to investigate," Carac lied. "Next thing I knew, I was being dragged in here."

She shrugged. "No matter. I have a use for you."

Carac knew what she was going to say before it came out of her mouth. He tried not to look at the arch and the awaiting darkness. It yawned like a great beast, waiting to devour its next victim.

Which would be him.

Of all the ways Carac had thought he might die, this wasn't one of them. On the battlefield, aye. But not by magic.

"I need what is inside there," Sybbyl said and pointed to the arch.

Carac looked around at the men. Some kept their heads down, some glared with utter contempt at Sybbyl. But their fear was palpable.

"Why not go yourself," he said as he returned his gaze to Sybbyl.

She grinned, though it didn't reach her eyes. "It requires someone without magic."

"Magic?" he asked, a brow raised.

She rolled her blue eyes. "Stop pretending that you do not know I am a witch."

"A witch?" Carac thought it better to feign ignorance than have her push for how he'd gained the knowledge.

He wasn't sure what kind of magic Sybbyl had, and he wasn't in the mood to have it tested on him. There were other —*bigger*—things to worry about.

"Get inside," she ordered.

Carac shook his head. "I think not."

Sybbyl's blue eyes blazed with fury. "You saw me pull you and the others in here. I can *make* you go through the doorway."

He glanced at the arch and twisted his lips. "If you could, why order me? Make me or one of the others do it." When her nostrils flared, he grinned. "You cannot. We have to go of our own volition."

"I may not be able to make you go through the doorway, but I can do other things," she threatened.

Carac took a chance, and it backfired. Now, it was Sybbyl's turn to grin.

"What?" she prodded. "No witty response?"

There were no words, but his hands itched to wrap around her throat and squeeze the life from her, to slowly cut off her air and make her feel as if her lungs were about to explode.

There had been many people throughout his life that Carac didn't like, but she was one of the few that he wholly detested.

"Ah. At last," Sybbyl said. "Now, I can finally see how you truly feel about me."

"Does it make you feel better to know that I detest you?" Carac asked.

"I have known it from the first moment we met, but you went out of your way to hide it. Why?"

"Because I do not feel the need to let others know my opinions," he retorted.

She smiled. "I prefer the opposite. I want people to know what I think."

"Because you are a witch?"

"Because they should fear me."

He nodded, disgust filling him. "How many innocent people have you killed?"

"How many have *you* killed?" she asked in response. "You,

who hire your services out to others. How many knights have you slain on the battlefield? You had no quarrel with them."

"Any man or woman who picks up a weapon knows they could die by one of the same. And anyone who goes onto a battlefield fully comprehends that that could be his or her last day. You kill for the pleasure of it."

Sybbyl's smile was slow and evil. "That is so true. Now, go through the doorway before I kill not only the knights around us but also your friend, Simon. And if that is not enough to get you moving, I will kill everyone inside the castle walls, as well as your army."

His options were gone. Carac only had one choice now.

22

The Abbey

The derelict state of the ruins was nothing compared to what Malene found as she and Armir were escorted through the arch.

It took a great amount of magic for Edra to keep the abbey and its occupants hidden from the Coven. But it took even more heart and love to make it into a home.

Malene stopped when she saw the extent of the repairs that had been done to the ruins. There were people of all ages who called the abbey home. Some with magic, most without.

But all were living together to fight the Coven and what the group stood for.

Her gaze slid to Edra and Radnar. "You both have done an amazing job."

"You have only seen a fraction of the abbey," Radnar said, pride in his voice.

He and Edra shared a smile before they joined hands. Edra then turned her attention on Malene. "It warms my heart to hear you say such words. I dreamed of this place for years, never thinking it would come to fruition. I could not have done it without Radnar and the others."

Radnar snorted. "She lies. She could have done it all on her own."

Their love was so tangible that Malene felt as if she could reach out and touch it. It made her smile and broke her heart at the same time because she knew she would never experience that kind of relationship.

She felt someone's gaze on her and swiveled her head, her eyes clashing with Armir's. His expression was unreadable, as it usually was.

"Come," Edra urged them. "I would like to introduce you to a few people."

Malene found herself becoming acquainted with a witch named Asa from Norway, who was able to communicate with animals. Malene was particularly fond of Asa's pet owl. The bird was small but beautiful, its large, yellow eyes taking in everything.

Armir remained indifferent to everyone until Radnar mentioned that Asa was the artist responsible for designing and giving the Hunters their tattoos. When Asa saw Armir's tats on the sides of his head, the two struck up a conversation.

Malene watched, mesmerized, as she was given a glimpse of another side of Armir that she had never seen before. He was friendly and interested in Asa. Engaging even. He smiled and nodded, freely talking with the pretty witch.

Malene was all too aware that while she considered her role as Lady a kind of prison, Armir experienced much the same thing as her commander—only he enjoyed his position.

However, her new edict allowed him to find someone. Who was she to stand in his way?

Malene turned to Edra and Radnar, then said in a low tone, "Let us leave them."

Edra glanced at the couple before she nodded and the three of them walked away. Malene met a hulking man named Berlaq who was the blacksmith. She got to see him design and craft a weapon before inspecting others. Once each piece was finished, Edra would spell it so it could kill a witch.

Next came three men who were from other parts of the world who'd come to help train those wishing to be Hunters. Malene watched their practice for a short time, awed by the way they moved, fighting with their feet as much as their fists.

"You have shown me much of your world without asking a single thing about mine," she said to Edra before turning to her.

Edra grinned, her bright blue eyes crinkling in the corners. "I wanted you to see that we are capable of pulling our weight."

"That was never in question. In fact, it is because of what your Hunter, Leoma, did that I knew we could have a fine partnership."

Radnar clasped his hands behind his back, his lips compressing. "While I share my wife's excitement in having outsiders joining us to fight the Coven, I worry about others learning of our location. The more people that know, the easier it will be for the Coven to find us."

"Armir and I will be the only ones to know the abbey's location," Malene promised. "I, too, believe that the fewer who hold that information, the better."

Radnar smiled, bowing his dark head to her. "Thank you."

"And while it goes against everything the Varroki are, I feel that the favor should be returned. I would like you and Edra to know where we can be found."

Edra's eyes widened. "Are you sure?"

"I am Lady of the Varroki. I make the decisions."

"Which means, she can do as she pleases," Armir stated as he joined them.

Malene met his pale green eyes and saw something flash in them before he looked away. If she weren't mistaken, he was angry. No doubt because she wanted Edra and Radnar to know the way to Blackglade. Well, he could just get over it.

She ignored Armir and kept her attention on Edra and Radnar. "I am sure you have many questions for us."

"Many," Edra said with a laugh.

Radnar nodded, flashing a grin.

Armir bowed his head. "And we will be happy to answer them."

"Follow me," Edra said.

Malene fell in step behind the couple. She was all too aware of how close Armir was walking to her. He normally kept a bit of distance.

Then he leaned down and said in a low tone, "I do not appreciate you leaving me."

"You were enjoying yourself. I wanted to give you time with Asa."

"Why?" he demanded in a hoarse whisper.

She gawked at him. "I saw your interest."

Armir merely made a sound at the back of his throat. When he refused to say more, she rolled her eyes. The man was infuriating.

They were led into a chamber that acted as a solar. After they'd all taken a seat, Edra licked her lips. "I wish I would have known of the Varroki when the Coven first approached me. I would have come to you over those seven years I ran from them."

"Blackglade is not easy to find," Armir said. "It is hidden like the abbey. But, had one of our warriors found you, they would have offered you aid."

Malene glanced at Armir before she said, "As Jarin told Leoma and Braith, the Varroki have been keeping the Coven contained for many centuries. Each time they gained power, one of our warriors was there to stop it."

"What happened?" Radnar asked.

Malene felt Armir's eyes on her. "The Varroki have strict rules. The warriors are trained to work alone, to have no attachments of any kind. It is why many of them travel with animals—like Jarin and his wolf and falcon."

"They do not take a mate?" Edra asked with a frown.

Malene shook her head, a sad smile in place. "That is not the only position that had such rules either. Over time, it has diminished our numbers to the point where the Coven was able to gain a foothold. We have been fighting to regain dominance ever since."

"Forgive me," Radnar said. "But you are very young to be in such a position of power."

"As I said, the Varroki have specific decrees that they follow. It has kept them secret and powerful for a long time. The Varroki are descendants of the First Witch and the Celtic tribes."

Edra grinned. "Now I know why you both have an accent."

Radnar's frown deepened. "Malene, you keep saying 'Varroki' as if they are not your people."

She swallowed and fought against looking to Armir. "Because they are not. Or rather, they *were* not."

"I am confused," Edra said with a shake of her blond head.

It was Armir who said, "Magic chooses who will hold the mantle of Lady. In all the generations we've existed, there have only been six chosen who were Varroki. Most are from the outside world."

Malene kept her back straight as Edra's and Radnar's gazes slid to her. "I will admit that it took Armir some time to convince me to return with him."

"What if she had not wanted to go?" Edra asked.

Armir shrugged, his lips twisting. "I could not return without her. The magic had already chosen her," he said, nodding to her hands.

Malene started to curl her fingers into a fist, but she left them flat on her thighs. For a short time, she had forgotten about the blue light. No one had commented on it while they were at the abbey.

She took a deep breath and lifted her palms face out so the couple could see the light. "I was not born with this. It appeared four days before Armir found me."

"And she had only one affected hand at the time. The second is a recent addition," Armir added.

Edra gazed at Malene's hands in wonder. "That is your magic?"

"Aye. I had none before it chose me."

"I thought I had seen everything," Radnar said in awe. His eyes lifted to Malene's face. "Do you remain in this position for a certain period?"

Malene lowered her hands. "Until I die. Most of the Ladies' reigns ended at about seven years."

"Why so short?" Edra wanted to know.

"The isolation," Malene answered honestly. "This is the first I have left my tower in five years. The only person I see or speak to is Armir. It is the way of the Varroki."

Radnar frowned again. "Does that mean you do not take a mate either?"

"It is forbidden for us to touch the Lady of the Varroki," Armir answered.

Malene swallowed and lifted her chin. "I struggled when I first came to live at Blackglade. To fill the hours, I asked Armir to teach me to read. There is an extensive library in my tower, and I wanted to know what was in the books. Once I could decipher them, I devoured every title at least once. It is how I learned that I could make or change laws. As of this morning, all the decrees to abstain from marriage or relations of any kind were overturned."

"Including yours?" Edra asked with a small smile.

Malene nodded. "It is time we rebuilt the Varroki. Besides, we have the Coven to battle. It took centuries for the laws to affect our population, and it will take nearly as long to rebuild. But it was the right thing to do."

"I agree," Armir added. "There will be some who do not think that, but most are eager to see us thriving again."

Radnar stretched out his legs as he slid down in his chair. "If your position can now marry, does that mean you might remain Lady longer?"

"We can hope," Armir answered before she could.

Her head jerked to him. His response was a surprise.

He met her gaze. "I told you that you were good for us. Too many others in your position faded away into nothing. You have a purpose. You have given the Varroki purpose."

Malene didn't know how to respond. Once more, Armir had astonished her. Would there ever be a time where she knew how he would react?

"Faded away?" Edra asked. "What do you mean?"

Malene saw how uncomfortable Armir was, so she looked at the couple. "I spoke of the isolation, and you heard Armir say how no one can touch a Lady. It can take a toll. It does not matter if the chosen wants her position or not, sometimes, the burden is too heavy. Some have taken their own lives. Some have simply withered away, their minds going."

"Did you know all of this before you asked to learn to read?" Radnar questioned.

She smiled sadly and shook her head. "I learned of it through the books. Each Lady's reign is recorded. Mine is being documented now."

"By who?" Edra wanted to know.

Armir said, "The Quarter. Three seers."

Malene knew the history of the Varroki was difficult to hear. "We may have strict rules and do things differently, but our warriors are exceptional. They have fought the Coven many times. Their knowledge will help your Hunters."

"Without a doubt," Radnar said.

"And not even those in the Coven know of our warlocks."

Edra smiled and said, "We are going to make great allies."

23

This couldn't be happening. Ravyn stared in shock at Carac facing the opening of the arched doorway. She wanted to knock the cocky smile from Sybbyl's face.

But Ravyn hesitated to make herself known. Sybbyl had said only one without magic could enter the doorway. That meant that no witch could get to the staff as long as it remained in there. But as soon as someone brought it out, then the Coven would take it.

Already, three men had died what sounded like horrible deaths. Though Ravyn couldn't see their bodies, their screams were proof enough that something was within the dark, waiting for anyone who dared to enter.

She wished it wasn't Carac. He was smarter than most, but that didn't mean he could survive whatever had killed the others. And, frankly, she didn't want him to die. She rather...liked him.

Too much, in fact.

Their earlier conversation about a future came back to her. Had he meant it? She might not have known him long, but

Ravyn didn't believe that Carac was the kind of man to blithely say such things. If he said them, then he meant them.

Could there be something that strong between them already? She didn't want to answer that, mainly because she thought there might be. She knew attraction. She even knew lust. Originally, she had believed that's all there was between them. But a night in his arms had proven it was something altogether different.

Something she was tempted to explore further.

Would they be happy together? The fact that he not only recognized her as a warrior but was also willing to fight along-side her said what kind of man he was. Carac accepted everything she was. They had similar lifestyles, and there was no denying the passion between them.

All that added up to one simple fact: she wasn't willing to let him go anytime soon. Which meant she didn't want him going through the doorway.

Just as she was about to make her presence known to take his place, Carac yanked a torch from the wall and strode beneath the arch.

Ravyn could only gape in utter astonishment as he faded into the darkness. A scream welled up within her to call him back.

Or race after him.

Then, her gaze swung to Sybbyl. Ravyn lifted her crossbow and took aim at the witch.

Carac had never been scared of the dark. He wasn't now, either. However, he *was* wary of what was *in* the blackness that was so thick the light of the torch barely broke through it.

It had taken every ounce of willpower for him not to turn

and look at Ravyn before he entered the doorway. He knew that the odds of his survival were slim—if the three dead men before him were any indication.

There was much he wanted to say to Ravyn. And more he desired to do to her...like kiss her for days at a time. Or make love to her every night for eternity.

Who was he kidding? That wouldn't be nearly long enough. With every step through the inky darkness, he thought of Ravyn and everything he wanted to show her. Like his home. He very much wanted to take her to his lands. More than anything, he wanted to see her face when she saw the impressive castle.

It was almost as if everything had changed once she came into his life. No longer did he want the glory that he had set out to find all those years ago.

Instead, he'd found something beautiful and rare in Ravyn. Thank the stars that he recognized it. Otherwise, he might have let her slip through his fingers. But he *had* realized everything she represented, and he hadn't run from her.

Nay, he had run straight *to* her.

He paused when his foot hit something. Carac went down on his haunches and lowered the torch in order to see. The flames flickered, showing the decapitated body of one of the three knights. With this corpse being so close to the entrance, it was probably the first man.

Carac moved the torch from one side to the other, turning all the way around as he searched for the head, but it was nowhere to be found. As if someone—or some*thing*—had taken it.

He glanced behind him. There was no light coming from the chamber or even the edges of a tunnel. Carac had no idea how big the place was. He assumed it was a narrow passageway, but perhaps it was time he found out for sure.

With the torch held high over his head to give as much light as possible, he walked to the right, one slow step at a time. He kept his sword sheathed despite his hand eager to feel its weight.

The dead knights were all the warning he needed to be prepared. So why didn't he reach for his blade? He wasn't sure. The darkness was eerie, the air stale and damp—and heavy—but he didn't feel threatened.

Yet.

After four steps, he saw the edge of a wall. With the torch held closer, he was able to discern the marks on the rocks from someone digging out the tunnel.

Carac turned around and counted his steps until he was back where he'd begun. Then he started walking to the left. He only took two steps before he met the wall.

He blew out a breath and faced forward. Something had beheaded the knight. Yet there was no sound of anyone breathing or movement of any kind.

The only sound was the hissing of the torch. The tunnel itself felt as dead and silent as a graveyard. But Carac knew something else had to be there, something that'd killed three men. It made him wish he could have read and understood the runes marked along the outside of the arch.

If he were going to find the staff, he needed to proceed. His gaze lowered to the dead man at his feet. Carac went down on one knee and inspected the man's wound. To his disbelief, the cut was clean, the skin seared.

Decapitation sometimes happened in battle, but not once had he ever seen such a thing. There were no jagged edges, no torn flesh. The blood that'd leaked from the body drained to the left and seemed to disappear into the ground.

Carac really wished he had more experience with magic and witches. He was completely out of his depth here. At least he knew a few things, but would it be enough to keep him alive? He really hoped so.

He stood but remained bent over to try and see where the knight's feet had been when he was struck down. Carac moved forward gradually, his gaze locked on the dirt floor.

With his eyes moving back and forth, looking for something he couldn't define, Carac discovered the top portion of a sword. He went down on one knee again and raised the torch higher for more light. If only he could see, he would be better able to determine what was going on. But that was obviously what the builders had intended.

He blinked to clear his vision and looked for the other half of the sword, which he found—still in the knight's hand.

Carac grimaced. The second man had also been beheaded, with the same clean wound. What was this weapon that could cut through bone and metal so easily? There was a very real possibility that he would find out soon enough.

He swallowed and once more thought about unsheathing his sword. Again, he decided against it. A look at the broken blade of the dead knight was proof enough that his weapon wouldn't help him.

Carac returned to looking for the place where both the knights had been standing when they were struck down. When he found it, he wasn't surprised to see that neither had taken a step back. They'd simply fallen backwards once they lost their heads.

He rubbed his forearm along his brow. It was becoming difficult to breathe. The air was oppressive, but more than that, it felt as if something were pushing on his chest, constricting his breathing.

Still, he continued onward. He needed to locate the third knight. If the man got past whatever had killed the other two, then there was hope for Carac.

But that was quickly dashed when he found the third man. He lay on his stomach as if he had been attempting to run back to the entrance. Same wound, same blood flowing to the left and disappearing.

"Shite," Carac murmured.

So much for the thought that one of the knights had survived. What Carac did find, however, was that all three had been struck down at different places. They were close to each other, but that meant that whatever the weapon was, it could move at will.

Or...even worse, there were many.

He closed his eyes and sighed. All of his training meant that he could outmaneuver most anyone on the battlefield, but this was something different, something he knew nothing about. Unfortunately, he would have to learn quickly. And adapt.

If Ravyn had shown him anything over the last few days, it was how she adjusted to anything. If he wanted to survive this, then he needed to think like she did.

He slowly stood. All three of the men had screamed in terror before they died. Had they triggered something? Or was something waiting for him? Either way, the knights had been truly petrified.

"*Caaaaaaaaaraaaaaaaaaac.*"

The whispered sound of his name came from all around him so he couldn't tell where it originated. His heart began to thump with dread.

"You know me?" he asked.

Silence met his words, and he began to think that he'd imagined someone saying his name. The place was unnerving, and combined with the three dead bodies, it bordered on peculiar.

He was one step away from being even with where the first

knight had died. Carac lifted his foot and moved forward a step. Nothing happened.

With his ears open to any sound, and his gaze darting around, he slowly took another step to put him even with where the second man had been cut down.

Once more, nothing.

Carac drew in a deep breath and lifted his foot. He hesitated in taking another step, but he couldn't go back. There was no other choice but to continue on. He gradually walked to the spot where the last knight was killed.

So far, he had come across nothing that would make him scream or that tried to attack him. If he were lucky, the dead around him had used up whatever had been added to the tunnel to keep others out.

It was a logical assumption. Still, he paused before he took another step. Blood pounded in his ears from his vigilance. And fear of the unknown. He tightened his grip on the torch and licked his lips. Then, he moved forward.

The scraping of metal on rock was faint behind him, joined by a second sound. Then he heard it in front of him. It was instinct that made him duck and roll forward.

He got to his feet and turned to find four huge double-edged axes coming from the wall, their blades horizontal to the ground. So that was what had taken the knights' heads. But what had made them scream?

Carac turned around and came face-to-face with a figure with hollowed-out eyes, sparse, stringy hair, a skeletal face, and long fingers that were reaching for him.

"Caaaaaaaaraaaaaaaaac," it whispered.

He wanted to run. He yearned to draw his sword and kill it. But, somehow, he remained still.

"How do you know me?" he demanded of the figure.

Its response was a laugh.

24

With the squeeze of a finger, this nightmare could end. Ravyn sighted down the crossbow. This was going to be the easiest shot she'd ever taken.

And one of the most fulfilling.

Ravyn's finger tightened on the trigger. Every bolt she had was imbued with Edra's magic. It didn't matter what type of magic a witch had, once the arrow penetrated skin, it would kill them.

She couldn't wait until Sybbyl's body disintegrated into ash. Then, she could rush after Carac and help him.

"I would think twice before you do that," Sybbyl said.

Ravyn frowned, wondering who the witch was talking to.

Then, Sybbyl slowly turned and looked at her. "I was beginning to think you lost your nerve, Hunter."

"Hardly."

Sybbyl's lips curved into a grin. "Or is it that you are worried about Sir Carac?" When Ravyn didn't answer, Sybbyl's smile widened. "I see."

Ravyn wanted to fire the arrow, but she was too far away.

The witch would be able to stop it. If only Ravyn had done it earlier while Sybbyl's attention was on the knights entering the doorway.

Instead, Ravyn had been too intent on what would happen. She'd lost her chance for a surprise attack. Now, she would have to face off with the witch.

"What are you waiting for?" Sybbyl urged. "Fire the arrow."

Ravyn took her finger off the trigger and lowered the weapon. The fact that the witch *wanted* her to use the crossbow was what made her put it down. For the moment. Once she got closer—because she would get close enough—Ravyn would use it.

Sybbyl shook her head of golden hair. "All this fuss over Hunters. I just do not understand it. I have finally met one of you, and you do exactly as I want. You will be my gift to the elders." Sybbyl then looked around. "Where is your servant?"

"She was never my servant," Ravyn said with a grin. She didn't have any idea where Margery was, but she knew her friend would find them eventually.

Sybbyl's eyes widened. "Another Hunter? Even better. Tell her to come out."

"Did you not hear me? I said, I do not know where she is."

"Come now. We both know you are the leader."

Ravyn chuckled. "We are equals."

"Nonsense," the witch scoffed. "If you were, you would have both come as ladies instead of her posing as a servant."

"You think you know what kind of people we are because of the roles we played?"

Sybbyl raised a perfectly arched blond brow. "Of course."

"Tell me, do you even know what she looks like?"

The witch opened her mouth to reply, then closed it.

"As I thought," Ravyn replied. "We each have our uses and special skills."

"What is yours?"

"I have many."

Sybbyl grinned as she eyed her up and down. "Oh, I imagine you do. How many men have you taken to your bed?"

"You assume because I am a woman that I use my body?"

"Please, my dear. Do not bother to lie to me. I know what I see, and I see a beautiful woman who knows how to charm a man. That means you have used your body."

Ravyn didn't see any reason to deny it. She wasn't ashamed of her life or the choices she had made. "What of it?"

"That's what I wanted," Sybbyl said. "For you to admit it."

"Why? You think to embarrass me somehow? Do not bother."

Sybbyl smiled suddenly. "Nay. I was not thinking about that at all. In fact, I have something else in store for you."

"Such as?"

"Why spoil it? I want it to be a surprise."

Ravyn tightened her hand on the crossbow. Sybbyl knew she was a Hunter, yet the witch didn't seem the least bit disturbed about it. Which meant that Sybbyl hadn't seen what the Hunters could do.

"I see you are as tough as I thought you might be," Sybbyl stated.

Ravyn frowned at her words. "Because I do not cry and beg you not to hurt me?"

"Aye," Sybbyl said with a nod. "Most women are annoyingly predictable."

Ravyn could say the same for witches, but she kept that bit to herself. "You seem very assured of your success."

Sybbyl shrugged, her gaze sliding to the doorway. "Carac seems extremely capable. He does not realize it, but I have seen him in battle before. Magnificent does not even begin to describe him."

How Ravyn hated that Sybbyl had seen him when she hadn't. "Does that mean you chose him to come here?"

"With the right words whispered into a man's ears, magic was not even needed. John was so easy to manipulate." Sybbyl grinned. "I am sure you know what I mean."

"Oh, I do. Why did you need Carac?"

Sybbyl's eyes brightened as her teeth flashed in a smile. "Is that jealousy I hear?"

"Curiosity," Ravyn corrected.

The witch shrugged indifferently. "I wanted him in my bed. And I will have him there."

"If he survives whatever is inside that doorway."

"He will," Sybbyl stated confidently.

Ravyn wished she had such conviction in Carac's survival. He was strong and cunning, but there was no telling what was through the arch. Already, it had killed three knights. Although, even she had to admit that he had been in there for nearly twice as long as the others.

But was that good news or bad?

"*Carac.*"

The orange light from the torch danced over the grotesque face of the figure before him. The clothes were in rags, hanging upon a skeleton that appeared ready to fall apart at any second.

Until you looked into its eyes. The black holes were like bottomless, soul-sucking voids. There was very little that scared Carac, but this...thing...certainly did.

He didn't know why it kept saying his name. It had yet to

reply to his questions. For all he knew, it couldn't hear him. It moved closer, and he fought not to take a step back. Or reach for his weapon.

As if reading his thoughts, the head shifted to the side and down, as if looking at his sword. He frowned. Surely, the thing couldn't read his mind.

Carac couldn't stand around staring at the being for the rest of time. He needed to retrieve the staff and help Ravyn, because if he knew the beauty, she was likely to go after Sybbyl while the witch was occupied.

"Who are you?" he asked.

The figure returned its gaze to his face.

He took a deep breath. Maybe if he attempted to talk to it... "I mean you no harm. If you wou—"

His words halted when the skeletal remains suddenly transformed into a beautiful woman with black hair and vibrant blue eyes. He could see through her body, and she hovered just off the floor. Her clothes looked to be made of the finest material but were obviously hundreds of years old.

"Carac, you are not a Bryce." Her gaze shifted over his shoulder to the others. "Neither were they."

He glanced at the knights behind him. "Nay, I am not. Lord Randall is in the chamber."

"He should have been the one to come." Her forehead furrowed. "But then, this tomb was never meant to be opened."

Tomb? Had she said tomb? Shite, just what had he gotten himself into.

"Is this your resting place?" he asked.

She blinked at him, her head cocked to the side as if she were debating answering him. "Aye. I guard this place for any who seek to walk this path."

"If you are here, why the blades?" he asked, referring to the axes.

Her lips turned up into a grin. "That was my brother's idea. As you can see, it works beautifully."

"Aye. So it does." He swallowed. "Are you a Bryce descendant?"

"I am."

"And your name?"

She paused as if considering his request. "Rossamond."

He rubbed his free hand over his jaw, his whiskers scraping against his palm. "I know what you guard here."

"Just as I know you have come to claim it."

"There are those who seek the staff."

She blinked. "The Coven."

It was his turn to frown. "You know of them?"

"They have been around for thousands of years. It was because of them that my brothers and I decided to put the staff in a place where they could not reach it."

"But they can force others."

"Which is why only a descendant can retrieve it."

He shook his head, his gaze dropping to the ground. "Sybbyl will not allow Randall in here. She knows he will destroy the staff or kill himself."

"There is only one way to destroy the staff, and there is no way Randall can do that."

Carac pointed behind him. "There is a member of the Coven here with elders on the way because of the staff. They knew the artifact was here, and Sybbyl has killed hundreds of Randall's people to force him to give up the location."

"That was to be expected."

"You do not sound worried that the Coven will claim the staff."

"Because I know they will not."

He blew out a frustrated breath. "If I do not return with it, Sybbyl will kill everyone in the castle as well as my men."

"Many have died to ensure that the staff remains hidden and safe. I was one of them," the woman said. "A witch cursed me to die a very painful, very slow death that could spread to everyone if I refused to tell her where the staff was. This was after she murdered dozens of our people—including my parents. We had already dug this place, so my brothers hurried to finish it. Then I took my place and was sealed inside."

It was a horrible way to die. Carac couldn't imagine the pain she must have endured. All to save a relic.

"It is more than a relic," the woman said.

Carac's gaze snapped to her face. "You know my thoughts?"

She shrugged. "The Staff of the Eternal holds the thigh bone of the First Witch. One bone from her can cause a multitude of problems for others if it falls into the Coven's hands. Then there are those few bones that have triple the power."

"The Blood Skull," he said.

There was a flare of surprise. "Aye. That is the most powerful piece. Does the Coven hold it?"

"Nay. They were thwarted by my friends. They are Hunters, and they spend their days tracking the Coven and stopping them."

Rossamond smiled. "If only we had such a group back in my day. I wonder if things might have turned out differently. But it does not matter. The staff holds significant power, and because of that, it must be hidden at all costs."

"Then why make it into a staff at all?" he asked without thinking.

The woman sighed, her eyes briefly closing. "Long, long ago, my family came to guard a bone from the First Witch. It remained buried for hundreds of years. Then, one of my ancestors dug it up to move it after a witch began looking for it. What he unearthed was a bone that resembled a piece of wood. He believed the best way to hide it was to keep it in plain sight. So he hollowed out a long piece of wood and put the bone inside it."

"It was a brilliant idea."

"It was," she agreed. "Until others began to realize that whoever held the staff also commanded power and wealth. People tried to steal it. And then the Coven returned to look for the bone."

Carac nodded. "That's when you hid it here."

She gave him a faint smile. "I like you, Carac. It really is too bad that I have to kill you."

25

Timing was everything. Ravyn had learned that lesson the hard way, but it was a mistake she didn't allow herself to make twice.

Sybbyl was confident in not only Carac's retrieval of the staff but also her success delivering the artifact to the elders of the Coven.

And Ravyn simply wasn't going to let that happen.

She didn't know how much longer she had before the elders arrived. What she did know was that she would have to fight Sybbyl. That was the main threat right now. Afterward, Ravyn could figure out where Carac was and get the staff. She refused to even think about coming up against the elders. Her mind had to be focused entirely on Sybbyl.

Ravyn glanced at Randall who hadn't moved from his position on his knees. His gaze was on her, a slight frown upon his brow. There was worry in the lord's eyes, and she understood his concern all too well.

Sybbyl walked to stand beside the man. She put a hand atop his head and forced it down until it was bowed. "Men have dominated women and ruled everything for many, many years. It is time for us to take their place."

"Witches?" Ravyn asked.

"Witches. Women," Sybbyl replied with a shrug. "Same difference."

Ravyn shot her a puzzled look. "I believe you are wrong on that point."

"Look at you," Sybbyl said as she motioned to Ravyn. "You dress like a man. You have trained as men do. You fight in the ways of men. And yet the knights in this chamber look down on you. They believe you inferior."

"I care not what they think."

Sybbyl's smile was slow. "It really is too bad that you do not have magic. You would make an excellent witch."

"Even if I did, I would never join the Coven," Ravyn stated.

Sybbyl waved away her words. "Oh, I think you would change your mind if your other option was death."

"Some might. I would not."

The witch eyed her for a moment. "I believe you would rather choose death. Your inner strength and courage are what sets you apart from others. Whether you admit it or not, we are very much alike."

"I disagree," Ravyn stated and turned slightly to look out of the corner of her eye at the knights behind her. "You like to murder innocents. I only kill those of the Coven."

"Ah, but you enjoy it," Sybbyl declared with a smile.

Ravyn shrugged and took a few steps before stopping and shifting the other way, once more taking note of the knights. Both groups stood as far from Sybbyl as possible on either side of the chamber, but Ravyn couldn't be sure if they would side with the witch or not. "I will not deny that I like ridding the world of evil."

"Evil." Sybbyl sighed loudly and glanced at the ceiling. "Why would you put us in such a category?"

Ravyn wasn't certain if Sybbyl was patronizing her or not. Then she saw the anger simmering in the witch's blue eyes as she turned on Randall.

"Men," Sybbyl all but spit the word. "They are the evil ones. They have taken it upon themselves to tell us how we should act and dress. They deem it their responsibility to sell us to other men as wives, to be nothing more than slaves. They rape and beat us without fear of reprisal. They claim we are not intelligent enough to learn to read or write. We are good for nothing but cooking and cleaning, bearing children along the way. Both men and the church tell us that we are naturally weak and have sinful natures." Sybbyl's head turned to Ravyn. "*Sinful.* How many men beat and rape women and children? How many *men* of the church disregard their vows and take others to their beds?"

Everything Sybbyl said was true. There was nothing Ravyn could—or wanted to—say to rebuke such claims.

The witch's lips twisted as her fury rose. "But we are deemed the weaker, wicked ones. All because men are guided by their pricks." She grabbed Randall by his hair and jerked his head back as she leaned down and put her face close to his. "Right?"

"Some, aye," he said, wincing at the pain.

Sybbyl shoved him away and spat on him. "When, in fact, males are the inferior sex. Women are the strong ones. We can fight just as well as men, and we bring life into this world. We were given that gift because God knew that men would not be able to handle the pain or endure the hours of labor. And it is women who raise the children because men cannot be bothered."

Sybbyl then looked around the chamber at the knights.

"We do not rape men. There is no need for such treatment. I have shriveled many a man's cock after they forced themselves on a woman. Why can men not understand the word *nay*?"

Ravyn was all for chopping off a man's privates if he forced a woman, but it bothered her greatly that she found herself agreeing with the witch...her enemy.

Sybbyl's blue eyes landed on her. "The time of men is coming to an end."

"You would willingly kill any woman without magic?" Ravyn asked.

The witch drew in a shaky breath as she struggled to gain control of herself. "Aye."

"So much for the time of women." Ravyn snorted in contempt. "What you really mean is it's the time of witches."

Sybbyl threw back her head and laughed. Ravyn's blood went cold, her body jerking as if hit. The laugh she had heard in her nightmares since she was a small child. To hear it again sent chills racing over her body.

As fury welled up.

After all this time, Ravyn had found the witch responsible for her family's murder. For a moment, all she could do was stare as fear of that terrible night mixed with resentment and the need for revenge. There had been times when Ravyn thought she would never be able to get justice for her family.

Now, she knew she could. And she intended to do just that.

Sybbyl's laughter died as she took notice of Ravyn. "So much rage inside you. Have you finally decided to join me?"

"Do you know how long I have looked for you?"

The witch raised a brow. "Me? Whatever for?"

"That horrible laugh of yours has haunted me for years."

Sybbyl's eyes widened as she grinned. "Did I hurt someone you loved?"

"You killed my family," Ravyn bit out.

There was a small frown on Sybbyl's brow before she laughed again. "What are you going to do about it?"

Ravyn was tired of words. She needed action. She needed death.

The witch's death.

Ravyn lifted the crossbow and took aim. Before she could fire off an arrow, Sybbyl raised both hands, palms out. Ravyn wasn't going to stand around and wait for whatever magic the witch released.

Instead, she darted back to the entrance where she dropped down to her knees and slid, turning her body so she could fire the arrows.

As soon as they were loosed, she got to her feet and shot another. She started running around the perimeter of the chamber. The knights near her scattered, wanting no part of the battle.

The wall near her suddenly exploded, sending Ravyn flying onto her back. Pain lanced through her as she landed on a pile of rocks, but there wasn't a spare moment to think about that. She rolled onto her side toward the center of the chamber and fired several more arrows.

This time, she watched as one of the projectiles skimmed Sybbyl's shoulder, only missing the witch because she turned away at the last second.

Ravyn continued to roll, firing each time. Never was Ravyn happier that she had a weapon that could fire multiple arrows without having to be notched each time. But she had to be careful. She was running out of bolts.

Sybbyl screamed her annoyance as she dodged a volley of projectiles aimed at her. Unfortunately, not a single one found its mark.

Not that Ravyn expected Sybbyl to be an easy target. She

jumped to her feet and then quickly turned and squatted as a ball of fire came at her. The fireball passed so closely that Ravyn felt the heat of it against her cheek.

Just as she straightened and prepared to turn and shoot the crossbow again, something struck her from behind in the back of her knee. She pitched forward, falling hard upon the scattered debris and slamming the side of her head against a rock. Her wrist landed on something hard, and it made her lose her grip on her weapon. She watched in dismay as it fell from her fingers.

Ravyn bit back a scream as another blow landed on her back. She was in agony, the pain sizzling through her body from her knee and head and shoulder blades. She had to get moving. Otherwise, she would be an easy target for Sybbyl.

No matter how she tried to make herself stir, her body wouldn't respond as it usually did. And that wasn't a good sign. In fact, if she weren't careful, it would mean certain death.

There was no way she had finally come face-to-face with her nemesis only to die at her hands. Nay. Ravyn would win this day. Once and for all.

Her family would get the justice they long deserved, the promise she had given as she gazed upon their ravaged bodies as a small child.

Ravyn finally scrambled over the rocks and got to her feet. She tried to retrieve her crossbow, but another fireball landed on it. Ravyn refused to lose her weapon to magic. She kicked the crossbow out of the fire and kept moving.

She reached down and took out the knife in her boot as she approached one of the knights. This one decided he would attempt to catch her. Apparently, he hoped by joining Sybbyl that she wouldn't kill him. Too bad he was mistaken.

Ravyn put her foot on the wall to launch herself upward.

She spun and came down before the knight, her blade piercing his neck before he could lay a hand on her.

She looked into his eyes filled with surprise. "Fool," she murmured.

Yanking out the blade, she shoved the dying man aside and quickly scanned the chamber for the best way to get to Sybbyl. Some knights tried again to leave while a couple of others decided to help Sybbyl.

The witch's laughter filled the chamber along with the crackling of the small fires. Ravyn stared at her adversary as blood trickled down the side of her face, imagining all kinds of ways she could kill Sybbyl. But all she needed was one—the one that would succeed.

"Get her!" Sybbyl demanded of the knights.

Ravyn ducked a meaty fist aimed at her head and kicked the knight's feet out from under him. She spun to the left and took out another dagger anchored at her waist. Then she slid on her knees between two of the men, making quick stabs as she skidded past them. They screamed in pain, each holding their legs as blood poured from their wounds.

But she wasn't done. Another, the biggest of them, was coming for her. And he wore armor.

She went straight for him, hoping to reach him quickly, but she wasn't fast enough. He pulled his sword and swung it at her head. Ravyn came to a halt and bent backwards. She watched the blade in slow motion as it passed over her face.

Before she could straighten, she found herself on the ground again, pain throbbing in her side. She didn't need to look at Sybbyl to know that the witch was responsible. No witch fought fair. Ravyn should have remembered that.

There was a shout from the door to the chamber, one that Ravyn recognized well. She tilted her head back and saw

Margery rush into the space with her sword drawn, Simon on her heels.

Ravyn had wondered where the couple was, but her attention was diverted to the knight and the sword bearing down on her. Ravyn rolled out of the way, right to her crossbow. Without hesitation, she grabbed the smoking weapon and fired two shots, each landing in the knight's eyes.

With Simon and Margery keeping Sybbyl occupied, it gave Ravyn the chance she needed to dart through the arch. She didn't think twice about going to find Carac or the staff.

Because as much as she wanted Sybbyl dead, defeating the Coven was a bigger priority. And if Ravyn could find the staff, then it would be a simple matter to end Sybbyl and any other witch who arrived at Bryce Castle.

26

Carac's head whipped around at the sound of laughter drifting from behind him. He couldn't help but wonder if it was the laugh Ravyn had been trying to find. If it was, that meant she was fighting Sybbyl on her own. He should be there with her.

He looked back at Rossamond. She gazed at him without any emotion. She was there for one purpose only, and no matter his wishes or desires or needs, she wasn't going to let him pass.

More sounds of bellows from knights, rocks tumbling, and even blasts could be heard. With each one, he became more and more antsy to return to Ravyn and the current skirmish.

"There is a battle behind you," she said.

He nodded.

She cocked her head to the side. "You wish to join in."

"I have a friend in there. She is fighting the others alone. I should be with her."

"Her?" the ghost asked. "A woman fights?"

"She is one of the Hunters I told you about."

Rossamond's eyes lifted to gaze over his shoulder. At almost the same moment, the axes returned to their hiding places within the walls. Carac turned and watched them, knowing that it most likely meant that someone was in the tunnel.

And since Sybbyl couldn't pass through the arch, then it could be Ravyn. His heart stopped at the thought of her rushing through the dark.

"Wait," he hurried to say as he faced the ghost again. "Please, just wait."

"Because you think it is the Hunter?"

"Aye. It could be."

"And if it is not?"

Carac ground his teeth together. "Then I will kill whoever it is if they are not a friend of mine."

Now, he could hear footsteps approaching. His heart was in his throat as he waited for the ghost to make up her mind.

"Please," he begged. "Take my life, but spare Ravyn's. She is on your side."

"Are you not?"

He wanted to shout his frustration. "I am. I have already told you that, but if someone must die, then let it be me. Spare her."

Now that he was accustomed to the tunnel's sounds, he could hear the blades getting ready to swing from their spots. He spun around and opened his mouth to shout a warning at Ravyn when his torch suddenly went out.

And then his voice was stolen.

Rossamond came up behind him and pressed her lips to his ear, making him shiver as if he stood in an icy river in the middle of winter. "You cannot lend any aid."

Standing idly by went against everything Carac was. He didn't think he would survive if Ravyn were beheaded. Then again, the ghost had already condemned him to death. So at least he wouldn't suffer long.

He was powerless to do anything but watch the darkness as his eyes grew accustomed, hoping the approaching person was not Ravyn. But he knew in his heart that it was. He then prayed that she would stop and listen and pay attention to the sounds of the tunnel.

He willed it with everything he was.

"Carac?"

His eyes closed when he heard Ravyn's voice, his heart catching when he realized how close she was. Any moment now, one of the blades would slide from the wall.

"I stopped the blades from taking you," the ghost whispered to him. "Shall I do the same for her?"

Carac nodded, hope filling him. But it was extinguished a second later when the first blade scraped against the rock. Even from a distance, he heard it like a whisper of death descending upon Ravyn.

He opened his mouth and shouted. It welled up within him with all the anguish, fury, and regret of twenty lifetimes.

But there was no sound. Nothing to commence such a fine warrior's death. Nothing to showcase the grief that was swallowing him whole for the beautiful woman who had stolen his heart.

His breath hitched when he heard the second axe. There was a whoosh of air and the soft sounds of feet hitting the ground. And then, Ravyn was there.

He dropped the extinguished torch and reached for her, yanking her out of the way of the third blade. It wasn't until she was in his arms and he was holding her tightly against him that he realized Rossamond had released the hold she had on him and his voice.

"Carac," Ravyn murmured and lifted her face to his.

He couldn't believe she was alive. Without the torch, he could only make out the outline of her body in the dark, but it was enough. He cupped her face with his hands before lowering his head to press his lips against hers. "You should not have come."

"Simon and Margery are fighting Sybbyl. We have no time to stand here. We must find the staff," Ravyn said.

No sooner had her words ended than he heard Ravyn gasp. There was also a faint glow coming behind him, bathing Ravyn's face in pale light. Carac didn't need to turn to know that the ghost was behind him.

"Carac," Ravyn whispered, alarm tingeing her voice.

A wry grin briefly passed his lips. His woman would stand against a witch and magic without hesitation, but a specter gave her pause.

He dropped his arm and linked his fingers with Ravyn's before he faced Rossamond. The ghost's eyes shifted from Ravyn to him. She said nothing. Merely gazed at them.

After several tense seconds, Ravyn kept her gaze on the ghost but turned her head toward him. "We need to get moving."

"That is not going to happen," the ghost stated.

Ravyn's fingers tightened around his. Carac gave her a squeeze of reassurance that he prayed wasn't a lie. "She got through your trap on her own."

The woman floated closer to Ravyn. "So she did."

Carac turned his head to Ravyn and said, "Rossamond was cursed by a witch from the Coven seeking the staff. She came down here to die in an effort to protect the artifact."

"Thank you," Ravyn told the woman. "Your sacrifice is appreciated."

To Carac's surprise, the ghost's attitude changed. She blinked as if unsure how to respond to Ravyn's gratitude. "I had no choice. I was dying, and it would have killed everyone else, as well."

"You had a choice," Carac said. "There is always another option. You decided to put yourself down here, away from family or anyone who might ease your comfort, to die slowly and in great agony."

Ravyn nodded in agreement. "What you did is remarkable. I do not believe anyone but the bravest and most valiant could have made such a decision."

Rossamond turned her head away and looked at something only she could see. "The Coven thought they could break me. They believed I was weak because I loved my family and people so deeply. The witch made sure that the affliction that she put on me would continue whether I had food or water. She knew that my brothers would see to me, and that I would spread the disease to them and more."

"The witch was wrong," Carac stated.

The ghost swiveled her head back to them. "I was terrified of dying alone. The disease lasted for weeks—or months, I know not—as I lost track of time. There were instances where the pain got so bad that I screamed for my brothers, begged them to let me out so I could feel a kind touch. I am grateful they never heard my pleas. With my dying breath, I went to the staff and begged it to allow me to remain here to protect it from intruders."

"And only allow descendants of family Bryce inside," Carac said, filling Ravyn in.

Ravyn's eyes widened a fraction. "Sybbyl will never allow Randall here."

"Carac said the same," Rossamond stated.

"He is not lying, and neither am I. Sybbyl has called in more witches. I believe the Coven elders are coming," Ravyn added.

The ghost shrugged. "No one with magic can get through the doorway."

"And if they tear down the castle?" Carac asked. "What if they come from above instead of through the doorway?"

The specter frowned before shaking her head. "My brothers and I never thought this place would be uncovered, but that was foolish of us to believe. It was only a matter of time before a member of the Coven returned to our family."

"They have always known there was a chance the staff was here," Ravyn told her.

"And now, they have come. In order to save others, they forced a descendant of my family to give up the location of the doorway, but it will be for naught. They will kill him and everyone else."

Carac shrugged and gave a quick shake of his head. "Randall no doubt knew that was a possibility, but he is a good man. He wanted his people to live."

"Instead, he is condemning the world to death," the ghost stated angrily.

Ravyn gawked at her. "Your anger being directed at Randall is wrong."

"Is it?" Rossamond demanded. "I gave up my life to protect the staff."

"Nay," Carac said. "Your life was already forfeit because of the witch. You chose to die here to save your family and others."

The ghost's eyes narrowed on him. "You think I cared nothing for the staff?"

"I think it was a bonus," he said, hoping his instincts were right. "The staff was in your family for generations. It was a problem that would not go away. It brought unwanted attention to your ancestors."

She cocked her head to the side. "That is a bold statement."

"But am I right?" he pushed.

Her face filled with sorrow. "It is true that I cursed the one who brought the First Witch's bone to my family. I railed at my ancestor for digging it up and making it into a staff. I loathed the Coven for continually attempting to find it. But I hated the staff the most. It ruined my life."

"You can think of it another way," Ravyn said. "You can choose to believe that the one who brought the bone to your family knew that you were honorable and trustworthy. You can believe that the Coven continued to be thwarted in their efforts because of the strength and ingenuity of your family. You can also choose to consider that the staff knew you would be the strongest in your family. It knew you would safeguard it at all costs—which you did. I believe all of that because when you asked it to allow you to remain and stop intruders, it granted your wish."

"You are attempting to sway me, to convince me to allow both of you to live."

Carac was growing weary of this conversation. "We are not part of the Coven."

"So you say," Rossamond interrupted. "I have no way of verifying your claims. You expect me to take your word for it."

"We do," Carac replied. "Just as we have taken yours. A witch killed Ravyn's family. Ravyn became a Hunter to fight them. And I joined her because it is the right thing to do."

"It's Sybbyl," Ravyn said in a low voice.

Carac's head whipped around to her. "What?"

"Sybbyl," Ravyn said as she met his gaze. "She is the one who murdered my family."

And she had learned that on her own. He should have been beside her. Carac released her hand and wrapped his arm around her shoulders to draw her close. "You thought it might be her."

"I could not kill her. She is too strong."

He tilted her chin up with his finger and grinned. "Then we do it together."

"If we get out of here," Ravyn said, her gaze darting to the ghost. "If not, then it is in Margery's and the other Hunters' hands."

Carac knew the chances of getting away from the ghost were slim, but he could make sure their deaths were not in vain. "If we cannot kill Sybbyl or the elders, at least we can make sure they never get the staff."

A slow smile spread over Ravyn's face. "Without the Blood Skull or the staff, their plans to kill off anyone without magic will be foiled."

"What do you plan, then?" the ghost asked.

Carac looked at Rossamond and cocked an eyebrow. "You would join us?"

"I wish to see the Coven defeated. Now, tell me your plan," she urged.

"Do it," Ravyn told Carac.

She would readily admit that speaking to a ghost was more than frightening, and knowing that Rossamond was also part of the reason the three knights died only made things harder to bear.

Then there were the blades that had come out of nowhere as Ravyn walked down the tunnel. It had been so dark that she'd had to sling her crossbow over her shoulder and make her way with her hands out in front of her, feeling her way along.

It had only been the soft scraping and a whisper of wind that alerted her. The sound had been near her head, so she rolled forward. Just as she was getting to her feet, she heard a second grating sound. She did two more rolls just to be sure. No sooner had she found her feet than she was pulled against a hard body.

The instant Carac's arms went around her, she let out a sigh of relief. Only then did she realize how close to death she had come, because with the ghost revealing herself, Ravyn was able to see the huge double-headed axes protruding from the walls.

She shivered as a chill raced down her spine as if the fingers of the dead had touched her. Ravyn didn't like the tunnel. It smelled of death—both old and new. The only thing that she did like about it was that witches couldn't get in.

Then again, they had mentioned that if the Coven really wanted to get to the staff, they could come in another way. And that sounded exactly like something the witches would do.

She looked at Carac's profile bathed in the light of the spirit as he turned toward Rossamond. He was strong and steady. And seemingly unaffected by the fact that he was speaking to a ghost that wanted him dead. All the while, he spoke to Rossamond calmly and rationally. Not once had he reached for his sword.

That made Ravyn frown. Why did she even contemplate attacking the specter? As a ghost, their weapons wouldn't harm her. And Ravyn wasn't sure if anything could.

Which left her and Carac utterly at Rossamond's mercy. A fact that Carac appeared not to mind.

His chest expanded as he drew in a breath. "We have little to work with. We can only consider the things we have here."

"Like?" the spirit asked.

"I suppose there is only one way in and out?"

The woman nodded. "Of course."

Ravyn glanced upward. "Unless they come in another way."

"True," Carac replied as he glanced at her. "For now, let us assume that they are focused on the arch. They will stand together, waiting for one of us to come out."

"Or send more in," Ravyn said. She hoped Margery would

get the upper hand on Sybbyl, but she was worried that the witch was too strong for her friend.

Ravyn shouldn't have left Margery. She should've stayed instead of rushing off after the staff and Carac. Margery wouldn't have abandoned her. What kind of friend did that make Ravyn? A lousy one.

Ravyn blinked and focused her gaze to find both Carac and Rossamond staring at her. "What?"

"I asked your opinion," Carac said.

She licked her lips and shifted feet. "I am worried about Margery."

"I thought as much, which is why I said we should return to the arch."

Ravyn gaped at him. "Go back to Sybbyl and most likely the elders without the staff? What good would that do?"

"She is here to stop anyone who comes in," Carac said, motioning to Rossamond.

Ravyn briefly met the woman's gaze and shook her head. "I got through, and so did you. Others will, as well."

"I only made it through because she allowed it," Carac confessed.

That made Ravyn frown. Her head swung to the spirit, who nodded in confirmation. Perhaps Ravyn hadn't made it through as she thought. "Did you help me?" she asked the ghost.

"I did not," the woman replied.

Ravyn considered Carac's plan. "Let us imagine that Margery wins against Sybbyl. There are still the other witches coming. We both heard Sybbyl send John to the great hall to await their arrival. If Sybbyl believes she is about to get the artifact, then she called for the elders."

"The elders are still witches," Carac said.

Rossamond snorted. "You obviously know very little about witches, or you would never make such a statement."

"He only recently learned of them," Ravyn said in Carac's defense.

Carac leaned back against the wall of the tunnel. "I suppose the elders have significantly more power than other witches."

"Aye," Ravyn and the ghost said in unison.

Unruffled at the news, Carac shrugged. "And with only your and Margery's weapons able to kill a witch, that puts us at a distinct disadvantage."

"I knew becoming a Hunter would likely mean that I died at the hands of a witch, but I did not want it to be today. Especially not at Sybbyl's hands." Ravyn squeezed her eyes closed for a heartbeat. "But if it means that the Coven will be defeated and not able to get to the staff, then I will do whatever it takes."

Carac took her hand again, his lips tilting in a lopsided smile. "I do not wish to die today either. I just found you, and I had plans for us."

That caused Ravyn to smile. "This is bigger than us, though."

"Aye," he said, his grin slipping. "Much bigger."

The ghost sighed loudly. "I have yet to hear a plan."

Ravyn adjusted her crossbow on her shoulder. "The tunnel is dark. I will stand as close to the entrance of the arch as I can and fire off arrows until I kill them all."

"I like this plan," Carac said.

Ravyn's chest puffed out in pride. Up until the ghost spoke.

"It will not work," the woman stated flatly.

"Why not?" Ravyn asked. "They cannot use magic."

A thin, black brow arched as the ghost stared at her. "No

one with magic can enter, but it will not stop a witch from directing her magic through the arch. They would find you quickly enough."

"I could still kill a couple of them."

"That will not be enough," Carac said. "Our options were slim to begin with."

Ravyn rubbed her thumb over the carved runes on her weapon, thinking about her family. "Whatever we do, the Coven will be waiting."

"But they are expecting the staff," Carac said with a smile.

Now Ravyn was confused. "That is something to smile about?"

"Do you know what it looks like?" he asked.

Ravyn shook her head. "As far as I know, no one does."

"I was hoping you would say that." Carac was still smiling when he turned to Rossamond. "Is there anything in here we could use as a staff?"

While the idea did have merit, Ravyn saw flaws, as well. "As soon as one of the witches gets ahold of the staff, they will know it is not the right one."

"Who said they would get ahold of it," Carac replied as he looked at her.

Ravyn had to smile. "That is a good idea, and the trick might work. But not for long."

"We do not need long. Just enough time to see if Margery and Simon survived, as well as determine how many witches are there."

"And elders," Ravyn added.

The spirit interjected. "There is something that might work. Follow me."

Ravyn and Carac exchanged a look as they trailed after the ghost. Ravyn's gaze lowered to see that the woman was floating. There were no feet touching the ground. Which was just as odd as being able to see through Rossamond's body.

With each step, Ravyn took in what little she could see revealed by the light from the woman. The tunnel narrowed suddenly, allowing only one person through at a time.

While she had to squeeze her shoulders in, Carac had to turn sideways and shuffle through. The spirit, however, didn't have such issues. She passed right through the rock.

Of all the magic Ravyn had seen in her life, she'd never thought to encounter a ghost. In fact, she'd always assumed that others' talk of such meetings were nothing but lies and proof that people were crazy. Now, she needed to rethink things.

Finally, Ravyn came out of the constricted tunnel and entered into a section that was as wide as the original passageway. She turned to get her bearings and saw the remains of a body curled up on the ground.

The ghost stood gazing down at the bones. Ravyn knelt next to the skeleton, the remnants of a gown hanging in tatters. Ravyn put her hand over the bones and sat silently for a moment.

Then, she looked up at Rossamond. "Shall we give you a proper burial?"

"This is my burial chamber," the ghost said and looked around. "The pain that body felt is long gone. As is my family."

"Not true," Carac said. He pointed back down the tunnel. "You have family currently being held by the Coven. Randall has been beaten and starved. He has had to watch his people being threatened and murdered. You remain here to guard the staff, but you are also guarding your family."

Ravyn slowly got to her feet and shot him a small smile of approval. If they were to survive this, it would be because they worked together. She couldn't do it alone, and neither could Carac.

They made a good team. Both in bed and out.

"What would you have me do?" Rossamond asked.

Carac drew in a deep breath. "Can you leave this place?"

The woman's head cocked to the side. "You saw me in the tunnel."

His lips compressed in exasperation. "I meant, can you go anywhere you want in the castle?"

"I can. I rarely do it, though. I do not like to see what has become of my home."

Ravyn saw an opportunity and took it. "But you do check in on your descendants every now and again, aye?"

"I have been known to make my way to the castle when I hear the cries of a baby," the ghost admitted.

Ravyn glanced at Carac while hiding her smile. "Which means you have seen new generations being born."

The ghost bowed her head in agreement. "I have also stood by the bedsides of some who died."

"You have witnessed what no one else is capable of," Carac said. "You have seen your line continue. You watched them from afar and saw that they held true to the honor of your family name by keeping the staff a secret."

Rossamond faced Carac and folded her hands before her. "You are attempting to convince me to help you."

"To help your family," Ravyn corrected her.

The spirit's cold blue eyes slid to her. "This body may no longer feel pain, but the emotions within me never halted. I was to be married. I wanted at least six children."

Now, Ravyn understood why Rossamond felt compelled to answer the cries of infants.

"I wept when my brothers died one by one, but I rejoiced in their offspring," the ghost continued. "I was there when

Randall was born, and when his wife and child died of a fever. And I will be by his side when he breathes his last." The woman paused and looked between them. "I envy the two of you and the love that blossoms. I regret that I was never able to experience it or hold my children in my arms."

Carac took a step toward the ghost. "Then take it out on the ones responsible. The Coven. They took your life. Your future. They have come into your home once again to threaten your last descendant."

"A compelling argument," Rossamond said. Then, she smiled.

Ravyn wanted to shout for joy, but she kept it contained. They still didn't have a plan, but they were much better off with the spirit helping them.

Maybe now, the Coven could be defeated.

Ravyn tried not to look around for the staff, but she couldn't stop herself. It was here somewhere. The Bryces had kept it safe for thousands of years, but now that the Coven had discovered it, more and more witches would come.

She didn't believe they could destroy the Coven that day. They might take out a few members, and maybe even an elder if they were really lucky, but that only meant that the Coven would return for the staff.

However, Ravyn would worry about taking the staff once the Coven was gone from Bryce Castle.

28

He should be happy that the ghost was agreeing with him, but Carac couldn't shake the feeling that it had gone too well. The spirit wanted him dead. Not once had she said that she would allow him to live.

Nor would he assume that she had changed her mind about ending his life. It was simply on hold while they dealt with the threat of the Coven.

Perhaps Rossamond knew that his chances of survival were slim and was allowing things to play out to see the end result. If he happened to live and defeated the Coven, then he might very well come face-to-face with the spirit again.

Carac glanced at Ravyn. More than anything, he wanted her to come through all of this alive and unharmed. She deserved to get retribution for what had been done to her family. And she was needed in the fight with the Coven. With her skills and knowledge of witches, she could inflict significant damage to the Coven. Now, all Carac had to do was convince the ghost of that.

How many times had he stood on a battlefield and

accepted that death might very well find him that day? Too many. Now, knowing that his time was likely coming to an end, he thought of all the things that he'd wanted in his life.

Each time he looked at Ravyn, he was reminded of what he'd found—only to lose so quickly. They would have been happy together. Of that he was certain.

In fact, he suspected that they could have the same kind of love that his parents had. His father used to tell him to settle for nothing less than the type of love that he would die for.

Carac had never expected to find such a woman. But he knew in his heart that, given time, that kind of soul-deep affection would develop with Ravyn. In fact, it had already begun without him even realizing it—or trying.

"You said there was something we could use as the staff," Ravyn reminded the woman.

Carac watched the ghost move through a wall. As she did, he saw the small section cut out of the rock. "There," he said to Rayvn and pointed.

They walked to it with Ravyn dropping to her knees first to crawl through it. Carac was right behind her, shifting his shoulders to get through the tight space. He didn't like being so cramped, and for a moment, he feared that the ghost might have led them into a trap. The next instant, he realized that was foolish. The spirit could end them anytime she wanted. There was no need for such an elaborate ruse.

All the witch and magic and ghost things were playing with his head. He had to push it all aside so he could do what he did best—strategize.

He spotted a light ahead, and soon, Ravyn was through the tunnel and standing. Carac drew in a deep breath when he was finally able to climb to his feet. He never wanted to go back through that space again. Unfortunately, from what he could gather from the four torches on the walls, that was the only way out of the chamber.

Carac raked a hand through his hair as he realized that Ravyn hadn't said anything. That's when he gazed around the circular area. His lips parted in shock when he turned and took in the dozens of staffs leaning against the walls.

His eyes landed on Rossamond. "The Staff of the Eternal is in here with the others."

"It is," she replied.

"I thought it would be something like what Leoma and Braith described for the Blood Skull," Ravyn said as she walked closer to the staffs. "It was the only one, though Braith did have to find the secret entrance."

"Why would we make it so easy?" the ghost asked.

Ravyn glanced over her shoulder at the woman. "Why make it this difficult?"

"In case someone who is not a descendant ever managed to get through."

Carac shook his head as he took in the various staffs, some with elaborate designs, some so simple they looked as if they could be reattached to a tree. "It is a good ruse, but you assume that a descendant would know which is the right one."

"Those living here would," Rossamond replied.

Carac turned to face her. "What about those who are descendants but do not reside here?"

"Hopefully, their families would have told the story."

"What if they didn't?" Ravyn asked.

The spirit gave them a flat look. "I suppose they would not know which is the correct one."

"Or likely even know the staff existed," Carac added. He ran a hand down his face. "We do not need the real one, so it does not matter."

Ravyn frowned at him. "But we do."

Carac had hoped she wouldn't bring up wanting to take the staff, at least not now. "The staff is safe here."

"We both know that is a lie," Ravyn said.

He shrugged and glanced at the ghost. "It was safe, and it can remain that way for a little longer. We need to send the Coven on their way."

"That will not work," Rossamond replied. "They will attempt to use the staff immediately."

That had certainly been something Carac was worried about. "Damn."

"What does the staff do exactly?" Ravyn asked.

The eyes of the ghost cut to Ravyn. "That does not matter."

"I would like to be prepared for whatever the Coven intends," Ravyn argued.

Carac twisted his lips at the spirit. "Ravyn has a point."

There was a long pause before Rossamond's shoulders slumped. "It magnifies the magic of the witch who holds it. If someone without magic has it, it tends to bring power, favor, and riches."

Shite. Carac pinched the bridge of his nose. This was not good news. Frankly, he was tired of all the bad. They really needed something good to come their way. Otherwise, he might begin to feel as if they were doomed from the moment they followed Sybbyl below the dungeons.

He looked into Ravyn's eyes. "There is a slim chance that we can make them believe we have the staff. It will only last a moment because they will force us out of the tunnel."

"You," Ravyn corrected. "I will remain hidden and maybe take down a few witches."

"Then you both die," the ghost said. "The Coven will stop Ravyn, and then they will take the staff from you, Carac.

Either they will kill you for bringing them the wrong one, or you will die when they force you out of the tunnel."

He nodded slowly. "Aye. That is how I see it, as well."

"That is an idiotic plan," Rossamond stated angrily. "It solves nothing. The Coven could still get into this chamber as you mentioned earlier."

Carac glanced at the numerous staffs.

"What are you thinking?" Ravyn asked as she walked to him.

He looked from Ravyn to the ghost and back to his warrior. "We destroy every staff. We will still die—"

"But they will lose the staff forever," Ravyn finished a smile growing. "I like it."

Carac then turned his head to the ghost. "What do you think?"

"If it were so easy to be rid of the bones of the First Witch, do you not think others would have burnt them before now?"

Just when Carac thought they had a plan, it fell apart. And quite frankly, he had no more ideas.

"But does the Coven know that?" Ravyn asked.

"I know not," the woman replied.

Carac walked around the chamber looking over the staffs. "I think we should take one of these and tell the Coven it's the Staff of the Eternal. Then we set it on fire."

"Any of the witches will be able to douse it," Ravyn said.

"So we toss several out and tell them to find the right one. Then we burn them and continue to throw more of them into the flames," he said.

The ghost looked away as if considering his words. "The Coven wants the relic badly enough that they will search through each one, burned or not. And when they do not find it, they will come looking for it."

Carac smiled. "Not if they believe that the fire destroyed whatever magic was within the First Witch's bone."

"That could work," Ravyn said, surprise making her smile. She then looked at Rossamond. "We will need help."

The specter bowed her head. "After all this time, I will finally get revenge upon the Coven. Aye. I will help you."

Now, they had to make sure that everything went according to their hasty and somewhat reckless plan. Then again, what options did they have?

"How many staffs should we use?" Ravyn asked.

Carac reached for the couple closest to him. Just start grabbing and tossing them through the entrance. We'll sort out the rest."

The ghost stood and watched as he and Ravyn chucked staff after staff through the small opening that he would have to crawl through again. Not once did the spirit tell them not to take one of the staves. Either that meant they hadn't come near the real one yet, or she didn't care if it was burned.

Surely, it would be in everyone's best interest to keep the Staff of the Eternal as far from the Coven as possible. Then again, the spirit was its guardian. She wanted to keep it from everyone.

Carac could only hope that the true staff would be one they left behind. He knew Ravyn wanted it, but in many ways, he agreed with the ghost. It would be better for all if the staff remained hidden and out of reach. But they may have come to a point where that was no longer possible.

If that were the case, then he would have to convince the spirit that Ravyn and the other Hunters were the ones best suited to keep it away from the Coven. And he hoped he was right.

Braith was now part of the Hunters, and that combined with what he knew of Ravyn gave him the ability to give his word and make such promises. He could only hope that the ghost would listen to him. If not, then Ravyn would have to do it on her own.

And he knew that she could handle it with confidence and ease. Because she was that kind of woman.

"What are you grinning at?" Ravyn asked him when they bumped into each other.

"That fact that I'm glad I met you."

She laughed and smoothed back a lock of his hair from his forehead, her dark eyes meeting his. "Are you sure? If you had not, you would not be in this situation."

"And I would not have such an amazing woman beside me. No, I would change nothing."

Her smile faded, and her gaze lowered to his lips and then his chest. "The odds are stacked against us. Most likely, we will both meet our end, and I think you deserve a better death."

He raised her chin with his finger and pressed a kiss to her lips. "Better than fighting against evil alongside a woman who makes my blood burn and my heart race? Nay. This is the death I would choose."

"I wish we had met years earlier," she said and wrapped her arms around his waist.

"A few days, a few years. It does not matter because it would never be enough for me."

She grinned seductively up at him, her eyes twinkling. "How long would be enough?"

"Twenty lifetimes. Forty. A hundred," he replied honestly.

"Maybe we will have better luck in our next life."

He ran a thumb over her bottom lip. "I have not given up on this one yet."

"Then neither will I."

Ravyn turned away to grab more staffs, and Carac shifted, his gaze colliding with Rossamond's. There was a peculiar look on the spirit's face. He couldn't quite name it, and he wasn't sure what to make of it.

To his amazement, her head turned to the side to look in the direction of a group of staffs they had yet to touch. He wasn't sure how, but he knew the Staff of the Eternal was in that pile.

And he was going to make sure that they left those alone.

29

Fury. It was the only thing that kept Sybbyl on her feet despite the agony that wracked her body. It had taken her longer than she expected, and there were a few close calls, but she finally had the other Hunter—Margery—and Simon on their knees beside Randall.

The chamber reeked of blood and burnt flesh. The few knights who'd joined her hadn't survived the skirmish. The other men who'd turned against her lay charred upon the ground. And, somehow, she'd survived.

She blinked, trying to stop the chamber from spinning. This shouldn't be happening. She was a witch, a powerful one at that. Many had attempted to slay her before, but they'd soon learned that it took much more than a random weapon to do the job.

Sybbyl's gaze slid to Margery's sword that lay on the ground. Simon's blade had also cut her, but she hadn't felt the same piercing pain as when Margery's weapon found its mark.

"Wondering why you are not feeling so well?" Margery asked, one side of her busted lip lifted in a smirk.

Sybbyl covered one of the cuts on her upper arm with her hand. She had discounted the Hunters, but it looked as if she would pay for such a big miscalculation. What little information the Coven had on the Hunters was missing a glaring detail—they had a witch helping them.

Because only a weapon imbued with magic could kill a witch.

"Who is the witch that you convinced to help you?" Sybbyl demanded to know.

Margery smiled. Sybbyl backhanded her so hard, Margery's head snapped to the side. There was a slight pause before the Hunter turned her head back to Sybbyl and smiled, blood coating her teeth from her lip splitting open again.

"Resorting to physical violence now, are we?" Angmar said as she walked into the chamber followed by the other councilmember, Matilda.

Sybbyl bowed her head in respect and tried not to look too long at the burn scars along the left side of Angmar's face from her fight with Braith for the Blood Skull.

The fact that no magic—not even Angmar's as the strongest of the council elders—could fix or hide the scars said much about what the relic could do.

And Sybbyl quite liked that Angmar's beauty was diminished by the burns.

Angmar strode into the chamber with confidence, wearing a blood red gown and a black girdle belt, her long, ebony hair hanging freely down her back. The witch's black gaze was locked on Sybbyl, assessing her with every step.

The other remaining elder came into view followed by John. Matilda with her flame red hair long enough to fall past her hips and amber eyes grinned brazenly at Sybbyl as she came to a stop beside Angmar and ran a hand down the side of her white gown.

"Well?" Angmar urged, one thin, black brow raised. "Why did you hit this woman with your hand when you could have used magic?"

Sybbyl lifted her chin. "Because I wanted to."

"Ohh," Matilda said with a laugh. "She is sassy today."

Angmar ignored Matilda and kept her focus on Sybbyl. "I do not like being summoned, but especially without knowing the reason. Telling me it is *important* is not enough."

"You came, though," Sybbyl replied.

Angmar's black eyes narrowed in anger. "And you did not even deign to meet us? You sent,"—Angmar glanced at John and twisted her lips in revulsion—"him."

"Because I was dealing with this. How long have you been at the castle?"

Matilda laughed and looked at her long, pointed nails painted blood red. "That is none of your concern."

Sybbyl had planned everything down to exactly what she would say to the councilmembers, but thanks to the Hunter, nothing was going right. But she wasn't going to let that stop her. This was her chance to become an elder, and she refused to fail.

Sybbyl dropped her hand from her wound and jerked her chin to Margery. "Before me kneels a Hunter."

That piqued Angmar's interest. She came around to stand before Margery. "Indeed?"

"Aye." Sybbyl pointed to the arch and whatever lay beyond. "There is a second in there."

Matilda rolled her eyes. "Then go get her."

Sybbyl glared at the elder, what little respect she had been able to muster earlier, leaving quickly. "If I could, I would not be standing here speaking with you."

Angmar walked to the arch and looked at the faded carvings. She then whirled around, her eyes wide. "Did you really?"

"Find where the Staff of the Eternal is?" Sybbyl asked with a smirk. "Aye. And it is inside. I sent men in after it. Three were killed, but then I sent another. He has been in there ever since."

Matilda frowned and tucked a strand of red hair behind her ear. "Why did you not stop the other Hunter?"

"I was doing that, and doing it well," Sybbyl said and pointed to Margery and Simon. "Then these two arrived and took my focus off the Hunter for just a moment. That's when she darted through the arch."

Angmar returned her attention to the doorway. "Is there another way out?"

"Nay," Sybbyl replied.

Matilda came up beside her and leaned her face close. "You appear very confident."

Sybbyl turned her head and looked into Matilda's amber eyes before pointing at Randall. "Because he told me. His family has been in charge of keeping the staff from us for generations."

Randall's head was down. He hadn't spoken or moved during any of the fights that had broken out, not even when someone bumped into him. She had well and truly broken him.

Matilda walked over to Bryce and grabbed his hair to yank his head back. He reluctantly met her gaze. "This...man was in charge of keeping the staff hidden?"

"He attempted to stand against me, but once I showed him my power and the extremes I was willing to go to in order to claim the staff for the Coven, he willingly gave me the information I wanted," Sybbyl explained.

"And all these years, we thought the Bryce family was

powerful enough to keep us out." Matilda shoved him so that he fell onto his back.

Sybbyl swiveled her head to Angmar. "I am going to deliver the staff to you. That is why I requested your presence. I am also going to hand over two Hunters so we can gain knowledge of the group. And the identity of the witch who is helping them."

Angmar turned to face her. "What do you mean?"

"That," Sybbyl said and jerked her chin at the sword. "A witch has spelled it."

Matilda grimaced as she raked her gaze over Sybbyl's body. "You are lucky none of the wounds were any deeper. Otherwise, you would be dead."

As if she didn't know that. Sybbyl stared at the elder for a long moment before she turned her attention back to Angmar. "Two of the councilmembers are gone. The spots need to be filled."

"And you want one of them," Angmar replied with a knowing look.

Sybbyl squared her shoulders. "Has any other Coven member given you a bone from the First Witch."

"You have not either," Matilda said. "You found its location, but nothing more. Eleanor found the location of the Blood Skull, too, but she could not get to it. And then she died."

"I will not perish."

Angmar laughed softly. "Bold words."

"Fine," Sybbyl said, keeping most of the heat from her voice. "I have produced a Hunter. That in itself should count for something."

"I agree." Angmar looked at Matilda. "You?"

Matilda curled her lip at Sybbyl. "Aye, but grudgingly. I do not like her."

Sybbyl opened her mouth to reply when a sound came from the darkness of the arch. She thought it would be Ravyn who appeared, but to her shock, it was Carac. And he carried a staff.

"What an audience," Carac said as he looked around. His gaze landed on Simon for a moment. Then his eyes moved from Matilda to Angmar. "I suppose the two of you are the Coven elders?"

"Aye," Angmar said. "Now, hand me the staff."

Carac remained just within the confines of the arch. "I think I will hold onto it for a bit longer."

"Carac," Sybbyl called.

He raised a blond brow. "Is this where you threaten my men and the others in the castle if I do not bring it out to you?"

She ground her teeth together. "Aye."

He tapped a finger on his chin, his face crinkling in thought. "I have been giving that some consideration. The way I see it, you witches want to kill off everyone once you acquire this," he said, pointing to the staff. "It seems that, in order to give others a fair chance, this should stay out of your hands."

"That kind of talk is foolish," Matilda said, her amber eyes narrowing on Carac. "We have immense power."

"Yet none of you can enter here to get the staff. Which," he said, accentuating the word, "means that it should remain out of your control at all costs."

Angmar held out her hand to Carac. "I give you my word that you and your men will not be harmed. *If* you give me the staff."

Sybbyl glanced at the three prisoners. Randall was still on his back, and Simon and Margery were on their knees. Their heads were turned toward Carac, but he paid them little mind.

Carac tilted his head slightly and grinned. "Being nice

after your counterparts threatened me... That might work on others, but not me. You see, I have used that tactic before. The problem is, I heard no sincerity in your voice."

"Oh, I like you," Angmar said with a smile, her arm dropping to her side.

Carac winked at her.

"Where is Ravyn?" Sybbyl demanded.

Carac's smile vanished when he looked her way. "How should I know?"

"She went in after you," Sybbyl snapped.

Frustration and irritation were rapidly taking hold of her. After all her careful planning. Sybbyl would be satisfied with nothing less than a seat on the council. She would be an elder.

Carac shook his head. "I have not seen Ravyn. Then again, it's dark in there."

"I do not believe you," Sybbyl said.

He smiled brightly. "I do not give a shite what you believe, you murderous, evil witch."

Carac bent and picked up a torch. As he straightened, it flared to life. He then touched it to the staff and tossed it into the chamber. Sybbyl, Matilda, and Angmar immediately used their magic to put out the fire.

"That was foolish," Sybbyl said and looked at Carac.

Only to find him holding another staff.

"Oh, did I mention that one was not the Staff of the Eternal?" he asked. "My apologies."

Angmar wasn't smiling when she faced him. "I am no longer amused. What do you want?"

"I want you all to die and rot in Hell," he stated.

Matilda took several steps toward him. "I am going to enjoy killing you."

Carac merely smiled and set the staff on fire. Once more, he tossed it into the chamber, and four more quickly followed.

There was a brief pause when the witches were putting out the last of the flames before another five burning staffs landed on the pile.

"What are you doing?" Sybbyl said and focused her magic again.

Carac laughed from within the safety of the arch. "One of those *is* the Staff of the Eternal."

It took several more minutes before the fires were contained. When Sybbyl and the elders turned to Carac, he was leaning against the wall, his arms crossed.

"Do you believe that fire can destroy the staff?" Sybbyl asked him.

He shrugged. "You tell me."

"It cannot," Angmar said.

His lips twisted. "Bloody hell. I really thought burning them would work."

Matilda rolled her eyes. "Hardly. And I will make you pay in blood and pain for what you have done this day."

Sybbyl touched each of the staffs and tried to use it, but nothing happened. Matilda and Angmar did the same.

"Which one is it?" Sybbyl demanded.

Carac shrugged. "Why would I tell you? Should you not be able to pick it out yourself?"

"Tell us!" Matilda shouted. Her eyes narrowed, and she pointed at him with a long blood red nail. "Or I will peel the skin from your bones."

Her hand was steady, her focus locked on Sybbyl as Ravyn aimed her crossbow from the comfort of the darkness. She hated that she only had two arrows left. One would find its way to Sybbyl's heart. Of that, Ravyn was certain. If it were the only thing she did that day, she would take the life of a witch.

She glanced at Carac as he shrugged indifferently at the wrath of an elder. Ravyn had listened intently to Leoma's and Braith's descriptions of the two remaining elders. She knew that the red-haired one with the long nails was Matilda. The leader, and the one with the black hair and the burns on one side of her face was Angmar.

Based on the little bit of conversation Ravyn had heard as she was taking her position, the two elders had yet to add any others to the council. And Sybbyl wanted one of the spots.

Ravyn couldn't wait to pull the trigger on the crossbow. So long ago, Sybbyl had shattered Ravyn's idyllic life in one night. Now, Ravyn had a chance to return the favor. After so long, justice would finally be served.

The witches were agitated. And that pleased Ravyn. For just a moment, she slid her gaze to the three being held prisoner. It warmed Ravyn's heart to see that Margery was still alive, and Ravyn knew Carac was glad to know that Simon was okay, as well.

Margery had done well in her fight with Sybbyl. The witch had sustained several cuts that might not be deep enough to kill her, but Ravyn knew she probably wasn't feeling so well. It was evident in how Sybbyl swayed from side to side.

It was all right, though. Soon, the witch would feel nothing but the fires of Hell.

Ravyn frowned. While Simon and Margery kept their eyes on the witches, they hadn't moved. But Randall had. It was barely discernable, and Ravyn might have missed it had she not seen his leg shift slightly.

She didn't know what he was up to, but she would be ready for whatever came. After everything Randall had endured at Sybbyl's hands, he deserved his revenge, as well.

Ravyn returned her gaze to Sybbyl, but her attention was on everyone in the chamber. The staffs had been burnt as per the plan. Now, it was time to see if Rossamond held up her end of things. Ravyn had her doubts, but she really hoped she was wrong.

In all of her training and her encounters with witches, not once had Ravyn been so calm. Without a doubt, she was in the right place at the right time.

Not even the knowledge that she would most likely die that day diminished the importance of the situation. Death was part of being a Hunter. Because to track witches, you courted death. It was a partnership Ravyn freely—and readily —embraced.

For her, there was no other option. The Coven was evil at its core. The fact that they believed their actions were done for the good of witches only made them more heinous. For how could anyone make those in the Coven understand that what they were doing was wrong?

A chill overtook Ravyn, the only warning she had that the spirit was making itself known. Unable to help herself, Ravyn turned her head to Carac.

Before he walked to the arch and made himself known, he'd kissed her with all the passion and longing of a thousand nights. It had left her breathless and craving so much more.

But it was the words he whispered in her ear that brought her the most joy.

"*I love you.*"

Ravyn held his declaration in her heart. She had been so shocked and overwhelmed and deliriously happy to hear his confession that she hadn't had time to say anything in return before he walked away. That would change as soon as she had the chance. There was so much she wanted to say to him. The first of which was that she returned his love.

Tears pricked the backs of her eyes when she thought about the life she and Carac could have, whether it was hunting witches or returning to his castle. An entire lifetime played out in her mind as he spoke to the elders and burned the staffs—a lifetime that would likely never happen now.

But they'd lived gloriously and loved hard in her dream.

He was the man she would have chosen above all others if she'd met him ten years before—or fifty years from now. He was the only one who had been able to touch her soul and claim her heart.

Carac, with his calm intensity and unwavering strength, his quiet authority and undeniable command. She knew he'd been born for her, and she for him. They were two sides of the same coin, and she couldn't believe that they had found each other.

There was no man on the Earth who could equal Carac. And together, they could be unstoppable. First, however, they had to get past Sybbyl and the elders.

Ravyn watched as Carac took a small step back, letting the darkness begin to surround him. He slowly lifted the leg closest to the wall and pulled her last arrow from his boot. She sent up a prayer that both of her arrows would find their marks.

With a deep breath, she once more put Sybbyl in her sights just as the ghost made herself visible, standing beneath the arch. Sybbyl took a half step back in surprise, but if Angmar and Matilda were shocked to see a specter, they hid it well.

"Leave," Rossamond told them.

Matilda looked askance at the ghost. "Why would we listen to you? What can you do to us?"

Suddenly, the heads of the three dead knights appeared in the spirit's hands. She tossed them toward the witches. "No one gets past me."

"But you allowed Carac to pass," Angmar stated.

Rossamond turned her head slightly in order to look at Angmar. "He was...compelling."

"We can be, as well," Sybbyl said.

The spirit gave a bark of laughter. "I doubt it."

Angmar walked a few paces closer to the arch. She pointed at the carvings. "It took someone with magic to spell this."

The ghost merely smiled in answer.

"That is what I thought," Angmar said. "If I cannot walk beneath the arch, then I will come from above."

"There is no need," the spirit replied. "What you seek is in that pile."

Matilda kicked at the scorched wood. "That is not possible. The Staff of the Eternal would not lose its potency with fire."

"Are you sure it was only fire?" Rossamond asked.

Ravyn had to hand it to the ghost, she was turning their questions in a way that made even Ravyn wonder what she knew.

Sybbyl shook her head as she strode to stand even with Angmar and stare at the spirit. "A bone of the First Witch is in the staff. Nothing can destroy it."

Ravyn shivered when the ghost turned her head to Sybbyl and stared at her for a long, silent moment.

Then Rossamond said, "You talk to me as if I do not know of the First Witch. I have been guarding this place for hundreds of years. My family was charged with keeping the staff out of the hands of anyone who sought it, but most especially, the Coven. I know more about the First Witch than you ever will. Just as I know that she put a spell on herself that if someone burned a bone to keep it from being used for evil, then the magic would leave."

"You lie," Matilda declared, looking at the ghost with contempt.

Angmar raised a hand to halt Matilda from saying more. Angmar's head cocked to the side as she studied the specter. "If what you say is true, why did your family not burn the staff long ago when the Coven first came for it."

"We thought we could keep it hidden," the ghost replied. "You have given me no choice."

Angmar was silent as she shifted to the side and looked at the pile of staves. "Why all the other staffs?"

"Ask him," the spirit said and motioned to Carac.

As Ravyn returned her gaze to Sybbyl, she was taken aback to find that she could no longer find Randall. Ravyn's attention then moved to Margery and Simon to see that they had shifted closer together while Margery slowly inched forward to get to her sword.

All hell was about to break loose. The tension within the chamber thickened with every heartbeat. The witches were suspicious and ready for blood. And Ravyn was set for vengeance.

Carac clasped his hands behind his back as he once more moved into the light. "The various staffs were put within the tunnel to throw off anyone searching for the Staff of the Eternal. They were scattered throughout, and if one did not know what the relic looked like, then they could easily take the wrong one."

Sybbyl wasn't going to give up that easily, however. "Where is the other Hunter? The woman?"

Ravyn's finger tightened slightly on the trigger of her crossbow. How she wanted to pull it, but it wasn't time yet. Just a few more moments.

"Dead," came the reply from Rossamond.

Sybbyl glanced at the three heads on the floor. "Where is hers? I want to see it."

"She has a point," Matilda said.

A smile pulled at Ravyn's lips as the ghost glowed brighter. She glanced at the specter, and the beautiful ghost she had spoken with was gone. In its place was a replica of the skeleton she'd found in the tunnel, complete with missing chunks of hair, torn clothing, and no skin.

The spirit let out a scream that made Ravyn's eardrums throb in agony. The shriek was so loud and long that it had everyone holding their ears—including the witches.

Ravyn tried to keep her gaze on Sybbyl. She wanted to rejoice at their suffering, but she couldn't when she, too, felt the pain.

Something brushed against her. Ravyn glanced up to see

the ghost right before she burst from the arch and into the chamber. The specter went by all three of the witches, scratching them in various places.

Ravyn tried to ignore the screaming and lined up her shot again. She steadied her hands. In the next moment, the shrieking halted, and she fired the crossbow directly at Sybbyl's heart.

The arrow flew through the air straight and true. Then, suddenly, Sybbyl grabbed Matilda and yanked the witch in front of her right before the arrow pierced the elder's heart.

Rage boiled within Ravyn. That arrow had been meant for Sybbyl. She had been denied her retribution. Ravyn retrieved her dagger from her boot and straightened at the same time Margery grabbed her sword and jumped to her feet.

Sybbyl pushed Matilda, who was already turning to ash, aside and bellowed, "Ravyn!"

For a heartbeat, Ravyn took in the scene as Rossamond, Simon, and Margery battled Sybbyl and Angmar. Her head turned, and she looked for Carac, but he was already rushing from the tunnel.

Ravyn followed him out and headed directly to Sybbyl. The witch whirled around as if sensing Ravyn's approach. Flames came at her, but Ravyn jumped, wrapping her arms around her legs as she tucked her body and flipped over Sybbyl's head.

When she landed, Ravyn turned and jabbed her dagger toward Sybbyl's back, only...the witch now faced her.

Sybbyl wrapped a hand around Ravyn's wrist as she smiled. "You cannot win against me."

"We shall see." Ravyn then jerked the arm that Sybbyl held upward and spun. She lowered her front half so that her back foot came up and connected with the witch's jaw.

The strike was hard enough to cause Sybbyl to loosen her

grip and stumble backward. Sybbyl rubbed her cheek and glowered. "Lucky hit."

Ravyn flipped the dagger end over end, grabbing it by the hilt. "Shall we try again?"

Sybbyl took a step toward her. Then everyone's attention turned to the doorway as Randall rushed into the chamber and ran straight for Sybbyl. He leapt over rocks and dead knights, his eyes locked on his target.

It all happened in slow motion for Ravyn. Her head swung back to Sybbyl just as Angmar wrapped an arm around the witch. Mist billowed up from the floor suddenly and swirled around them.

When it finally cleared, the witches were gone.

As was the ghost.

31

"**I**s it over?" Simon asked after John had scrambled from the chamber, tripping over his feet in his haste.

Carac looked around until his gaze landed on Ravyn. Without another word, he strode to her and grabbed her shoulders. "Are you injured?"

"Nay," she said tightly. Ravyn sighed and glanced away. "I did not get to kill her."

"There will be another day. And I will hunt her down with you."

At Ravyn's smile, the tightness around Carac's heart lifted. "Is that a promise?" she asked.

He nodded. "It is. The victory is ours," he told the others. "We are alive, the Coven is gone, and the staff is secure."

Randall's lips curled into a sneer. "Do you really believe that? The Coven will be back with more witches."

"Did you not hear the spirit?" Simon asked Randall. "The staff is no more."

Randall snorted. "You believe that because you know little of the First Witch, but I know the truth."

"It does not matter," Ravyn said. "We convinced the Coven."

But Randall didn't seem to hear them. "I was unprepared this time. I will not be again," he mumbled to himself as he left the chamber.

Margery was holding her left arm against her, her face white with pain. "Now what?"

"We see to your injury," Carac said. Then he noted the blood dripping from Simon's fingers. "And Simon's."

Ravyn went to Margery and put her arm around her. "I am ready to leave this place."

As the women left the chamber, Carac remained behind as Simon walked to the doorway before stopping and looking back at him.

"Go on," Carac urged.

Simon shook his head, laughing softly. "I know you better than that. Why do you stay?"

"The spirit intends to kill me."

"And you want to wait around for her to do it?" Simon asked with a frown.

Carac looked out the door. What he wanted to do was rush after Ravyn and take her hand, never looking back. He wanted to think of the future and all that could be theirs. "Nay."

"Then come on," Simon urged. "There is no one here."

Carac nodded in agreement and started toward the doorway. Simon continued on, but when Carac reached the door, a blast of cold air hit him from behind.

He halted and took a deep breath. Then he turned to face the specter. Rossamond waited beneath the arch, her appearance once more that of a beautiful woman. He swallowed, unsure what to think.

"Thank you for your help," he told her.

She continued to stare at him.

Carac looked down at the arrow in his hand that he hadn't gotten to use. "You were convincing. I do not believe the Coven will be back for a while."

"Their damage to Randall is already done. The line of Bryce will end with him."

"Maybe not. But you will remain to protect the staff?"

She looked around the chamber. "I will."

"Is this where you tell me you are going to take my life?"

"I thought about it," she admitted. "But too many have died this day. I also realized that you did not seek the staff on your own."

"Neither did the other knights who died."

Her gaze grew stony. "Do you pass judgment on me?"

"Nay," he said, shaking his head. "Just stating a fact."

"The truth, Carac, is that whether you intended it or not, I saw many things in you. First and foremost, honor. You remind me of my eldest brother, who was loyal and as solid as an oak. I see the same attributes in you."

He was stunned by her words.

But she wasn't finished. "Not once did you attempt to draw a weapon on me. You used your head and your heart in our discussions. Yet, it was not until the Hunter came that I saw a side of you that I believe you have kept hidden for years. You love Ravyn. Deeply."

Carac bowed his head at the ghost. "I am flattered by your words. I believe I would have liked your brothers. If they were anything like you, they were fair individuals. And, aye, I love her deeply."

"Then go find her and the life that awaits."

He bowed again and turned to go. But just as he took a step, she said, "Forget the Coven if you wish to live a long life."

Carac halted and looked over his shoulder at her. "Ravyn is a Hunter. Braith, the one who found the Blood Skull, asked me to join their fight against the Coven. And there is nowhere else I would rather be than beside Ravyn as we battle this evil."

"You never asked which one of the staffs was the one you sought."

He sighed and faced her once more. "Because I understood why Ravyn sought it, and I recognized why you protected it. In the right hands, the staff can do good, but in the wrong hands, it can be devastating. As long as it is out there, the Coven will seek it."

"All of that is very true, but there is something I did not share with you or the others."

Carac frowned, wondering what it could be. He waited expectantly.

She smiled then. "The staff was never in the tunnel."

He blinked, thinking he must not have heard her right. "I do not understand. You gave me the impression that it was. Even Randall led the witch here."

"Of course, he did. Everyone, from my brothers on, has believed the staff was where they put it in the tunnel with all the others. But in the weeks that I was dying, I moved it."

Carac's brow furrowed. "But you were walled up. You could not leave."

"Exactly," she said, a small smile on her lips.

His gaze went to the arch. "Why do you tell me this?"

"I know not."

He ran a hand over his jaw. "You will move it now. It is logical that you are the only one to truly know where it is hidden."

"Farewell, Carac."

"Wait," he called.

But the ghost was already gone. He looked at the archway

again. Then he turned on his heel and hurried up to the great hall only to find it empty.

Sounds from outside drew his gaze to the open door of the castle where sunlight was pouring in. Carac walked to the entrance and looked out into the bailey where Randall had John on his knees along with his knights. Surrounding them was the remainder of the servants and people who lived at the castle all shouting for John's head.

Randall had his sword at John's neck, but he didn't kill him. Instead, he lowered the weapon. "What would you do to save your own neck?" he asked John.

John shook, sweat running down his face. "Anything. Name it."

"Sign over your land and castle to me."

Carac smiled and crossed his arms over his chest as he leaned a shoulder against the door. He wasn't surprised when John readily agreed, asking for ink and parchment.

While the items were brought to him and John used the ground to write out his agreement, something caught Carac's attention out of the corner of his eye. It was Ravyn, looking at him while a dozen of his knights stood behind her.

Carac pushed away from the door and dropped his arms as he went to her. Her smile was bright, her eyes clear. And she looked amazing in the morning sun.

"There is much I would say to you," she said.

He raised a brow. "Is that right?"

"Aye. But I think you need a bath first."

He laughed and pulled her against him for a quick kiss. "I agree. As well as some food."

"Your men have been searching for you. A group has already taken Simon and Margery back to your camp, and there are more standing guard to make sure things do not get out of control here."

"They are good men," he said, nodding to his knights.

Ravyn pulled his head down so their gazes met. "They have a good leader."

He kissed her forehead and took her hand as he faced his men. "I believe our time is finished here."

"Your and Lady Ravyn's horses are waiting," one of the men said.

Ravyn grinned. "I am not a lady."

The men all looked at her with frowns before one of them replied, "You are to us."

Carac walked her to their horses, smiling at how he had managed to get out of another tight spot with the witches and Rossamond. One day, his luck would run out.

"How do they know my name?" Ravyn leaned close to whisper.

He shrugged as he released her to grab the reins of his horse. "Simon, probably. Or Margery."

They mounted and rode through the bailey. Carac met Randall's gaze, and they nodded to each other. With his men at his back, Carac and Ravyn rode to his camp.

It felt as if it had been years since they left early the previous morning, not just a single day. So much had transpired, that he had yet to take it all in.

Once they reached the camp, they dismounted before his tent and handed the horses off to Rob. Then Carac said to Ravyn, "We probably could have stayed at the castle."

"Which one?" Ravyn asked with a grin.

Carac chuckled. "Either."

She shook her head. "I prefer this."

"Then it is all yours."

Ravyn licked her lips and looked around. "Your men are watching."

"Aye."

"I do not care if they talk about me."

"But I do," he told her. "The tent is yours."

She put her hand on his cheek for a moment and smiled. "I will accept only because I long for a bath."

"I could have some men fetch a tub from John's castle," he offered.

"The river is fine for me." With one last look, she walked into the tent. A second later, she shouted his name.

Carac rushed inside and came to a halt beside Ravyn at the sight of a staff, twisted and slightly bent, lying in the middle of his bed.

"Is that...?" Ravyn trailed off.

He shook his head. "I have no idea."

Carac turned and hurried to find his squire to make sure Rob hadn't put the staff there. When Rob asked what staff, Carac questioned his men. No one knew anything about it.

He returned to the tent where Ravyn stood staring at the relic. Then he said, "I had another conversation with Rossamond after all of you left."

Ravyn turned her head to him. "What did she say?"

"That I reminded her of her brother. And that the staff was never in the tunnel. She moved it."

"To where?" Ravyn asked in shock.

Carac's lips twisted. "Think. She was walled up with nowhere to go."

"The arch," Ravyn said with a laugh. "The one place a witch would not look. No one would think to look there."

"I know. It was perfect."

"Why tell you that at all? And is she the one who gave it to you now?"

He shrugged helplessly. "We can go back and ask her."

"Nay. I would rather not."

They both returned their gazes to the staff. Carac blew out a breath. "I am not sure how since the Coven had the upper hand, but we not only survived, we also have the staff."

"And another elder is dead," Ravyn added.

32

With her stomach tingling with excitement and the hope of a future, Ravyn combed out her wet hair with her fingers. The bath had felt amazing, even if it was in the cold waters of the lake.

To her surprise, she returned to Carac's tent to find him gone, but the gown she had worn at John's had been laid out for her. No doubt, Margery was responsible for that.

She smiled as she thought of her friend. Ravyn had gone to find Margery before her bath to see to her wound, but it wasn't a woman in pain she found. Instead, Margery and Simon were locked in a tight embrace as they kissed.

Ravyn had missed all the signs. She had been so wrapped up in her passion and concern over the staff that she neglected to see that Margery and Simon were finding a deep affection.

With her hair untangled, Ravyn glanced down at the gown she now wore. It wasn't that she disliked such clothes, but after the freedom of trousers, it was difficult to be so...encumbered. However, it was also nice to be in something clean while her other attire dried after being washed.

She stood and found her gaze drawn to the staff. Upon her return to the tent, she had set it in the corner. It made her uncomfortable. Not just because she was baffled about why it was in Carac's dwelling, but also because she knew the ghost hadn't meant for her to have it. Rossamond had chosen Carac.

And quite frankly, Ravyn agreed with her.

There was no one else Ravyn would trust with such a weapon than Carac. That didn't mean she no longer yearned to bring it to the abbey. It didn't matter who delivered it, as long as the Coven did not get their hands on it.

"Cannot take your eyes off it, can you?"

Ravyn whirled around at the sound of Margery's voice. She smiled at her friend and walked to her, taking her hands. "I wondered if you would tear yourself away from Simon."

"I take that to mean you saw," Margery said, a blush staining her cheeks.

"I am deliriously happy for you."

Margery smiled widely. "I cannot stop grinning. And when Simon is near, I just want to touch him."

"And to think, you both could have died at Sybbyl's hand." Ravyn shook her head. "I was overjoyed to see that you cut her."

"Not deeply enough," Margery replied with a frown.

Ravyn waved away her words. "It is over."

"Is it?" Margery asked, her russet gaze filled with worry.

"You see the staff here. And the Coven is gone."

Margery shook her head. "I have a bad feeling. It is why I came to see you. I cannot shake this worry that Sybbyl is not done with us yet."

"And I am not done with her," Ravyn stated. "I vowed to kill her for what she did to my family, and I will carry out that promise."

"I know."

Ravyn looked askance at Margery. "Do you think I will fail?"

"It is not that." Margery glanced away and sighed. "You are like a sister to me, and while I do not have the heart to hunt witches as you do, that does not mean I am unaware of the danger."

"Whether as a Hunter or someone at the abbey, the fact that we oppose the Coven puts everyone in danger," Ravyn stated.

Margery swallowed. "But you did not see the way Sybbyl looked at you. She wants a seat on the council, and in her eyes, you took that from her."

"It is payback for the slaughter of my family."

"I fear that Sybbyl is not finished with you."

Ravyn snorted. "Then let her come after me. I do not care."

"That is the problem. It is not just you. It is every soul in this camp, including Carac." Margery smiled sadly. "Aye, I know about the two of you. It is hard to miss."

Margery had a point. A very valid, concerning one. Ravyn looked over her shoulder at the staff for a long moment. Had the ghost also recognized the danger Carac would be in by associating with her? It was certainly a possibility.

"I have spoken to Simon about this," Margery continued. "He does not believe that Carac will shy away from the risks of contesting the Coven. Especially when he is smitten with you."

Ravyn wasn't sure how to reply. Carac had given his word to fight against the Coven, but it was more than that. Ravyn wanted to be with him. His whispered words of love wrapped her in comfort and light. Now that she'd experienced it, she couldn't just walk away.

The tent flap opened, and Simon stuck his head in. His

dark gaze landed on Margery with a smile before turning to Ravyn. "Carac awaits you."

She shook her head with a grin. Carac had been serious. He didn't intend to enter his tent while they were unwed. Ravyn hurried past Margery and Simon, who held open the flap. Once her gaze found Carac, everything else disappeared.

Carac's smile was wide as he looked her up and down. "By the stars, you are beautiful."

She couldn't help but laugh. She wanted to reach up and touch the golden strands of his damp hair. He hadn't shaved his beard, and she found she quite liked it. He wore a simple white tunic and brown leather trousers with a white padded jerkin.

And he was stunning.

"I love you," she said.

His green eyes widened before a sensual smile pulled at his lips. "You are all I can think about. And, you are all I want." He took a step toward her. "I gave you my word that I would fight by your side for however long it took to end the Coven, and I will do it."

Her eyes lowered, and she saw an emerald ring with a family crest upon his right index finger that hadn't been there before. As if he were ready for everyone to know his true identity. She returned her attention to his face. "What of your castle and people?"

"We will visit as often as we can."

She raised a brow. "If the Coven learns who you really are —and that is only a matter of time—they will destroy all of it."

"Not if we stop them first. I know the risks involved by aligning with you, but I accept them."

"And your men? Simon?" she asked.

Carac's head cocked to the side. "Are you trying to dissuade me?"

"I am merely pointing out facts."

"Simon and I have already spoken. We both agree that fighting the Coven is important. I intend to give my men the option of going their own ways or coming with me. I hope that Edra will be able to use her magic so that every man here has a way to kill a witch."

"A Coven witch," Ravyn corrected.

Carac frowned. "Of course. Braith asked me to join him because he knew I had an army. And an army is what is needed."

Ravyn let her gaze move around the camp. Even if only a fraction of the men decided to fight the Coven, that was much more than what they had now. Yet she and the other Hunters had undergone years of training to fight the witches. It took much more than lining up on a field and standing behind a shield or riding toward an enemy with a sword drawn.

However...with more men that could be trained, no longer would the Hunters have to go out on their own to track the witches. They could lure the Coven witches into traps.

"I love you," Carac said as he closed the distance between them.

She looked into his pale green eyes and reached for his hand. "I came to kill a witch. I never expected to find you."

"I know we can have a good life, Ravyn. I want you with me always. I want to share my bed, my home, and everything I am with you. So, I am asking you to be my wife."

The joy within her was so consuming, she thought she might burst from in. She wasn't nobility, but she didn't care. When it came to love, there were no boundaries. "Aye."

There was a shout of joy behind them from a group of

knights she hadn't known was there. Within moments, the entire camp knew of their engagement.

The others pulled her away from Carac as music began playing. Ale was passed around as the cheering continued. She was handed from one man to another, and each twirled her around to the music.

Until she managed to break free. Ravyn moved to the sidelines, laughing as someone pushed a cup into her hands. She caught sight of Carac on the other side of the camp, smiling as others congratulated him. He waved away a mug of ale, a reminder of the story he had told her about his father.

"He is one of the best men I know," Simon said.

Ravyn looked to her left as he walked up. "I agree with that statement."

"But there is something about him you should know. Do not ever betray him."

"I know about his uncle and the betrayal," she stated.

Simon shook his head. "Carac has much mercy and love in his heart, despite the fact that he leads such an army and fights many battles. He can forgive many things, but never betrayal. Once someone deceives him—however trivial or insignificant —he will never forgive. Ever."

"You tell me that as if you expect me to betray him."

"On the contrary," Simon said. "I believe you would stand beside him always."

She stared at him a moment. "Then why tell me that as if it is a warning."

"Because it is. Never try to dissuade him once he cuts someone out of his life for a betrayal."

"All right," she said with a nod.

"I am glad he found you. He tried to hide it, but there has been something missing in his life. It was you."

She turned her gaze to Carac once more, her heart swelling. "I need him, too."

"I know."

Ravyn's head swung back to Simon. "If we are sharing, then let me say that I am delighted that you and Margery are together. She is amazing."

"Aye," Simon said, his gaze going to the ground as he smiled. "She is."

"Did she tell you that she is not going to be a Hunter anymore?"

Simon met her gaze and issued a single nod. "She mentioned it. She would rather protect the abbey and those that seek its comfort."

"You are a good match for her. In every way. Like it was destined."

"Fate." He chuckled. "Despite the Coven having the proverbial blade at our throats for a while."

Ravyn frowned at his words. "It is not like the Coven to leave anyone alive. I still do not understand why Sybbyl did not kill Randall."

"I wondered the same. He did not seem to care about anything when Margery and I fought Sybbyl. He did not even attempt to escape."

The more Ravyn thought about it, the more that worried her. Something was nagging at the back of her mind, but she couldn't put her finger on it.

"I know why Sybbyl wanted Margery alive," Simon continued. "Margery is a Hunter, and therefore, a great prize for the Coven."

Ravyn met his dark gaze. "Why did they keep you alive?"

"I know not," he said with a shake of his head.

Too many years of training pushed Ravyn to her next question. "Where did you and Margery go when you left the camp yesterday? I know we split up, but it was hours before I saw either of you."

"Margery and I got separated for a bit," he admitted. "It took me some time before I was able to find her again. Then we continued to hide so none of the guards would see us."

"You and Margery were parted? Neither of you mentioned that."

Simon chuckled and lifted his mug to his lips, draining the ale. "There has not been much talking. I am sure there is a lot we four have to share with each other."

"Of course," Ravyn said with a smile.

She had spent too much time doubting everyone. That was in the past now. She had Carac and Simon and Margery to put her faith in.

They had survived the Coven.

And she was getting married to the most wonderful man ever.

It was time to celebrate, not to try and find something bad in all the good that was raining down upon her.

33

Lucky. That's exactly what he was. Carac's gaze sought out Ravyn again and again as the celebration continued throughout the day.

A few times, he was able to get close to her and share a kiss or two, but then someone called him away or pulled her aside. It was all he could do not to throw her over his shoulder and take her into his tent to make love to her all night.

He craved her body once more. Wanted to hold her against him, to taste her lips. To hear her cries of pleasure.

When night finally fell, he could no longer wait. As soon as he could, he caught Ravyn's attention and motioned to the tent with his chin. Then he extracted himself from the group he was talking to and made his way to the pavilion.

He finished lighting the last candle when the staff caught his eye. Carac was walking to it when the rustle of the tent flap halted him. He turned just as Ravyn straightened.

Their gazes met, locked. They started toward each other, meeting halfway in a tangle of arms and lips. Their kisses were hungry, their fingers needy as they hurried to shed each other's clothes.

Finally, they were skin-to-skin. Carac couldn't believe this woman was going to be his wife—and maybe even one day the mother of his children. But that thought was for another time.

Right now, it was all about her.

Or so he thought until she pushed him back onto the bed. He grinned at her as he rose up to his elbows. She leaned over him, her long hair grazing his chest. He reached for her, wanting to pull her down atop him, but she pulled away. Then she knelt between his legs.

Carac's breath locked in his throat as he watched her take his cock in her hand before bringing it to her lips. Her sweet mouth parted and took him into her mouth.

He let out a moan as he fell back on the bed, pleasure enveloping him. Between her hand moving up and down his arousal, and her wet mouth sucking him, he was on the verge of orgasm in no time.

And he wasn't going to wait to be inside her any longer. Carac sat up and pulled her mouth away from his cock before he tossed her onto the bed. She spread her legs and reached for him.

He thrust into her and sighed, his eyes closing at the exquisite feel of her surrounding him. This was where he belonged. With Ravyn. It didn't matter where they lived or what they did as long as they were together.

She wrapped her legs around him, locking her ankles. Carac opened his eyes and looked down at his beautiful warrior. He pulled out of her slowly until only the head of his cock remained, then he pushed back inside. Again and again, he thrust—harder and deeper each time until they were clinging to each other.

Ravyn's nails dug into his arm as she arched her back. She

cried out as the orgasm took her. He watched the pleasure fall over her face while her body clamped hard on his cock. His hips moved faster as his own climax rose up. He welcomed it, giving himself over to the ecstasy.

When the last of his seed was drained from him, he pulled out of her and flopped onto his back. He reached for Ravyn the same time she rolled toward him.

He couldn't begin to describe the peace he felt just holding Ravyn in his arms. And to think, he might have gone the rest of his life without ever knowing such a woman existed.

"I did not think you would share the tent with me," she teased.

He kissed her forehead and held her tighter. "It seems I cannot stay away from you."

"Or I, you. I think we have a problem."

"I like it, though."

She laughed. "Me, too."

"Where shall we go from here? I assumed you would want to go to the abbey to hand over the staff."

Ravyn shifted her head to see him. "I do want to go to the abbey. I think Braith will want to see you, as well. That is if he and Leoma have not left for his castle."

"It will be on the way. We can stop there first."

"I have been thinking about the staff."

Now that intrigued him. He put his free arm behind his head. "And?"

"Rossamond had plenty of opportunities to give it to us while we were with her, and she did not. She chose to make sure everyone understood that she was handing it off to you and entrusting *you* with the right to guard it."

Carac stifled a yawn. "Perhaps, but she also knows that I have combined my forces with yours. We work together. And that means the staff is both of ours."

"I want you to give it to Edra and Radnar."

He lifted his head to look at her. "Really?"

"Really," she replied with a smile.

Carac laid his head back, his eyes drifting closed. There was so much more he wanted to talk to Ravyn about, but it would have to wait until morning because sleep would no longer wait.

Ravyn didn't know what woke her. She had been sleeping deeply on Carac's chest. She yawned and rolled onto her back only to grin at the sound of Carac's soft snores.

She listened for the noises of celebration, but there was only silence. Had they slept all night? That was odd since she was a light sleeper and would have known when the reveling halted.

After slowly rising so as not to wake Carac, she walked to the flap and peered outside to see the sky beginning to turn gray. So they had slept the entire night. She shook her head and returned to the bed and Carac's arms.

But she couldn't go back to sleep. After several attempts, she gave up and finally rose to dress. She put on her Hunter attire and was just pulling on her boots when she heard someone whisper her name.

Ravyn grabbed her crossbow and looked for the last arrow she had given Carac, to no avail. Frustrated, she set aside the weapon and made sure to put her dagger in her boot before stepping out of the tent.

She glanced around for signs of movement. All she saw was smoke from fires that were burning out. There were loud snores from the knights, and grunts as they turned over in their sleep.

Still, she didn't move for long moments. Someone had said her name. It had sounded like Margery, but she couldn't be sure.

But nothing was happening there. If she were going to find out who had called to her, then she would have to search for them. Ravyn walked silently away from the tent toward where the horses were kept. The animals were calm, still.

She then made her way through the camp to Simon's tent. After whispering Margery's name a few times, she poked her head inside to find the couple sleeping soundly.

If it hadn't been Margery who said her name, then who was it? Immediately, Ravyn's thoughts turned to Sybbyl. It also could have been the ghost.

Ravyn turned back in the direction she had come and retraced her steps. There were a few copses of trees in and around the camp, but the forest was a ways off. Yet the sound of a twig snapping echoed like thunder and brought Ravyn to a halt.

She turned her head to the forest. Whatever had come for her was in there. She faced the trees. A predator could lay in wait anywhere in the woods. It would be absolutely foolish for her to venture in alone. She might want the Coven annihilated, but she wasn't stupid enough to go into what was obviously a trap on her own. She was going to get Carac.

As Ravyn turned away, something moved out of the corner of her eye. She gasped when she saw Margery rushing toward the forest as she withdrew her sword.

Ravyn opened her mouth to call out to her friend, but she hesitated. Instead, she hurried after Margery, hoping to catch her before the Coven—or the ghost—did.

As soon as Ravyn entered the forest, a chill overtook her. Where she'd once thought it a good place to hide from John and even Carac, something had changed. It was silent as a tomb. Danger throbbed like a heartbeat, palpable and conspicuous. Death was there, waiting to take someone.

How she yearned to have her crossbow. Now, Ravyn wished she had listened to Radnar when he urged her to always carry a sword no matter what other weapon she favored. She'd had plenty of arrows before, but now she was learning firsthand what it felt like to be at a disadvantage.

She walked slowly through the trees, her gaze moving over everything as she searched for Margery and anything else. There wasn't even movement within the leaves. Everything became oppressive and bleak.

"I knew you would come."

She halted at the voice behind her. "Sybbyl."

Ravyn slowly turned around to find Margery kneeling with Sybbyl beside her. And on Margery's other side was none other than Angmar.

"You were right," Angmar said to Sybbyl.

Sybbyl smiled while glaring at Ravyn. "I cannot believe you doubted that I could get these two here."

"But they do not have the staff," the elder stated.

Ravyn didn't take her eyes off Sybbyl. They had been celebrating their victory over the Coven by making them think the staff was out of reach. She should've known the witches wouldn't accept such a story.

"Oh, she will get it," Sybbyl declared with a smile.

Ravyn's heart sank. But she would try to dissuade them again. "Did you not hear us at the castle? Even the ghost told you the staff is gone."

"Angmar believed your story might be true, but I was not so quick to believe," Sybbyl said. "We know you have the staff. And you are going to bring it to me."

Margery tsked. "Or you will kill me... The same old threat."

Ravyn glanced at Margery when Sybbyl's smile turned truly evil. "Or what?" Ravyn asked the witch.

"Do not do it," Margery said.

Before the last syllable had left her mouth, Sybbyl held out her hand and said two words. Ravyn could only stare in shock as Margery's clothes melted away and her chest burst open so that her heart flew into Sybbyl's hand.

After Margery had fallen forward, Ravyn lifted her gaze to the witches. "There is no staff," she said again, trying not to look at the fear and pain on Margery's face.

Her friend would not die in vain. Not after everything they had done and sacrificed. The staff would remain out of the Coven's hands.

"You had quite a party yesterday," Sybbyl said. "And are soon to be married I hear."

Even before Sybbyl said the words, Ravyn knew what was coming. But that didn't make it any easier to hear.

"Did you see Margery's face before her heart was torn from her chest?" Sybbyl asked with a fake shudder. "It was excruciating. Trust me when I tell you that Carac's death will be ten times worse."

Angmar smiled coldly. "Nay, we will not kill him. Instead, I will force him to kill everyone at John's and Randall's castles. Can you imagine a man like Carac carrying the weight of those murders around?"

It would kill him. The only thing Ravyn could be grateful for was that his death would come soon after.

Sybbyl shared a grin with Angmar. "Making Carac live with the knowledge that he is a murderer will be worse than killing him."

Angmar shook her head as she laughed. "We're making him work for us."

That would destroy him. Everything that Ravyn had fallen

in love with would be stripped away piece by piece. It would be a hellish life for a man like Carac. And he deserved more.

She couldn't do that to him. Her love was too great. Besides, the abbey had the Blood Skull. So what if the Coven had the Staff of the Eternal?

"Or," Angmar began.

"I will get it," Ravyn interrupted her.

Sybbyl laughed and lifted her chin. "Bring it to us. Now."

Ravyn didn't even bother to try and get a promise that the witches would leave everyone alone because they couldn't be trusted. Her knees knocked together as she walked past Margery's dead body and back to camp.

With every step, she prayed that Carac was still asleep. Mercifully, he was. She stood beside the bed and gazed down at him, tears gathering in her eyes at what could have been.

Then she took the staff and her crossbow and walked away without looking back.

34

Something was wrong. Carac knew it from the moment his eyes opened. He lay still upon the bed, listening. The faint stirring of the knights as they rose to meet the new day reached him. Then he turned his head to the side.

His heart leapt in his chest, fear coiling like a snake when he found the bed empty. The spot where Ravyn had slept was vacant—and cold. She had been gone for some time.

Carac sat up, his gaze scanning the tent as his mind raced with possibilities. As soon as he thought of Margery, he breathed a sigh. No doubt Ravyn had gone to visit her friend to see to her wounds.

He rubbed his chest and swung his legs over the side of the bed. Yet he couldn't shake the feeling that something awful had transpired. After everything that had happened over the past several days, it had become a common occurrence. He needed to accept that things had changed.

Maybe then, he wouldn't wake with the fear that something had been taken from him. Namely, Ravyn. Of all people, he knew she would never do anything dishonorable. He had seen the kind of woman she was firsthand in the midst of turmoil and the heat of battle. Once you saw that side of someone, you recognized their true selves.

Carac rose, raking a hand through his hair. He dressed while sorting everything that would need to be done that day in his mind. There was no reason to remain. It was time to head to the abbey.

But first, he needed to speak with his men. They deserved to know the truth and learn just what they would be fighting if they decided to remain.

There would be some who wanted no part of such conflict. Carac had several men he knew would lead them well. They would no longer be able to carry his banner or fight under his name, but they could still do well on their own.

Carac tore off a piece of bread and put it into his mouth as his gaze went to the bed. He wished he could have woken with Ravyn by his side. But there would be years for such things.

He swallowed and took a long drink from the waterskin before taking the rest of the bread and exiting the tent. He straightened and breathed in the morning air. The sun was streaked a vibrant red and pink with the sun rising on the horizon.

Carac had seen many sunrises, but this was the first in his life with Ravyn. It didn't matter that they weren't yet man and wife. Their hearts were bound, and that united them deeper than any vows ever could.

There was a smile on his face as he strolled through camp and watched his men wake up with hangovers. When he reached Simon's tent, he stopped near the entrance and stoked the dying fire. The morning air was cool. It wouldn't be long before the first snow fell. Simon always woke before sunrise, but after the following night, Carac gave him some time.

After finishing his bread and waiting thirty minutes, Carac

called his friend's name. There was no response. He scanned the camp, wondering if he'd missed Simon as he walked to the tent.

Carac's head turned to the shelter. He called Simon's name again. This time, when there was no answer, he pulled the flap back and peered inside. Simon was on his side, but he was alone.

That horrible feeling tightened like a steel band around his chest. Carac strode into the tent and shook Simon's shoulder. It took several attempts, which wasn't normal, before Simon finally stirred.

He blinked and looked up at Carac before rolling onto his back. "What is it?"

"Do you feel all right?"

Simon shrugged. "My head aches, and I crave more sleep. Why are you up so early?"

"It's dawn."

That had Simon frowning. He rose up on one elbow and ran a hand down his face. Not once did he look or reach for Margery. The longer Carac watched his friend, the more concerned he became.

"Where is Margery?" Carac asked.

Simon finally looked over his shoulder before he shrugged. "She is about somewhere."

"I would like to find her and Ravyn."

Simon chuckled as he stood and pushed Carac out of the way so he could dress. "They can take care of themselves. They are Hunters."

"You are not acting yourself."

His friend paused in tucking his tunic into his trousers. His brow puckered in a frown. "I know I should care about where Margery is, but I do not."

Something was definitely wrong. Carac had to find the

girls. He stalked from the tent and went to where the horses were corralled. Ravyn's mare was gone, but Margery's still stood with the others.

Carac rubbed his chest again. His head swung to his tent. With wooden legs, he made his way to it. Once inside, his eyes went straight to where the staff had been the night before. It was gone.

Just as Ravyn was.

The betrayal cut so deeply, he couldn't catch his breath. It felt as if someone had pulled open his chest with their bare hands and ripped out his heart.

Ravyn, the woman he loved, had deceived him in the most heinous of ways. It was worse than what his uncle had done. Worse than...anything. It would have been far simpler had she just killed him.

His first thought was to track Ravyn down and take back the staff after he gave her a piece of his mind. But he wouldn't. She'd left him because the staff was more important than their love. If *anything* she said had been the truth. He'd promised to take the artifact to the abbey, and she'd said he should be the one to present it to Edra.

Had that all been a lie, as well?

Nay. That wasn't possible. He had seen her fighting the witches. That wasn't feigned. Neither was her hatred for Sybbyl and the Coven. So, why?

Why!?

Carac curled his fingers into fists. He wanted to throw back his head and bellow the word until he could no longer speak. But he locked it inside.

Just as he sheltered what fragments remained of his heart. He had thought the world bitter and cold when his mother died, and his father became a drunk. He'd once thought himself broken when his brother died.

But none of that compared to the hollowness that resided in him now.

How could he have been so deliriously happy just hours earlier, only to suffer so now? It would have been better never knowing the love or contentment within Ravyn's arms.

"Sir?"

He closed his eyes and refused to turn around at the sound of Rob's voice. "Aye?"

"Some of the men are wanting to know whether we are going or remaining?"

"Tell them to start packing. I want to leave immediately."

"Aye, sir," the boy said hesitantly. "Where are we going?"

Carac opened his eyes to look at the bed. "Home, Rob. We are going home."

He'd had enough of blood and death for a while. Possibly forever.

Each time his thoughts turned to Ravyn, he cut them off. He exited the tent. Being inside it made him nauseous. He would sleep beneath the stars until he returned home.

He walked to the horses as the men started to tear down the camp. Carac stroked the neck of his stallion. Somehow, being with the animal helped to calm the rising tide of anger and resentment within him.

A shout from the trees drew his attention. He looked over the horses to see two of his knights come running out of the forest. One bent over and emptied his stomach while the other looked as pale as death.

Carac made his way to them along with others. He stood back as the two men were repeatedly asked what they'd seen, but neither could answer.

"Sir Carac, what is it?" asked his squire.

He looked down at the young lad and put a hand on his shoulder. "Stay here. I aim to find out."

Carac glanced at the knight who continued to dry heave and decided to talk to the other. He paused beside the man. "What did you see?"

The knight's eyes swung to him. All he could do was shake his head, refusing to speak.

Carac glanced into the woods. "Where?"

The knight pointed behind him before stumbling away. Before Carac could take a step, three of his knights stood on either side of him. He nodded to them, and then they began walking into the forest.

They didn't have to go far before Carac saw the boot sticking out from behind a tree. He walked closer and caught sight of long, blond hair tangled in the leaves. He knew before he saw the body that it was Margery.

His knights halted in shock at the heart lying several feet from the body. But that wasn't what disturbed everyone—including Carac. It was the fact that it appeared as if the organ had burst from Margery's chest.

Carac walked to her and slowly went down on his haunches near a dark stain on the ground. The first two knights must have turned her onto her back, revealing the hole in her chest.

He swallowed when he looked into her face. Margery's eyes were open, staring into nothing. Carac reached up and put his fingers on her lids before pulling them closed.

Ravyn was gone with the staff. Simon wasn't himself. And someone had murdered Margery.

Had Margery's death happened any other way, Carac might have suspected Ravyn. But this kind of torture was something that witches did.

He stood and faced his men. "I need something to cover the body."

A knight turned on his heel and rushed away.

Then Carac looked at the man nearest him. "Get two groups together. You take one to Bryce Castle, and send the other to John's keep. I want to know that everything is as it should be."

Carac looked through the trees to the camp. Simon should be with him. Simon was never far, always there when Carac needed him the most. Where was his friend now?

The first knight returned with a cloak that Carac draped over Margery before lifting her into his arms. The news had already traveled through the camp by the time he returned. His gaze locked with Simon's before his friend turned and walked away.

Carac had nowhere else to take Margery but into his tent. Rob brought in a bucket of water and rags, and to Carac's surprise, the boy helped him clean Margery's body.

If Carac knew how to get to the abbey, he would return the Hunter's body to them. Since he didn't, he had no choice but to bury Margery there.

When they finished readying her, Carac once again carried her to the grave his men had dug. He jumped into the hole and carefully laid Margery down. Then he reached up and took her sword that Rob had carried.

Carac was helped out by one of his men. There was a moment of silence before they began covering the body with dirt. Carac looked behind him and saw Simon, who stood off to the side as if a stranger.

He stalked to Simon and glared at him. "You should have carried her."

"I barely knew her."

"You told me you cared for her."

Simon began to answer before he hesitated. "I thought I did."

Carac cocked his head to the side and narrowed his gaze at his friend. "What is wrong with you?"

"I...I do not know," Simon said before his face crumpled. "I want to care about Margery, but I...cannot."

"When did you begin realizing something was different?"

Simon shrugged, shooting him a helpless look.

"Tell me everything that happened from the time the four of us left the camp the day before yesterday and headed to Bryce Castle," Carac demanded.

He listened intently as Simon detailed everything. Right up until he and Margery were separated. Simon couldn't answer a basic question about that time. Which left only one explanation...witches.

35

To have held everything. And now to have nothing.

Ravyn knew death was coming, and she welcomed it with open arms. The moment she'd taken the staff from Carac, her soul had withered and died.

It didn't matter what Sybbyl and Angmar did to her now. The one thing she hadn't known she wanted or needed was gone. She had betrayed Carac. The very thing Simon had told her never to do.

Carac would not forgive her. Not that she would be around to ask for his mercy. She heard the witches, but she didn't pay them any heed. Her mind was on Carac and Margery. Poor Margery. Ravyn wanted to cry for her, but the tears were locked away, shed only in her mind.

Because she would not show such weakness to the Coven.

"Praying?" came a voice close to her ear.

Sybbyl. Hatred for the witch ran thick and pervasive in her blood. But part of Ravyn's training had been to withstand any kind of assault a witch would launch at her—physical, emotional, and mental.

Ravyn opened her eyes and looked around at the Witch's Grove. The area was permeated with evil. It seeped from the ground and from the leaves of the trees to swirl in the air. Every fiber of her being screamed for her to get away from the moment Sybbyl pulled her across the invisible barrier of the Grove.

The circular area was larger than the previous Witch's Grove she had ventured into, but what kept her on her knees was the sheer number of Gira surrounding them.

The nymphs looked like the trees they remained close to. Their skin was like bark, their hair branches. But it was their whispers that led others into a Witch's Grove where the Gira would entrap the terrified person within the trees and tease and torment them for days before killing them.

The Gira were drawn to Witch's Groves, but they could be anywhere. If someone disappeared in the woods, Ravyn always suspected that a Gira was responsible.

"What is the matter?" Sybbyl asked in a voice filled with false sadness. "Do you not wish to talk? Do you mourn your friend? Or your lover?"

Ravyn kept her gaze straight ahead on Angmar, who stood in the center of the Grove with her arms out and her head back. Mist suddenly rose up from the ground and began rolling toward the elder as if it were alive.

"Scared?" Sybbyl asked with a small chuckle. "You should be. There is much information we want from you. And you will give it to us."

Ravyn drew in a deep breath and mentally readied herself for the torture that she knew was about to begin. Yet, nothing could prepare her for the pain of the silver lash that came from Angmar's hand and cut across her arm.

Her entire limb exploded with agony. Ravyn gritted her teeth and fisted her hand to keep from screaming, but she couldn't stop her body from jerking at the contact with such malicious magic. It burned through her, spreading from the cut outward until she shook with it.

They had yet to ask a question, and that was the first strike. Already, she felt as if she were dying. How much could she endure?

Then she thought of Edra and Radnar, of Asa and Berlaq, and all the others at the abbey. She thought of Margery and everything Hunters trained for.

"Who is the witch that helps you?" Angmar demanded.

Ravyn lifted her chin and smiled. She braced herself when she saw the whip come for her again.

Carac looked out over his men, each staring back at him with a mixture of disbelief and fear. Five hundred men that trusted him. Followed him. Telling them about the witches had been the easy part. The hard part came when they wanted proof.

"Your evidence came in the battle with Lord Randall's men. How many of you actually left the field with blood on your swords?" he asked. "It was magic that prevented those men from being able to defend themselves and their lord."

He swallowed. "Some of you saw Margery's body that we found this morning. No one's heart goes flying out of his or her body. A witch was responsible. And all of you saw her. Sybbyl."

A murmur went through the men. He imagined that he'd worn that same shaken, stunned expression when he learned about witches. "Margery and Ravyn are witch hunters."

"Where is Ravyn?" someone asked.

Carac rubbed a hand over his mouth and shifted his feet. "I have no idea." His head swung to the side where Simon stood, guarded by two men. His friend had no idea that his mind had been altered with magic. And Carac didn't know how deeply the spell went. Or what the witches wanted in Simon's head.

But Carac could guess.

"I tell you all about this group of witches known as the Coven because there are witches who do good. But the Coven is something altogether different. We were packing up today to return to my home."

At the men's expressions, which had now turned confused, Carac glanced at the ground. "My name is Carac, but I am more than a knight. I am Duke Carac de Vere. I have discovered that magic has been used on the man I consider my brother, Simon. I do not know what exactly was done to him, but he is not the same. I intend to track Sybbyl down and make her pay for this slight."

"We will join you," came a shout from the back.

It was followed by more than half of his men shouting in agreement.

Carac raised his hand for silence. "Before you agree to come with me, know that witches cannot be killed with our blades. Only those weapons spelled with magic can kill them. But I have one," he said and raised the single arrow from Ravyn's crossbow. "And I intend to use it."

The army gazed at him silently. He smiled, understanding their hesitation. "You are the best men I have ever had the pleasure of fighting beside. We had many victories and made a lot of coin in the process. I will not think less of any of you if you choose another path. I know mine, but I do not expect any of you to accompany me on it."

The hush that followed was broken by a horse stomping its hoof. Then, one by one, men turned and walked away. Five hundred was soon only twenty. And Rob.

"Lad," Carac said with a shake of his head. "This is no place for you."

Rob squared his shoulders. "I want to be a knight. That means I will follow you into all situations, Your Grace."

He ruffled the lad's hair and looked up at the men who remained. "We ride out in ten minutes."

Though Carac had known many of his men wouldn't fight the Coven, he was disheartened that so few would stand beside him. At least, he wasn't alone.

While the last of the camp was taken down, Carac made his way into the forest where Margery's body had been found. So many had trampled through the area that whatever footprints had been there were now erased.

It took some time, but he located three sets of tracks headed northwest. One of them had a small round impression next to it every other step.

"The staff," he murmured as he pressed his finger into the indentation.

He straightened and tucked the arrow into his boot next to his dagger. It was the only weapon he had that could kill the witches, and he wasn't going to lose it.

When he returned to get his horse, the men, including Simon and Rob, were mounted and waiting. He put his foot in the stirrup and threw his leg over the stallion. "I found tracks. We're headed northwest."

They rode hard, stopping often to check tracks. Carac wondered who the third set of footprints belonged to. He would think they belonged to Ravyn if he didn't know that her horse was gone.

And yet, the Coven seemed to have the staff.

Nothing was adding up. Everything pointed to Ravyn being with the Coven, but after hearing her story, he couldn't imagine her joining them for any reason.

"You know you can talk to me," Simon said as he came up beside him.

Carac hesitated, but he and Simon had shared confidences for over a decade. He took a deep breath and told Simon everything that had happened leading up to entering the castle with Ravyn, during their time with the ghost, and right up to waking this morning and everything he had found in the forest since.

"Did you ever think that maybe the witches are holding Ravyn against her will?"

Carac frowned because he hadn't thought along those lines. "Ravyn would fight them."

"She may have been there when they killed Margery," Simon said.

Carac accepted a waterskin from him. "I wish I knew what the witch did to you."

"I know."

They rode in silence for some time until the tracks suddenly vanished. Carac and his men spent the next hour searching the area to see if they could find them again. Finally, Carac made the decision to continue in their current direction.

And so on they traveled until nightfall. They stopped to bed down for the night against a lone tree, but every time Carac closed his eyes, he saw Ravyn's smiling face. So, instead, he stared up at the stars until it was his turn to stand guard.

He rose to exchange places with one of his men for the last watch. No sooner had Carac gotten settled than he felt a chill overtake him. The night was cool, but not that cold. The only thing that came close to that sensation was when the specter at Bryce Castle was near.

Carac looked around, but he saw no sign of a ghost. He settled against the tree and let the night surround him.

Inevitably, his thoughts turned to Ravyn. Again and again, he cut them off, but they kept returning.

And each time was like a knife twisting in his heart.

He squeezed his eyes shut for a moment. When he opened them again, he found a woman standing about fifty feet from him. He jumped to his feet and slowly approached her. The moon shed enough light that he was able to see her face.

She gave him a small smile and tucked a strand of dark red hair behind her ear. "You have no cause to trust me, but I have information for you."

"Who are you?" he asked.

"I saw what happened at Bryce Castle. I watched how you stood against John and the witch. I saw you fight alongside the Hunters."

He took a step toward her. "Ravyn? You know her?"

"I do not know her name, but I know what she is. You were all inside the castle for a long time. I feared the Coven had won. Then I saw you emerge."

Carac gave a shake of his head. "Who are you?"

"My name is Helena. The Coven tried to recruit me not long ago. I was aided by another Hunter named Leoma, which allowed me to get free. I owe the Hunters a debt. That's why I am here."

"To fight with me?"

She gave a little snort and glanced around nervously. "I tried to stand against the Coven once. That did not turn out so well."

"So you will allow them to win? It is because witches like you decided not to pick a side that the Coven will get the victory they seek."

Helena lowered her gaze to the ground briefly. "You are following the two witches, aye?"

"I am. One did something to my friend's mind. I would have it reversed."

"You will likely grab the moon before you ever convince a Coven member to undo what has been done. However, I might be able to help."

Carac knew he was taking a risk by trusting her. For all he knew, she was the third person with Angmar and Sybbyl. But what if she could help Simon?

He gave her a nod and turned on his heel. Together, they walked to the camp where he knelt to wake Simon, but Helena stopped it.

"It will be easier this way," she whispered before putting her hands on either side of Simon's temples.

Carac wrapped his fingers around the arrow in his boot, ready to plunge it into the witch if she made a false move. He studied her as she sat there with her eyes closed for a long time.

Finally, she dropped her arms and opened her eyes. "It was Angmar's magic. She was using Simon to see through his eyes to learn what you were doing and to, eventually, turn him against you. She knows everything in his mind. His past, the present. And she's aware that you are following her."

Carac ran a hand through his hair before propping his elbow on his knee. "Is the magic gone?"

"A Coven elder has significant power. I have removed all that I can, but I can never erase it all. There will be parts of his memory missing, but he will at least be his old self once more."

"I hope you are right."

She rose and went to each knight, touching their weapons and saying something before returning to Carac. She held out her hand, and he handed her his sword. After whispering something he couldn't understand, she gave him back the weapon and motioned for him to follow her. He kept the arrow in his hand, the shaft against his arm—because while he wanted to believe her, he couldn't.

Helena stopped and faced him. "I have ensured that each of your men now has the ability to kill a witch. You no longer have to carry a single arrow."

"Thank you." He put the bolt back into his boot and slid his sword into its scabbard.

"I know that you love Ravyn."

He didn't reply. There was nothing to say. He wanted to deny it, but the words locked in his throat.

"I was too late to stop them from killing the other Hunter, but they have Ravyn."

Carac took a step back, shaking his head. "Nay. She would fight them."

Helena smiled, her gaze dropping briefly to the ground. "Angmar was in your friend's mind. They knew you had the staff. And they wanted a Hunter. Neither Ravyn nor her friend stood a chance."

Carac rubbed his chest where a pain had begun again. He'd intended to abandon Ravyn because he stupidly believed she would betray him. Even when everything pointed to the fact that she had no reason.

The witches knew exactly what to do to turn him against Ravyn.

"Keep on your course," Helena said. "You will find them soon enough. But hurry. I do not know how long Ravyn will survive."

He began to turn away when she added, "And be careful. Not all is as it seems."

S he wanted to die. Actually prayed for death.
   But Ravyn knew such relief wouldn't come anytime soon.

No longer did she attempt to hold back her screams. The witches took turns torturing her. She lost count of the various ways their magic had been used on her. She had been burned, frozen, choked, stabbed, had bones broken, and felt as if she were being ripped apart limb from limb.

The entire time, they repeated one question: "*Who is the witch helping the Hunters?*"

No matter what they did to her, Ravyn would never give them the answer they sought. Because she feared the witches getting into her head, she didn't even refer to anyone by name in her thoughts. She put up a mental wall in her mind and kept laying stone after stone to keep anyone from busting through.

The passage of time was irrelevant. Ravyn didn't know how many hours or days had passed. All she knew was the constant, unending agony.

She fell back on the ground as Sybbyl relented with her most recent torture. Ravyn pulled the sweet taste of air into her lungs and gloried in the short respite from the pain as the witches spoke.

"She is tougher than I expected," Angmar stated.

Ravyn didn't have the energy to raise her eyelids to look at them. Her mind retreated from the anguish that assaulted every part of her body. If she could find the tears, Ravyn would cry. But even that part of her was wounded.

She winced as the breeze passed over her many injuries. Whatever fight had driven her all those years had been ripped out and hacked to pieces. She desperately wanted to go to a place in her mind where she had tucked Carac and their unexpected, extraordinary love.

He no doubt hated her now. Maybe that was for the best because he would have no desire to be anywhere near her, which meant that he wouldn't seek out Braith and join the fight against the Coven. So there was a good chance Carac would live.

"I think it is time for something more," Angmar said, yanking Ravyn from her thoughts.

More? What more could there be?

And then it dawned on Ravyn. The Staff of the Eternal.

Ravyn forced her eyes open and looked up at the sky. Dawn was breaking. How many more days could she survive the constant torment? She feared the answer.

There was a soft *thunk* as Angmar stabbed the staff against the ground. "This can all end, Hunter. All you have to do is give me a name."

Ravyn slowly turned her head to the last Coven elder. "Mary."

Angmar frowned and looked at Sybbyl. "Do you know a Mary?"

"Many," Sybbyl replied with a shrug.

"Edgar," Ravyn continued. "Robert. Jane. Angus. Elizabeth."

Angmar's face mottled with rage as she realized what Ravyn was doing. Ravyn laughed as Angmar's fingers tightened on the staff as she whispered something.

The laugh was cut short as a scream locked within Ravyn as she writhed upon the ground while it felt as if she were burning from the inside out. With every breath, every movement, the agony doubled.

It lasted a moment...or an eternity. Ravyn did not know which. All she knew was that the pain finally relented. But if she thought she would get another respite, she was wrong.

Sybbyl squatted down beside her, a smile on her face. "I should have known it was you. It is so obvious now. You have believed all these years that your mother saved you by hiding you behind her skirts. I saw you, Ravyn. I saw your little hand and the way your mother refused to run and expose you."

The tears Ravyn hadn't been able to shed earlier filled her eyes. "Nay."

"Indeed." Sybbyl laughed and straightened. "I waited the entire day for you to get out from beneath your mother's dead body. But I grew tired of waiting and left." She bent forward, putting her hands on her knees. "I gave you your life. And now, I'm going to take it away."

Ravyn took a deep breath as Angmar handed Sybbyl the staff.

Carac pushed his horse hard. As soon as Helena walked away, he roused the others and told them about her visit, her gift of spelling their blades, and her warning. They were riding within moments. Carac kept a close watch on Simon, and it appeared as if his friend was back to his former self.

And Carac was thankful for that.

He had no idea where he was going, but the witch had said he would know it when he found it. His gut twisted with fear each time he thought of Ravyn in the clutches of the Coven. He had been so quick to judge that he'd never considered she had been taken.

Carac finally slowed when they crested a hill, and all that was before him was a thick forest to his front and right and a village to his left.

He glanced over at Simon to find his friend's face crumpled. Simon then turned his head to look at him, and a tear fell down his face. Carac clamped his hand on Simon's shoulder.

"I did no—"

"Do not," Carac said over him. "You had no control. The witch took it from you."

Simon rubbed his eyes and swallowed as he looked forward. "I cared deeply for Margery. They did not make me feel that. But they took it away. She is gone, but we can still find Ravyn."

Carac hoped his friend was right, but his gut told him that the chances of Ravyn remaining alive were slim. But he would hold out hope until he saw her body.

"The trees," Carac said as he pointed to them.

Simon raised a brow. "Are you sure?"

"Helena said I would know."

"Then we go." Simon looked behind him and motioned the men to follow.

Carac clicked to his horse and galloped over the rolling terrain until he reached the forest. He then slowed his stallion to a walk.

The only sound was the horses' hooves as they clopped along the ground. The deeper into the woods Carac traveled, the more everything felt...wrong.

Suddenly, his horse slid to a halt and reared up. When he came down, the stallion was throwing his head and trying to run away. It was everything Carac could do to hold him steady. But his men had no such luck.

Carac finally allowed his horse to back up, but the animal was shaking and breathing hard. He dismounted and patted the stallion's neck, talking low while others watched their horses run off.

He exchanged a worried look with Simon, who was also able to manage his mount. Carac looked back at the spot where the horses had gone berserk.

"We go on foot," Carac announced and gave his horse another rub along his neck.

Simon came to stand beside him as he started forward. They had only gone a few paces before a bird flew right at his head. Carac ducked, his eyes going skyward to the animal. And when he faced forward again, a hooded figure stood there.

"You enter a place you know nothing about," the man said and set the end of his staff on the ground while a wolf came out to stand beside him.

And then the bird—a falcon—landed on top of the staff.

Carac studied the man. "Who are you?"

"My name matters not. You should turn away from this place."

"I cannot," Carac said. "I search for two witches who have taken my friend prisoner."

The man raised his free hand and pushed back the hood of his cloak to reveal long, blond hair and eyes so pale a blue they were nearly white. "Well, then. That changes things."

"How so?" Simon demanded.

The wolf sat beside the man. "It means that instead of warning you off from this place by saying it is evil, I will have to tell you what you will find if you venture within."

"I am going in," Carac declared. "You will not stop me. If you are working with the Coven, you can tell them that."

One side of the man's lips lifted in a grin. "I do not work for the Coven. I fight them."

"Then we are on the same side," Simon said.

The man looked from Simon to Carac. "I do not think so."

Carac was losing patience. "I do not have the time to stand here and argue with you. Move aside, or I will go through you."

"You can try," the man said calmly.

Carac withdrew his sword from its scabbard and widened his stance. "So be it. I have stood against a ghost and witches and survived. I will get through you."

"I can kill you without moving," the man said. "Or send my animals to attack. I am trying to warn you away to save your lives. You may know of witches, but you do not understand what awaits you inside."

Carac lifted his sword. "The Coven. And they have my woman. A Hunter."

The man frowned before giving a short whistle. The falcon flew away, and the wolf ran off. "I have been tracking the two Coven elders."

"One," Simon corrected him.

Carac nodded. "We killed one of the elders, the red-haired one."

"My name is Jarin," the man said. "I am part of a race of witches and warlocks who have been fighting to control the

Coven for thousands of years. I recently aided a Hunter against the elders."

"Leoma," Carac said as he lowered his weapon. "She was with my friend."

Jarin grinned. "Braith."

"Aye. Thank you for helping them."

Jarin shrugged and changed his staff to his other hand. "I will warn you that it is not a good sign that Angmar has a Hunter."

"Her name is Ravyn," Simon said.

Carac looked at the trees ahead. "We found the Staff of the Eternal. I thought we'd kept it out of the Coven's hands, but I was wrong."

"It is not your fault," Jarin said. "The only reason the Coven did not acquire the Blood Skull was because it did not want to be with them. The other relics will not do the same."

Simon grunted. "So whoever has them, controls them?"

"I am afraid so," Jarin replied and looked to the men behind Carac. "You know your weapons will not kill witches."

"Actually, they will," Carac said with a grin.

A warlock. Carac stared at Jarin. Just when he'd begun to think there were no more surprises, Carac was hit with another. But they were going to need the man.

"You are about to enter a Witch's Grove," Jarin told them. "Magic binds it. Once you cross the threshold, you will hear the witches. And Ravyn."

Carac looked at the woods. He had thought because there were no screams that Ravyn wasn't being hurt. What a fool he was.

"There are also...other things within," Jarin continued. "Do not stray from the path I set. Walk in pairs. And if you want to come out alive, do not follow the whispers."

Carac's gaze swung to Jarin. "You have not told us what to do to get out."

"That will depend on whether we survive the battle. Angmar is the strongest of the elders. She is a formidable opponent," Jarin replied.

"What are the whispers?" one of the men asked.

Jarin stared flatly at the knights. "Not something you want to discover. Trust me."

Carac turned to Simon. "I think half the men should remain out here."

"Carac," Simon began.

But he talked over him. "Braith and those at the abbey need people who know how to fight. We cannot lose everyone inside."

A muscle flexed in Simon's jaw, but he gave a nod after a pause.

"Good. You will stay to lead them," Carac stated.

Simon gave a shake of his head, frustration and anger mixing. "I should be with you. We have never gone into battle without each other."

"I know, but this war is greater than any we've ever fought. If I do not make it, Braith will need you."

It was only after Simon had agreed that Carac turned to the men. "I will need half of you with me."

After the men had stepped forward, Carac looked at Jarin. "Ready?"

"I was born to hunt the Coven. I am the one who should be asking if you are ready."

Carac shrugged. "I suppose we will find out."

"I imagine we will," Jarin mumbled. Then he looked at Simon. "My companions will be around. Do not attempt to harm them. They will kill you."

"How do we know which animals are yours?" Simon asked.

Jarin grinned. "You will have to guess."

Carac and Simon exchanged a nod. Carac then walked to Jarin.

"The terrain is rough, and the slope up the hill steep. We move fast. Prepare yourself," Jarin said as he took a step.

The moment Carac crossed the indiscernible line, it was like stepping into another world. Though the sun had been shining just a second ago, it felt as if it shrank behind layers of clouds. Evil pervaded everything. But it was the screams wracked with pain that brought him to a halt.

He knew they belonged to Ravyn. And it broke his heart that he had almost left her to the Coven. Had Helena not found him, he would have tried to forget Ravyn.

"Come," Jarin said and took his arm, pulling him forward.

Carac was almost immediately nauseous. He struggled to breathe, wanting clean air that wasn't doused with wickedness. He wasn't sure how the plants could grow in such an atmosphere. Then he heard the whispers.

"Steady," Jarin said without looking at the knights behind him.

Carac continued the climb upward, only to jerk when he felt something next to his cheek. The whisper was right in his ear. But he didn't look at what it was. He didn't want to know. The fact that Jarin kept his gaze forward was enough for Carac.

Whatever the things were, they left the warlock alone. It must have had something to do with magic. They continued through the trees, their pace slow and steady.

Carac hated not being able to see clearly. What light made it through the trees was so dim that it was almost like hunting at dusk. His eyes kept playing tricks on him because he was sure he saw a tree move. Or a portion of a tree break away from itself.

There was a shout from behind them. Carac turned around in time to see one of his men dragged off into the shadows. Another knight ran after him and disappeared.

Jarin gripped Carac's arm. "Remember what I said."

He looked at the warlock before motioning his men to continue upward. Then, blessedly, Ravyn's screams stopped.

The relief he felt was short-lived because he knew she could be dead.

Finally, Carac saw an opening through the trees ahead. They reached the top of the hill to find a flat, open area. But he didn't see the witches.

Jarin turned to face him, his pale gaze intense. "They know we are here."

Carac stared at the warlock for a moment before his gaze slid back to the clearing. He scanned the area. That's when he saw the still form lying on the ground. "Ravyn."

"It is a trap," Jarin warned.

"It will not be the first I've stepped into." He moved his gaze back to Jarin and gave a nod.

Carac shifted to his men and mouthed *trap*. They all knew what to do. He motioned for them to spread out and stay alert. Then he returned his attention to Jarin.

"What will you do?"

Jarin grinned. "What I do best."

Carac watched the warlock walk away to be swallowed by the shadows. At least near the center of the Grove, the whispers weren't so prevalent. Carac felt something brush along his back. He gripped his sword tighter but didn't turn around. He walked from the tree line and into the clearing.

It took everything he had not to rush to Ravyn. As he drew closer, he saw the torture she had been put through. Her clothes were shredded, her face was bruised, one eye was swollen shut, and she had cuts everywhere.

His chest tightened as he knelt beside her and lifted a matted tangle of her long, midnight locks. He had been subjected to torture once, so he knew the wounds reached much further than just skin-deep.

He smoothed her hair back from her face, his throat clogged with emotion. Had they entered her mind like they had Simon's? When she woke—*if* she woke—would she be the same warrior that he'd fallen in love with?

Carac reached for her hand. Before he could touch it, he was flying through the air. He managed to hold onto his sword, even when he landed so hard that it knocked the breath from his body.

He rose up on an elbow and watched as Sybbyl and Angmar, who held the staff, walked from mist that had suddenly appeared. As if it were their doorway somehow. He had seen the same fog at the castle.

"What a surprise," Sybbyl said as she sauntered toward him.

Carac managed to get to his feet. "Is it? I thought whatever was done to Simon would tell you what we were doing?"

Angmar's blue eyes narrowed. "Who helped you?"

"Does it matter?" he taunted. "I bet it irritates you to know that there are witches who continue to stand against you."

"Not for much longer," Angmar replied.

Carac raised his brows. "Really? How do you expect to get the Blood Skull if you burn every time you touch it? That is what happened to your face, aye?"

He didn't hide his smile when Angmar's hand immediately rose to touch the scars.

Sybbyl tsked. "Did you learn nothing from our encounters, Carac? You cannot best us. You lack...well, everything."

He raised his sword. "Did you miss the part where a witch helped us?"

"Or you could be lying."

"Why would I lie about that?"

Sybbyl shrugged and tossed her blond hair. "To try and make us believe that your weapon can hurt us."

He looked at the new gown she wore. No longer could he

see the cuts Margery had inflicted, but he bet they were still there. "How are your wounds, by the way? The Hunters are formidable, are they not?"

"I would disagree with that," Angmar said and looked at Ravyn. "It was easy to break her."

Carac was no fool. He wouldn't believe anything the witch said. Especially when it was about Ravyn. Instead, he smiled. "You are going to die today."

"Me?" Angmar said with a laugh. She raised a dark brow and motioned to the staff. "Did you forget what I now hold?"

"Did *you* honestly think I came alone?"

Sybbyl let out a bark of laughter before it grew. She covered her mouth with her hand and gave him a pitying look. "Call your men out, Carac."

Unease coursed through him. He stared at the witches. They couldn't know how many of his men he'd brought with him inside the Grove. Yet he gave the signal for them to come out. And none did.

"They will not be joining you," Angmar said. "They are now in the hands of the Gira."

Sybbyl laughed again. "It looks like it is just you and us. Too bad the fight will be over before it even begins."

Carac glanced at Ravyn to find her eyes open and focused on him. He didn't know if she was aware that it was him. It didn't matter. He would fight for her, for everything she stood for.

"What are you waiting for?" Carac demanded.

Suddenly, the temperature became frigid. And to Carac's shock, the ghost from Bryce Castle appeared. Rossamond pointed a finger at the staff and told Angmar, "That is not yours."

"Yet I am holding it, and there is nothing you can do about that," the witch announced.

Carac didn't wait to hear what the ghost might say. The witches' attention was elsewhere, and he was going to take advantage of it. He rushed toward the center of the Grove where they stood.

He only took two steps before Sybbyl raised her hand and locked her eyes on him. He flew backwards, slamming into a tree before crumpling to the ground.

Carac raised his head to see that Rossamond's beautiful face had been replaced by the skeletal figure. The specter was flying around Angmar, skimming through the witch's body again and again. All the while, Angmar kept throwing magic at the ghost.

Carac jumped to his feet and once more faced off against Sybbyl. Except, this time, he wasn't alone. Jarin strolled from the trees. Sybbyl smiled when she saw him, but it quickly faded when she realized he was something more.

Sybbyl looked between him and Jarin. "Just two of you? Really?"

"I hear a tremor in your voice," Jarin replied.

In response, Sybbyl raised her hands and sent a blast of magic. Jarin merely raised his staff and blocked it. Carac grinned and twisted his wrist to twirl his sword.

Was she dreaming? Surely, she was. Ravyn had drifted into a corner of her mind where she kept her memories of Carac. She was reliving them when she thought she heard his voice.

It was a trick. It had to be. But then she opened her eyes and saw him.

Before she could fully grasp his appearance, the ghost was there, attacking Angmar. And then another man appeared, easily deflecting Sybbyl's magic.

He was obviously Varroki. But how had he and Carac met up? Ravyn rolled onto her side, wincing at the pain. It didn't matter how or why any of them were there. A battle was taking place, and she was meant to be in it.

She could only watch as Carac and Jarin attacked Sybbyl at once. The witch was having a difficult time dodging Jarin's magic and Carac's sword.

Ravyn tried to push herself up. It took several tries before she was able to get into a semi-seated position. Pain vibrated through her every time she breathed, so moving was excruciating.

She glanced at Angmar and smiled to find that the ghost was doing considerable damage to the elder. But Ravyn's gaze returned to Carac. This might only be his second time fighting a witch, but he learned quickly.

He moved often, never remaining in one spot. His sword work was mesmerizing as he got closer and closer to Sybbyl each time. Then he got too near, and Sybbyl knocked him back so that he flipped head over heels.

As soon as he landed, though, he was back on his feet, returning to the battle. But Ravyn's gaze was on what had fallen out of his boot. Her last arrow.

With her teeth clenched, Ravyn crawled to the bolt and wrapped her fingers around it. Sybbyl had shattered her crossbow, but that didn't matter. Ravyn didn't need it.

Though it took several attempts, she eventually got to her feet. Ravyn's gaze locked on Angmar. She was the last elder. Without her, the Coven would crumble. But Ravyn's eyes slid to Sybbyl.

She'd promised her family she would kill the witch that slaughtered them. Yet, she only had strength enough to take out one.

With a sigh, she focused on Angmar. Then, with measured steps, she began making her way to the elder. Halfway there, Ravyn's knee gave out, and she fell to the ground, the arrow slipping from her fingers.

Tears gathered. She had trained to battle the witches. But nothing could have prepared her for the endless torture and the things witches could do with their magic.

She felt hot tears on her cheek and dug her fingers into the ground, pulling herself slowly and painfully toward the arrow. Finally, she had it in her grasp again.

It would be so easy to lie down and let the others fight. It was what her body wanted. She hurt so badly. If she allowed sleep to claim her, the agony would stop, if only for a little while. Didn't she deserve it?

An image of Margery dying filled her mind. Then she heard her family's screams. Ravyn squeezed her eyes shut and drew in a shaky breath. When she opened her eyes, she pushed herself up as far as she could. It was only to her hands and knees, but she could crawl.

She didn't know how far she'd gotten before she heard Carac shout her name a second before she was tossed into the air. Ravyn landed and rolled several times before she came to a stop.

When she looked up, she was farther from Angmar than before. And she wasn't sure she had the energy to get up again. Her tears fell against her split lip, stinging it as she peered at the arrow in her grasp.

How confident she had been that she could take out any witch. How utterly ridiculous she must have seemed to everyone. A few victories did not make her special. There were endless witches in the Coven. Instead of thinking about a single witch who had killed her family, Ravyn should have been focused on the bigger picture.

And now, she was paying the price.

She looked at the elder again. Ravyn blinked because it looked as if Rossamond were pushing Angmar backward. Right to Ravyn.

This propelled Ravyn. She knew she had one chance. Sybbyl's back was to her, and Angmar had no idea she was there. All Ravyn had to do was get to her feet. But could she? She glanced at Carac fighting with everything he had.

She swallowed and bit back a cry of pain as she rolled onto her stomach. Her arms shook as she pushed herself up onto her knees. Getting to her feet wasn't easy. She fell twice, and each time, she felt more of her blood running from the cuts along her body.

But then she was standing. She was so unsteady that a breeze could knock her over, but she remained upright. Her gaze slid to Angmar as the elder was pushed back again, coming closer and closer to Ravyn until she could almost reach out and touch the witch.

Then Angmar whirled around, her eyes widening when she saw Ravyn. She smiled and thrust the arrow between the elder's two ribs, right into her heart.

Ravyn reached for the staff the same time the ghost went through Angmar once more. The staff flew through the air, glowing with magic. Ravyn could only watch as time slowed to a crawl and Sybbyl spun around.

She and Jarin leapt for the staff at the same time. There was a bright flash, and then Jarin fell to the ground on bent knees.

"It is lost," Rossamond wailed. "The staff is in the hands of the Coven!"

The world began spinning then. Ravyn felt herself falling. Then she was caught in strong arms and held against a hard chest she knew well.

"I have you," Carac said. "I have you, love. It is going to be all right now."

She wanted to answer him, but she could no longer hold back the darkness that dotted her vision.

The first thing she heard was chirping. Ravyn slowly came awake and opened her eyes. She had to blink against the sunlight pouring through the window. She recognized the ivy on the windowsill and the circlet of flowers hanging on the wall that Leoma had made for her when they were just children.

Somehow, Ravyn was back at the abbey. She took stock of her body and felt no pain, which was a relief. Her head turned on the pillow, and her eyes landed on a blond head near her hand.

She threaded her fingers through the golden locks. Immediately, Carac raised his head, his green eyes meeting hers.

"I thought I'd lost you," he murmured.

She choked up when she saw the emotion filling his eyes. "I am so sorry I left."

"Nay," he said with a shake of his head. "I know you did not willingly do it."

Ravyn closed her eyes, but a tear escaped anyway. She sniffed and looked at Carac. "How did you find me?"

"I was going after the witches because I knew they were responsible for Margery's death."

Ravyn blinked rapidly at the reminder of her friend's murder, but the tears flowed anyway.

Carac took her hand and kissed it, enfolding it between both of his. "There was a memorial here, and we buried Margery at the camp." He paused a moment. "Another witch found me. Helena. She told me that the Coven had you. Then she freed Simon from the magic they had put on him and spelled our weapons. When I reached the Witch's Grove, Jarin was there."

Ravyn swallowed and licked her lips. "Did I see things right? Did Sybbyl get away with the staff?"

Carac glanced away. "Aye. Jarin healed your wounds before we left the Grove, but you did not wake. As we made it out of the Grove, there were others waiting for us. Edra and Radnar."

"How?"

"It seems that Asa's owl was following you. It returned and told Asa that the Coven had you. Edra and Radnar went to aid you, and they had help."

She raised her brows. "Who?"

"A woman named Malene, who is Lady of the Varroki, and her commander, Armir."

Ravyn couldn't believe she'd missed that. "You met them?"

"Aye. They have a way of...jumping...long distances with magic," he said with a twist of his lips and distaste on his features.

"You do not care for it?"

He shot her a flat look. "You were the only one not sick. Though not everyone traveled in such a way. Edra wanted you returned quickly, and Malene agreed. I would not be parted from you, so they reluctantly allowed me to come along, as well. Radnar, Simon, and what remains of my men returned on horseback."

Her fingers tightened on his. "How many men did you lose?"

"Of the twenty? Half."

"I am sorry."

He shook his head. "I wish Jarin would have returned with them, but the warrior set out to look for Sybbyl."

Ravyn pushed herself up. "How long have I been asleep?"

"Over a week. I feared you might never wake. I cannot live without you."

She threw her arms around his neck and held him tightly. His arms locked around her. It felt amazing to be in his embrace again because, for a moment, she had thought he was lost to her forever.

"I love you," she murmured.

He leaned back and cupped her face. "And I love you. I will never doubt you again."

"And I will never leave you again."

He smoothed his thumb along her cheek. "Do you still wish to be my wife?"

"More than anything?"

"So you will not mind if we join in the hunt for Sybbyl."

Ravyn laughed. This was one of the many reasons she loved Carac. Their life together would be full of adventures, and no doubt some quarrels, but it was their love that would hold them together.

Not just in this life, but in the next.

EPILOGUE

Two weeks later...

"I am not calling you Duchess," Leoma said with a smile as she hugged Ravyn before moving off.

Ravyn beamed at Carac as more well-wishers came to congratulate them on their nuptials. Happy didn't even begin to describe how she felt.

"Are you sure you want to go?" Carac asked when they had a moment to themselves.

The plan was to travel to his castle with Asa and gather more men, both to defend his lands and also to join in the war against the Coven. Asa would spell any weapons while there, and Ravyn would help with the training.

"Aye, it needs to be done," she replied.

He put an arm around her and pulled her against him. "We will return here."

"I know."

"And we will find Sybbyl."

She looked up at him and smiled, looking into his green eyes. "Together, we can do anything."

"Exactly."

"We might get lucky," Ravyn said. "Without any elders, maybe the Coven will fall apart. They will be easier to take down then."

"We can certainly hope." He grinned down at her. "Did you not promise to show me your favorite place in the forest."

Ravyn smiled as she thought of the waterfall. She took his hand as they made their exit from the abbey for some time alone.

Sybbyl didn't know where she was. For a long while, she didn't remember *who* she was. But bits and pieces were returning. She stood in the middle of a clearing with mist so thick she couldn't make out anything else.

But she feared nothing.

Because she had the Staff of the Eternal.

Her gaze moved to the relic. Magic beat like a heart through the wood. The remnants of the First Witch were still so strong, even after all these centuries. The power was unmistakable. And it was all hers.

Sybbyl's mind turned to the Hunters. One in particular —Ravyn.

She wanted to thank the woman for giving her the ultimate power. Then, Sybbyl was going to take her life. The Hunters and the witch who helped them were a nuisance that needed to be stamped out quickly.

An image of a blond man with pale blue eyes and a staff filled her mind.

"Warlock," she mumbled.

He would be hers. Because where there was one, there were more.

The staff warmed in her hand as if responding to her thoughts. She was unstoppable now. Nothing would stand in the way of her finding the rest of the First Witch's bones and ushering in the time of women...the era of witches.

COMING SOON

Look for the next Kindred book
EVERBOUND
Winter 2018

THANK YOU!

Thank you for reading **EVERWYLDE**. I hope you enjoyed it!

If you liked this book – or any of my other releases – please consider rating the book at the online retailer of your choice. Your ratings and reviews help other readers find new favorites, and of course there is no better or more appreciated support for an author than word of mouth recommendations from happy readers. Thanks again for your interest in my books!

Donna Grant
www.DonnaGrant.com
www.MotherofDragonsBooks.com

NEVER MISS A NEW BOOK

FROM DONNA GRANT!

Sign up for Donna's newsletter!
http://eepurl.com/bRI9nL

Be the first to get notified of new releases and be eligible for special subscribers-only exclusive content and giveaways. Sign up today!

ABOUT THE AUTHOR

New York Times and *USA Today* bestselling author Donna Grant has been praised for her "totally addictive" and "unique and sensual" stories. She's written more than seventy novels spanning multiple genres of romance including the bestselling Dark King stories. Her acclaimed series, Dark Warriors, feature a thrilling combination of Druids, primeval gods, and immortal Highlanders who are dark, dangerous, and irresistible. She lives with two children, a dog, and three cats in Texas.

Connect with Donna online:
www.DonnaGrant.com

www.facebook.com/AuthorDonnaGrant
www.twitter.com/donna_grant
www.goodreads.com/donna_grant
www.instagram.com/dgauthor
www.pinterest.com/donnagrant1